WHITE WITCHMAS
A WICKED WITCHES OF THE MIDWEST MYSTERY BOOK 23

AMANDA M. LEE

WINCHESTERSHAW PUBLICATIONS

Copyright © 2023 by Amanda M. Lee

All rights reserved.

No part of this book may be reproduced in any form or by any electronic or mechanical means, including information storage and retrieval systems, without written permission from the author, except for the use of brief quotations in a book review.

Created with Vellum

PROLOGUE
14 YEARS AGO

"We have a checklist, girls," Aunt Tillie announced as she paced in front of the door that led to the backyard, a football helmet firmly in place on her head. "Does everybody have their checklists? Do you know what you're supposed to do?"

I glanced at the piece of paper she'd supplied us with five minutes earlier. A laundry list of tasks had been laid out—some more absurd than others—and she seemed serious about tackling everything on the list before the blizzard of the century hit. That's what she was calling it anyway. I, Bay Winchester, assumed it was going to be just another snowstorm. If we were lucky, this one would get us out of a day or two of school.

"Do you really want us to carry enough wood into the house to get us through the rest of winter?" my cousin Thistle demanded. She was younger than me, louder than me, and sometimes I wondered if she was smarter than me. She was definitely snarkier than me, which was why she always fought with Aunt Tillie the most. At least that's what my mother said. She was a firm believer that people who shared common personality traits hated one another because they were two sides of the same coin, and it was impossible for people to see—and thus accept—the worst in themselves reflected back from other people. After watching Thistle and Aunt Tillie go at each other for weeks, I understood what Mom meant.

"Yes," Aunt Tillie replied.

"No," my mother snapped as she walked into the room. The flour on her nose indicated she'd been baking up a storm in preparation for the blizzard. We were witches; we could survive almost anything weather related. My mother believed surviving wasn't good enough. We needed fresh baked goods—a lot of them—to be comfortable while surviving. I knew my mother and aunts had baked a cake and were preparing to frost it, so was more than happy with her method of storm survival preparation.

Aunt Tillie's method was another story.

"So you don't want us to get wood?" Thistle asked my mother. She didn't wait for an answer before unbuttoning her coat. "You heard her. No wood."

Aunt Tillie glowered at Thistle. They'd taken to torturing each other to alleviate winter's inevitable boredom. The "games," as they called them, were starting to get out of hand. With a blizzard barreling down, I didn't think it was going to get any better in the next few days.

"You're doing what I say," Aunt Tillie shot back. "I'm the boss."

Mom looked as if she wanted to argue, but she was more diplomatic. "We need wood, Thistle." She was matter of fact. "We need to make sure that we can keep warm in case the power goes out."

"Why not just use our magic to make the power come back on?" my other cousin Clove asked. She was short, dark hair offsetting porcelain skin, and she looked even less thrilled than Thistle about going out in the cold. If that were even possible.

"Magic should be a last resort," Mom replied. "We can't use it as a crutch."

Aunt Tillie screwed up her face. "Don't listen to her. She's a lazy witch. We'll totally use our magic if the power goes out. I'm not going days without my shows."

"Yes, let's teach them that television is more important than common sense," Mom shot back.

"I'm glad you agree." Aunt Tillie was haughty as she turned back to us. "We're getting wood."

"We're not getting all the wood in the shed," Mom countered. "There's no way we'll need that much."

"I don't know," I replied. "Aunt Tillie told me just last week that wood was necessary for all the important things in life, including orgasms."

Mom's mouth dropped open. "You told her what?" she screeched.

Since my lone goal in uttering the words had been to get Aunt Tillie in trouble, I wasn't surprised when she extended a warning finger in my direction.

"You're on my list," she hissed.

I was expecting that too. "Can we just get this over with?" I asked. "The storm is almost here. If we're going to do this, let's do it before it gets bad."

"I don't think we should go outside," Clove argued. "I saw a documentary that showed pioneers were lost in blizzards all the time."

"You saw a documentary?" Thistle challenged dryly.

"I did," Clove confirmed solemnly.

"A documentary?" Thistle challenged.

"Fine!" Clove's eyes flashed with distaste. She was thirteen going on thirty, my mother said, and she—of all of us—had a flair for the dramatic. "It was an episode of *Little House on the Prairie*. What does it matter?"

I had to bite the inside of my cheek. She loved watching reruns of *Little House on the Prairie* on WGN when we came home from school.

"Was it the one where they got so much snow, they could walk on it from a second-story window?" Thistle demanded. "Because I've got news for you, that's not a real thing."

"It could be." Clove turned her sad gaze to my mother. "Tell her that could really happen."

Rather than acquiesce, Mom rolled her eyes. She could take only so much Clove. "Don't push things, Clove. We have enough to deal with as it is."

"I hate this family," Clove grumbled.

"I heard that Bigfoot does almost all of his errands during blizzards," Thistle offered. She was the picture of innocence—if you didn't know her—but there was a sly tilt to her head. "Maybe we'll luck out and run into him."

Clove's eyes widened. "I don't want to run into Bigfoot!"

The look Mom shot Thistle could've peeled paint. "Just get enough wood for three days. We'll be fine." She surprised me when she handed me a rope. "Tie this between the back door and the shed. Tie it tight. We need to be able to follow it from building to building in an emergency."

"So it *is* like *Little House on the Prairie*," I said. I wasn't prone to theatrics like Clove, but I found myself feeling uneasy. If my mother felt a rope was necessary, she expected trouble.

"It's going to be fine," Mom replied, almost as if reading my mind. "Don't work yourself up over nothing. As for you, Clove, suck it up. If Bigfoot is out there, he doesn't care about you. He'll be too interested in stocking up for the storm."

"What if he's lonely?" Clove pressed. "You know darned well he'll want to take me instead of the others. I'm a better talker, and I'm cuter."

"You're definitely on top of my list," Aunt Tillie grumbled.

"If we're bringing in wood, can we leave Clove when we come back?" Thistle asked.

Mom shot her a quelling look as Clove's lower lip—like clockwork—started to tremble. "No shenanigans," she snapped. "The storm is almost here. We need enough wood for three days. We also need some canned goods." She was all business now as she started rattling things off. "Grab a couple jars of tomatoes and vegetables. We stocked up on meat earlier and are handling the bread and everything else right now. Can you handle that?"

It took me a moment to realize that the question was directed at me. "Oh, um ... sure."

"What about our presents?" Clove asked. "Christmas is in a few days. What if it's still snowing and Santa can't find us."

"Oh, give me a break," Thistle intoned, throwing her hands in the air. "You're thirteen years old. How can you still believe in Santa?"

Clove's glare could've been convicted of murder on circumstantial evidence alone. "It never hurts to cover all your bases."

Clove wasn't an idiot—all evidence to the contrary—and there was no way she still believed Santa Claus existed. However, when she pretended to believe it, adults went out of their way to spoil her because they thought she was precious. She used that to her advantage--constantly.

"Nobody has time for this," I insisted as I tugged on my gloves. "Let's get the wood and get this over with."

"You're going to be popular in high school with that mentality," Thistle drawled.

This time I didn't have to think too hard about the double entendre. "You suck," I muttered as I glared at her.

She blew me a sarcastic kiss. "That will make me popular in high school too."

"That will be enough of *that*!" Mom exploded as she jabbed a finger in Thistle's face. "I knew letting you read those Stephen King books was a mistake. Your mouth has been out of control ever since."

"Stephen King?" Clove shook her head. "She found the VC Andrews stash and has been reading those."

"Yes, I've learned all about attic incest," Thistle confirmed. "I have questions. The biggest is: what sort of sick freak would just have those books lying around?"

"I believe those are your mother's books," Mom replied. "If they bother you so much, stop reading them."

"I didn't say I was bothered."

"Obviously you are if you can't stop talking about wood," Mom replied. She wasn't about to let Thistle embarrass her into silence. "Perhaps it's time we get out the book again."

I froze in place. Not *the book*.

"No." Thistle vehemently shook her head. "Nobody needs the book."

"Definitely not," I croaked.

"What book?" Aunt Tillie asked.

"It's a lovely book we found about five years ago," Mom explained. "It shows girls—with age-appropriate illustrations—how the changes in their bodies are normal. It also breaks sex down into basic terms so they can understand it."

Aunt Tillie blinked twice before speaking again. "In my day, we didn't use books."

"In your day, women got married at fourteen and cranked out kids and then died as ladies old and worn out before their time," Thistle fired back.

Aunt Tillie's mouth fell open. "Oh, you're on my list." She bobbed her head. "Just how old do you think I am?"

"We watch *Little House on the Prairie* to get perspective on your childhood, so take from that what you will," Thistle replied sweetly.

"This conversation has gone completely off the rails," Mom complained as she pinched the bridge of her nose.

"You shouldn't have brought up *the book*," I complained.

"It's still better than that book we found two years ago," Clove argued. "The one with the hairy people in all those weird sexual positions."

Ah, yes, *The Joy of Sex*. For some reason, my mother and both of my aunts all had copies. We'd found them when we'd been snooping for Christmas gifts two years ago. We were still traumatized. "Let's talk about something else," I blurted.

"Yes." Clove agreed. "Let's talk about the cake. I smell it from here. Can we have it tonight?"

"Sure," Mom replied automatically. She seemed to be dealing with the fact that we'd found her copy of *The Joy of Sex*.

"I want to know about this book you got for them," Aunt Tillie insisted. "What kind of book shows little girls the proper way to address sex? Is it a dirty book?"

"It's no VC Andrews," Thistle shot back.

"Hey, those were your mother's books," Aunt Tillie argued. "I didn't read them. I'm a nonfiction girl for reading and get all my sex information from television, like you're supposed to."

"I cannot believe we're having this conversation," Mom growled.

She wasn't the only one. "Can we focus on the wood?" I exploded.

"Speaking of perverts," Thistle drawled.

"Just get the stuff for the storm," Mom ordered, sweeping out her arm. "Don't forget to tie the rope."

"Whatever." Aunt Tillie rolled her eyes. "Let's go, girls." She prodded us toward the door. "We'll talk about the book later," she warned Mom.

"I can't wait."

"Have fun scavenging up your copies of *The Joy of Sex* so you can burn them," Aunt Tillie sang out.

"You gave them to us for our eighteenth birthdays!" Mom's tone was scalding.

"And I stand by it. I want to review the new dirty book. I don't want their little minds warped by anybody but me."

"Oh, whatever."

The air on the other side of the door was a bitter blast when it smacked me in the face, but I was grateful, because it allowed me to forget the conversation we'd been mired in for what felt like years. Perhaps, if we were stuck outside long enough, I would be able to forget everything that I'd been picturing.

"I'll handle the rope," I volunteered as I tied one end around the fence right by the door. "Then I'll come help with the wood."

Aunt Tillie nodded. "Tie the rope tight, Bay." She was serious now. Apparently, embarrassing the three of us and my mother wasn't enough to relax her. "When it's done, I'll reinforce it with magic just to be on the safe side."

I nodded. "Okay, I—" A shadow passed between us and the shed. It happened so fast I doubted my eyes, but Clove had been looking directly at the shadow, and her scream was earth-shattering.

"What was that?" I asked in a shaky voice.

Aunt Tillie was calm. She'd seen the shadow, but barely reacted. "Don't worry about it."

How could I not worry about a shadow running through the yard? "What was that?" I repeated.

"It was Bigfoot!" Clove screeched. "He's running errands and decided he needed company. I'm the best company in the house. Oh, I don't want to die." She threw her arm over her face in dramatic fashion.

"If you don't want to die, stop acting like a ninny," Thistle shot back. "You're in greater danger from me killing you than whatever that was." She sounded sure of herself. Mostly. There was worry in her eyes, though. "What was it?" she asked in a low voice.

"What did I just tell you?" Clove snapped. "It was Bigfoot!"

Aunt Tillie growled. "Your cousin is right. You're being a ninny. That definitely wasn't Bigfoot."

"Then what was it?" I demanded. My heart was threatening to pound out of my chest, and I wanted to run back into the house.

"It wasn't Bigfoot," Aunt Tillie assured me. "It was ... something else."

"What?" I had to know.

"Sometimes the snow brings forth different sorts of trouble," Aunt Tillie replied evenly. "One day, I'll tell you about it. We're perfectly safe. Trust me."

I wanted to trust her—and, honestly, I had no choice—so I nodded. "I'll handle the rope."

"We'll handle the wood and food," Aunt Tillie said. "Ten minutes." She lifted her face and stared at the sky. "That's all the time we have. The storm will be upon us."

And the thing in the storm, I wondered, would that be upon us too? I redoubled my efforts tying the rope. "Let's get through this. I want that cake."

"Yeah." Thistle nodded. Even she was done being a pain, some sort of miracle. "Let's finish this and get inside. Cake sounds good."

We worked as a team, moving fast. All the while I felt the shadow in the trees beyond the shed watching us. There was definitely something new in this storm.

I wasn't certain I wanted to know what it was.

1
ONE
PRESENT DAY

"Slave to Your Man, what's your twenty?"

Aunt Tillie's voice crackled through the radio my cousin Thistle held as we crouched behind the wide hedge that served as a fence of sorts in Mrs. Little's backyard. We were supposed to be flying under the radar, but the radio made that hard because Aunt Tillie was constantly shouting orders through it from somewhere on the other side of the house.

"Is that supposed to be me?" I demanded as I ran the call sign through my head. Aunt Tillie had demanded that we all have call signs—she said it was imperative so people couldn't recognize us if they recorded our radio chatter and arrested us after the fact—but I hadn't agreed to this call sign.

"Who else falls all over herself for her man?" Thistle demanded.

I narrowed my eyes. "I don't fall all over myself for a man. Besides, he's my husband, and it's Christmas. I delivered his dessert to him last night because he was tired from a long day at work. That hardly makes me his slave."

"It kind of sounds like you were his slave," Thistle argued. "I had to hear all about it when Aunt Tillie picked me up downtown after work this afternoon. She said she was embarrassed for you."

"Because I got Landon a slice of pie?"

Thistle shrugged. Her hair was bright red with white highlights this week, a nod to the Christmas holiday right around the corner. She kind of looked like a candy cane because she was the thinnest of us all and had almost no curves. I didn't point that out, however. I valued my life too much.

"I don't care if you got Landon a slice of pie," Thistle replied. "I'm too mature to get worked up over that sort of thing. Aunt Tillie feels differently."

"You're too mature, huh?" I was close to the edge, debating whether to jump. Ultimately, I went for it. "We're hiding behind hedges because our great-aunt decided that we're going on daily—or nightly—missions to torture her arch nemesis this Christmas season, but you're too mature to get worked up about a bad call sign?"

"I don't know what you want from me. I'm an adult. I can't be bothered with something so ridiculous."

I tackled her before I could think better of it and shoveled a pile of snow in her face as she sputtered and fought back.

"Don't!" Thistle slapped at my hand. "Stop it!"

Clove, who had been hunkering behind the hedges one row over, lifted her head. "Hey! You can't have fun without me," she whined. She'd only recently rejoined the antics after giving birth to her first child and taking it easy for several months. "I told you it wasn't fair that I was over here alone and you two were over there."

"Yes, this is so much fun," Thistle groused as she fought against me. "What did I say?" she demanded when I threw more snow in her face. "You have no idea where that snow has been," she sputtered.

"It's not yellow," Clove said philosophically. "You're fine."

"Even if it was yellow, you'd be fine," I added. "We turned all the snow in her yard yellow yesterday."

"Not *all* of it," Clove argued. "Just enough to spell out 'Margaret

Little is the tinkle stain of life' in the front yard, like Aunt Tillie wanted."

"Ah, yes." I rolled back on my haunches. "One of the sayings Aunt Tillie wants embroidered on pillows and delivered to all the businesses before Christmas."

"Too bad none of us can sew," Clove mused.

Thistle propped herself on her elbows and glared at me. "I can sew, but I refuse to waste my talents on pillows that are going to be thrown away after a few laughs."

"If that pillow magically appeared on your front porch as a Christmas gift, would you throw it away?" I challenged.

"Good point. I'll make some pillows for her."

I left her on the ground rather than help her up—she would take advantage of my soft heart—and moved back to the hedge to look for movement inside Mrs. Little's house. We'd been torturing her for days—it was our Christmas gift to Aunt Tillie—and she was riding a very fine line of sanity these days.

"Anything?" Thistle asked as she regained her footing.

I shook my head. "Not yet."

"I still don't understand why she's bringing all of Mrs. Little's Christmas decorations to life," Clove lamented. "That sounds fun."

"She got the idea when we needed an army to fight the lamias in Hawthorne Hollow last week," I replied. "She enchanted all the lawn gnomes in the area and essentially drafted them. They were a big hit ... and they sang."

"See, that sounds cute," Clove argued.

"It's terrifying when they're rushing at you with little knives and singing *Who Let the Dogs Out* while ripping you to pieces," Thistle replied. She, unlike Clove, had been present to witness some of the fight.

"That sounds less cute," Clove acknowledged.

"These lawn ornaments won't kill anyone," I assured her, my eyes going to the sky. Aunt Tillie insisted that revenge be doled out under the cover of darkness. All I could think of was that my husband was home, warm in our bed, and I wanted to be with him. We'd committed to a plan of chaos, though. Mrs. Little deserved it. I refused to be the first to bow out. "They're just going to run around town and terrorize Mrs. Little."

"How?" Clove looked dubious.

"For starters, they're going to sing Christmas carols," I replied. "Not the good ones. We're talking every ear worm known to man. They're going to follow her and sing until she loses her mind."

"It's sort of a genius plan," Thistle admitted. It was always hard for her to admit when Aunt Tillie came up with a good idea. The older she got, the more like Aunt Tillie she became, although I valued my life too much to ever say that to her face. "It's one of her better revenge schemes."

"It's pretty good," I agreed as I scanned the darkness for our great-aunt. She'd ordered us to specific positions and told us to wait until she was ready to launch her spell. "I kind of saw it coming when she cursed every lawn gnome in Hawthorne Hollow to go to war. She'll beat this prank into the ground."

"Compared to some of her other pranks, it's harmless," Thistle argued. "These are the sort of pranks we should be encouraging. These, the farting unicorns in Mrs. Little's store, and I was also a big fan when she enchanted every chair in town to fart whenever Mrs. Little sat down for three straight days."

I smiled at the memory. Mrs. Little had been mortified. "That was a fun one, although I'm a little worried that so many of Aunt Tillie's pranks involve farts. I mean ... isn't she a little old to be laughing at fart sounds?"

Thistle shrugged. "There are worse things."

"Seriously," I muttered as I scanned the yard for her yet again. "Where is she?"

"She's close," Clove replied. "I feel her in my bones."

"Oh, geez," Thistle said. "Is this like when you decided that you had a trick knee and could predict the weather because you read about it in a book?"

"I still maintain that I'm right about the weather fifty percent of the time," Clove shot back.

"So are the weather forecasters."

"See." Clove preened. "I could do it professionally."

I made a face that she couldn't see because of the darkness. Maybe Thistle wasn't the one most like Aunt Tillie after all.

"That jail warden was in the bakery when the fart spell started," Thistle said. "He saw the whole thing."

Brad Childs, the former warden of the Antrim Correctional Facility, had been hanging around Hemlock Cove a lot the last two weeks, ever since he'd lost his job after a magical prison escape that left the community reeling. I'd been instrumental in helping to find all the prisoners. Childs had been suspicious ever since. Not that I could blame him. The fact that I single-handedly found more escaped prisoners than the other law enforcement groups combined was bound to draw attention. Because Childs had lost his job, his attention felt somewhat nefarious.

"Did he say anything?"

"He laughed with everybody else," Thistle replied. "Then he asked some pointed questions of the regulars. But he didn't ask me."

"He knows who you are." I had no doubt that Childs had done his homework regarding my family. "He will have researched my immediate family because he's suspicious about how I pulled it off."

"You didn't have a choice," Clove said. The prisoners were dangerous. You couldn't let them wander around hurting people."

"We kept bringing in the prisoners. Just our little group," I said. "We pretended it was Landon and Chief Terry doing all the work, but he didn't believe us."

"Do you blame him?" Thistle was serious. "The stories have been flying fast and furious about our family for years. Not just in Hemlock Cove either. I'm sure the second he started asking questions people were more than happy to provide some surprising answers."

"There's nothing I can do about it." I held out my glove-covered hands. "He's going to ask questions. He lost his job, and the explanation for how those prisoners escaped wasn't satisfactory. It's not as if we could explain about the Happy Holidays Players and how they were involved."

"They're still under memory spells?" Thistle asked.

I nodded. The acting troupe hadn't been far from my mind. "If all goes as planned, they'll always be under memory spells. It was the easiest way to handle the problem and not drop a bunch of bodies."

"Then we'll just have to wait it out." Thistle was surprisingly pragmatic when necessary. "He'll give up eventually. Even if he does manage to assign blame for some magical pranks to our family, that's a far cry from masterminding a prison break."

"To be fair, I'm not sure he thinks I masterminded the prison break," I said. "It's more that he needs something to focus on now that his career path has been upended. He thought he was going to retire from that job and have a nice pension to fall back on."

"Technically, the prison break wasn't his fault," Clove argued. "I feel sorry for him. He didn't really deserve to lose his job."

"Didn't he?" I'd gone back and forth on the subject for weeks. "He had lax rules in place that allowed the prisoners and the Happy Holidays Players to plot the breakout. If he hadn't been falling down on the job, that wouldn't have happened. One of his guards facilitated the escape, and that took months of grooming. Nobody ever said a word about it, even though they knew the guard was having sex with an inmate. They stood back and did nothing."

"Yeah, that was weird," Clove agreed. "Still, it's not as if he was the bad guy."

"He was lazy," I said. "I wish I could've saved his job for him, but that wasn't an option. There's nothing I can do to help him."

"I'm not worried about you helping him," Thistle said. "I'm worried about him hurting you."

There was nothing I could do about that either. I opened my mouth to say just that, but my attention was drawn to the yard as the Christmas lights Mrs. Little had turned off before bed flared to life ... and the Christmas lawn ornaments started swaying.

"Here we go," I muttered. I had no idea why Aunt Tillie had insisted we accompany her. She hadn't needed our magic. Still, with the reds, blues, greens, and yellows illuminating the yard, there was something magical about the moment.

Then the lawn ornaments started to sing.

"Dashing through the snow, in a one-horse open sleigh, O'er the fields we go, laughing all the way."

"Ha, ha, ha!" Multiple lawn ornaments joined in and bellowed at the house.

"Ah, and she started with a classic," Thistle mused as she popped up her head to take a look at the huge inflatable Santa dancing in front of Mrs. Little's house. Aunt Tillie had managed to turn him so he faced the house ... and he seemed to have pretty good rhythm with his hips.

"Bells on bobtails ring, making spirits bright, what fun it is to ride and sing, a sleighing song tonight."

At least ten voices joined in for the chorus, singing loud enough to make me pull my shoulders up around my ears. I was amused, and even a little surprised, at the fortitude with which the ornaments were singing.

"That's kind of nice," Clove argued. "It's not even a bad prank."

That's when Aunt Tillie appeared behind the hedge with her. "Yeah, say that again at three o'clock," she suggested. "They'll still be singing then. I cursed them to stick to seven songs—all in the public domain, so I don't steal anybody's intellectual property. She'll want to deafen herself with Q-tips by dawn."

It was diabolical really. Aunt Tillie had come up with more ingenious plans, but this one was guaranteed to drive Mrs. Little bonkers without causing property damage or risking exposure for us. It really was a Christmas gift for everybody concerned.

"Should we leave now?" I asked Aunt Tillie. I wasn't sure of protocol, but it was getting late, and I needed my beauty rest.

"Not quite yet." Aunt Tillie raised a finger to keep us in our places. Then, like clockwork, the front door to Mrs. Little's house burst open, and she appeared in the doorway.

Margaret Little was old school. She still wore housecoats and wrapped her hair in those old-fashioned curlers every night. While most women of a certain age had outgrown the Golden Girls House of Style, Mrs. Little embraced it, complete with head wrap over the curlers.

She was furious, but the string of curses she let loose could be heard over the singing lawn ornaments.

"Tillie!" she bellowed.

The look of triumph on Aunt Tillie's face would be emblazoned in my mind forever. She was thrilled with how things had turned out. To be truthful, so was I. This was only the beginning, though, I realized. Aunt Tillie was nowhere near done with Margaret Little. This was just the start of a very merry Christmas.

"Just one more second." Aunt Tillie waited for Jingle Bells to die down. Then, to my utter horror, the lawn gnomes launched into the same refrain, the lyrics ten times dirtier.

"Oh, you included the filthy Batman Jingle Bells?" I asked.

Aunt Tillie shrugged. "That one should only happen out here, not downtown. I don't want to traumatize any parents if their kids start spouting it."

"Are you ready to go home?" I asked. I wanted my warm bed more than anything. I also wanted to think about the Brad Childs conundrum. I couldn't do that when tinsel reindeer were kicking up their heels and singing about Robin laying eggs.

"Sure." Aunt Tillie beamed at me. "The spell is just starting to ramp up. It will be even better tomorrow."

2
TWO

Thistle and Clove left for their homes from The Overlook's parking lot. We'd grown up in the old family living quarters of what was now the most popular inn in town. Clove had moved to the Dandridge, the lighthouse on the far side of town, and Thistle lived in a converted barn with her boyfriend, Marcus. I lived in the guesthouse with my husband, Landon Michaels. We had privacy—of a sort—and access to home-cooked meals twice a day. The tradeoff was worth it, especially if you asked Landon.

I remained in the parking lot until I was certain Aunt Tillie was safely inside the inn. Then I drove to the guesthouse. Earlier, Landon had been watching hockey as I dressed in all black, complete with a ski mask. He lifted the mask and turned it into a hat before giving me a kiss. He didn't seem bothered in the least that I was about to go out and break the law.

"Don't get arrested," he warned before handing me my gloves. "Don't wake me when you get back. You know how I am if I don't get a full eight hours."

"Yes, you're a big baby," I'd replied.

"I'm your big baby." He gave me another kiss and then flopped on the couch. "See you tomorrow morning, sweetie." With that, he turned his attention to the hockey game on the television, unleashing me on the world with my great-aunt and cousins. How far we'd come that he didn't insist on accompanying us, and then lambasting us for breaking the law the entire trip.

I killed the engine of my car and slipped into the guesthouse. Landon had left the front porch light on, and I killed it once the door was shut. I padded into the bedroom and stripped at the end of the bed—leaving my clothes in a big heap to be dealt with the following day—and crawled under the covers.

Even in sleep, Landon knew I'd joined him. He tugged me close, his snoring never breaking, and I passed out with him as our hearts fell into sync.

When I woke, Landon was already awake and alert. He grinned when I reached up to rub my eyes. "How was your terrorist mission last night?"

"You smell like happiness," I murmured as I cuddled closer to him.

"Happiness?" Landon's hand moved over my back. "Does that mean I smell like you? Because you're my happiness."

"Cute," I teased. "Right now, happiness smells like chocolate and marshmallows."

He stiffened. "How did you know?"

"Know what?"

"That I ate a marshmallow candy. I was very quiet taking it out of the nightstand."

My eyes popped open. "You keep candy in the nightstand?"

"Maybe." When I tried to reach around him to check, he stopped me. "That's my candy."

"You just told me I'm your happiness," I argued. "Don't I get some of your candy?"

"Oh, you're cute." He kissed the tip of my nose. "And no. That's my candy."

"I'm wounded," I complained. "I thought I was the thing you loved most."

"Baby, I would die for you. That doesn't mean I'm sharing my candy."

"Ugh. You're the worst."

He kissed me again. "Did something go wrong with your terrorist attack on Margaret Little last night?" He was aware that I'd been going out with Aunt Tillie to wreak havoc every night this week. He'd been careful not to request details.

"Actually, it was fine."

"Then why do you need my candy so early in the morning?"

"Why do you need candy?" I challenged.

"Because my greatest joy in life is watching you sleep while eating candy."

The fact that he could say that with a straight face was unbelievable. "I kind of want to hurt you sometimes," I groused.

"I know." He kissed me again and then flopped on his back. "You slept late. Breakfast is in twenty-five minutes. As much as I would like to spend the morning cuddling with you, I need my bacon."

He was unbelievable. "You said we would always be gooey and in love," I complained as I rolled away from him. "You said it the day we married, which wasn't all that long ago."

"We are gooey and in love," he replied as he followed me toward the bathroom. "We're taking the gooeyness to the inn so we can be in love over eggs, hash browns, bacon, and toast."

I cast him a dubious look over my shoulder. "If you had to choose between loving me and losing your sense of taste, which way would you go?"

"I'll always choose you, Bay." He was sincere. "But if I lose my sense of taste, you might decide you don't want to be with me because I'll be a monster."

"I could use some breakfast," I admitted. "You burn a lot of fuel trying to keep warm while waiting for Aunt Tillie to spring a trap. I guess I can be gooey with bacon."

"You are the perfect woman for a reason," he said.

"Let's hurry up. Now I want breakfast."

"Your wish is my command."

WE DROVE TO THE INN INSTEAD OF WALKING BECAUSE the weather had turned bitterly cold. We used the front door rather than entering through the family living quarters, and therefore, it was easier to sneak up on my family. This morning, unless we'd brought a bomb with us, they wouldn't have noticed our arrival. They were too busy yelling at one another.

"I don't know why you're blaming this on me," Aunt Tillie screeched. "You have no proof this is my fault."

"Excuse me?" Mom boomed. "Are you seriously going to sit there and claim that someone else magically caused all of Margaret Little's Christmas decorations to get up and walk away?"

I darted a look to Landon to gauge his response. He'd tried to keep from learning the details about our nightly excursions.

"Seriously?" he asked. "You stole her Christmas decorations?" He made a tsking sound. "That's kind of disappointing, Bay."

"Hey, it wasn't my idea!"

"And the decorations weren't stolen," Mom offered. "They were enchanted to sing a few songs and then got up and walked away under their own power."

"I didn't know you were going to enchant them to wander away," I said to Aunt Tillie.

"Yeah, I didn't realize I did that," Aunt Tillie absently scratched her cheek. Then she realized Mom was still staring at her. "Not that I did it. You can't go around accusing people of things they didn't do, Winnie." She used her most imperious voice. "That is slander, and I'll sue if you continue."

Mom wasn't having any of it. "Why don't you sue me and see what happens?" She shot Chief Terry a significant look. They'd been dating for months now. Heck, as far as I could tell, they were basically living together.

"It's not my fault you two play fuzzy handcuff games, and he's forgotten how to be impartial," Aunt Tillie fired back. "I'll sue."

Chief Terry remained calm as he sat at the table and sipped his coffee. He used to get agitated during these morning scenes. Now he let them wash over him like waves over beached seashells. "There is no law that says Winnie can't accuse you of something you clearly did."

Aunt Tillie shot him a look that promised retribution. "Do you want me to make her smell like oysters?" she demanded.

Chief Terry grimaced. "Why would you do a horrible thing like that? I hate oysters."

"I believe that's why she's threatening it," Landon replied as he pulled out my chair for me. He waited for me to sit before settling next to me. "Coffee or juice?" he asked.

"Both," I replied.

He poured coffee for both of us, and I handled the juice. I wanted tomato, but he was an orange juice drinker. Mom and Aunt Tillie were still going at one another.

"Prove that I did it," Aunt Tillie insisted when Mom folded her arms across her chest.

Mom angled her head toward me. "Were you out with Aunt Tillie last night?"

There was no way I was answering that. "Landon smells like happiness in the morning because he keeps candy in the nightstand, but he won't share with me," I announced.

"Why would you be that mean to her?" Chief Terry demanded.

Landon's eyes were narrow slits when they landed on me. "That was cruel, baby." He turned to Mom. "She did indeed sneak out of bed last night. I thought maybe she was up to no good with another man. I had no idea she was breaking the law. Like you, I am horrified."

"You're sleeping on the couch tonight," I blurted.

"Please." Landon didn't look bothered in the least. "We both know you need someone to put those ice-cold feet of yours on. I'm your only option, so you're not kicking me out of bed. Besides, I'm the one with the candy."

"Candy you won't share."

"I might if you're nice to me." His smile was playful.

I turned my full attention to my mother. "You're getting worked up over nothing. The caroling lawn ornaments were a delight."

"That's not what Margaret said," Chief Terry replied. "She's called three times since midnight."

"You should learn to turn off your phone," I suggested.

"I'm the chief of police."

"Then just block Mrs. Little," I countered. "Send her straight to voicemail."

"Or you could stop torturing her," Mom argued. "You've been going at her for more than a week straight. Don't you think that's enough?"

As far as I was concerned, given all the things Mrs. Little had done to us the last year, it would never be enough. "No."

"Bay, she's a sad old woman who hates us because she's afraid and envious of what we can do," Mom started.

"Her actions could have killed any one of us more than once," I shot back. "We're not done."

Mom opened her mouth to argue further, but there must have been something about the tilt of my head that made her rethink her strategy. "Fine." She held up her hands in supplication. "Do whatever you want, Bay."

"That's the plan," I agreed.

"Just stop stealing her lawn decorations."

"We didn't steal them," I snapped. "They were there when we left." I turned to Aunt Tillie. "Where did they go?"

"How should I know?" Aunt Tillie asked. "I'm innocent in all of this. In fact, this is the first I'm hearing about it." She clucked her tongue. "Really, Bay, she's an old woman. I can't believe you're getting your jollies messing with her like that. It's so wrong."

"You are the worst," I muttered.

"You should punish her," Landon told Aunt Tillie. "A week of smelling like bacon could be just what the doctor ordered."

"Maybe I'll make her smell like something else instead. How would you like that?"

"If you want me looking the other way when my wife sneaks out of bed every night during the run-up to Christmas, it must be bacon," he fired back.

Aunt Tillie pursed her lips. "I'll consider it."

Landon leaned closer to her. "If she were to taste like bacon—you know, for kisses and stuff—I'd look the other way into next year."

Aunt Tillie's eyes gleamed with interest. "I believe we can come to an agreement."

"No, you can't," Chief Terry boomed. I felt bad for him to a certain extent. The problem was easily fixable, however, so my sympathy extended only so far. "You're done," he insisted.

"Fine, we're done," I said automatically.

Chief Terry's eyebrows moved toward one another. "Are you lying to me?"

"Are you forcing me into a position to lie to you?" I countered.

"My little sweetheart is not supposed to lie to me."

I felt guilty again, but not guilty enough to stop. "Let's talk about something else," I suggested. "Thistle said Brad Childs has been hanging around downtown. Is there a way we can force him out of town?"

Several expressions washed over Chief Terry's face before he got control of his emotions. "He's here because of you, Bay. He's convinced you did something magical to capture all of those prisoners."

"I *did* do something magical."

"Which is why we're in this predicament." He held up a hand to stop me from jumping in. "You did what you had to do, Bay. I'd never say otherwise. My problem is that we are now at the mercy of a man who thinks he's lost everything and that perhaps you're the only possibility to get it back."

"How can I possibly help him?" I demanded.

"I don't know. Heck, he doesn't know. He's grasping at straws. We have to ride it out."

That was easier said than done. "What do you suggest we do?" I asked.

"I suggest no more shenanigans against Margaret Little."

"Suggest something else," I ordered.

"Bay, you're making me tired," Chief Terry said. That might've been enough to get me to stop—he had a way of wearing me down nobody else could claim—but his phone alerted with an incoming call. "We're not done," he warned me before answering. I could tell the call was serious, because he hopped to his feet and headed out of the room.

"Breakfast," Landon said. "We need it now. We'll have to head out soon."

"Fine." Mom headed into the kitchen to get Marnie and Twila so we could eat. She returned with the food before Chief Terry did with his phone, so Landon was elbow deep in eggs and bacon before Chief Terry delivered the bad news.

"They found a body at Stonecrest Academy," he announced.

I paused with a slice of bacon halfway to my mouth.

"What's Stonecrest Academy?" Marnie asked between bites.

"The private school between Hemlock Cove and Shadow Hills," I replied. "It's on the old Catholic school campus."

Chief Terry nodded. "It's for children with behavioral issues."

Now it was my turn to make a face. "I thought it was for girls who couldn't be controlled by their parents."

"I believe that's what I said."

"Stonecrest is for girls who have gotten pregnant, or whose parents are worried they're going to get pregnant," I argued. "The kids at the high school are threatened with it all the time. They told me when I was interviewing them for the fall edition of the school newspaper. That's how the parents are trying to keep them from having sex these days."

Chief Terry scalded me with a look. "Minors should not be having sex."

"Give me a break. Kids shouldn't be having sex," I argued. "Older teenagers always have sex. What do you think we were doing out in the fields when we were partying as teenagers?"

"I won't listen to that story again," Chief Terry warned. "It doesn't matter what the school is. What matters is that someone is dead."

"A student?" Landon asked before shoveling more eggs into his mouth, determined to get his breakfast in before heading out.

"I'm not sure," Chief Terry replied. "Nobody's going near the body until I get there. You're coming with me."

It wasn't a question, so Landon nodded. He was an FBI agent with a lot of leeway. He could pretty much pick his own cases.

"Of course you're coming with me," Chief Terry said on a sneer. "I was talking to Bay. I want you to talk to the girls if necessary. You'll be a friendlier face."

"I'll gladly go with you," I said. "Just as long as you stop harassing us about Mrs. Little. We won't stop."

Chief Terry, exasperated, sighed heavily. "We'll have that conversation later."

"Fine, but I'm serious. She has it coming."

"As I said, we'll talk about it later." Chief Terry sat. "We have ten minutes to eat, and then we're out of here."

3
THREE

Mom filled insulated cups with coffee for the three of us and caught me at the front door to give them to Landon and Chief Terry, who were already warming up the truck.

"You really need to stop encouraging Aunt Tillie," she said in a grave voice. "It's a bad idea to get her going like this. It only feeds her ego."

That very well might have been true, but I didn't care. "Mrs. Little has it coming," I insisted.

"That's neither here nor there. That warden in town changes things. Do you want to risk exposure?"

Two years ago, that would have been the worst thing in the world. Not any longer. "It's a town full of witches, Mom. We're supposed to do magical things."

"We're supposed to be humans pretending to be witches. There's a difference."

"People want to believe," I countered. "It's fine. If he wants to expose us, I guess that's his right. I'm not backing down."

Mom studied my face. There was surprise, maybe even a bit of awe. "Most of the time I'd say that an inflated ego was a bad thing," she noted. "In your case, it's good. I'm glad you're feeling full of yourself of late."

There was a "but" in there somewhere, so I waited.

"But you need to make sure you don't cross the sort of line that can't be uncrossed," she continued. "We need balance, Bay. We don't need you turning into Tillie Jr. and terrorizing the county because you're bored."

"I guarantee that will never be me," I promised as I took the drink carrier. "But I'm not backing down on this. Mrs. Little needs to be put in her place."

Mom's forehead filled with lines. "What does that mean? What's her place?"

"She needs to mind her own business and stop trying to hurt our family. If she had carried on just running her mouth, I wouldn't have liked it, but I would've lived with it. But she crossed the line when she tried to physically hurt us. I'm going to make sure she doesn't get another chance."

Mom sighed. "I have to take Aunt Tillie to Traverse City today. Her plow truck needs a tune-up so we're hitting the mall over there while we wait. Do you need anything to finish your Christmas shopping?"

It was a weird transition, but it made me grin. My mother was good at picking her battles. "I'm good for now," I replied. "Everything I have left to get for Landon is a local pickup, I'm done with everyone else. I do need to get some wrapping time in. I have everything shoved in a closet at the guesthouse. I enchanted it so Landon can't open it, but he won't fall for the 'It's jammed' excuse much longer."

"I'm sure he'll live." Mom patted my shoulder. Her face was still lined with tension, but she'd decided to let the Mrs. Little conversation go for now. "Where do you think he's hidden your Christmas gifts?"

"The police station," I replied without hesitation. "In Chief

Terry's office. I tried to go in there the other day, and they both acted weird. I'm sure your gifts are in there too."

"Okay, well, maybe we'll stop by Terry's office on our way out of town. We know he'll be at a scene with you, so it's perfect timing."

I was caught off guard. "You're going to invade his office?"

"I need to make sure that I get him more gifts than he got me." Mom suddenly looked angelic. All she was missing was a halo. "It's about balance in a relationship."

"Uh-huh." I didn't believe her for a second. "You'd better hope his nosy receptionist doesn't tattle on you. He'll be mad."

"You let me worry about her. You should get going. If one of those students at Stonecrest is dead..." She trailed off, looking troubled.

"Thanks for the coffee. Don't worry about Aunt Tillie's vendetta against Mrs. Little. We're making her keep her shenanigans within reason."

"Never once has Aunt Tillie kept her shenanigans within reason," Mom argued.

"There's a first time for everything."

IT TOOK TWENTY MINUTES TO GET TO the school. It was located on the opposite side of town, and even though Hemlock Cove didn't have a rush hour, early mornings were still busy in a one-stoplight town.

"If anybody asks, you were already with us, and we didn't have time to take you back to town," Chief Terry said to me as he pulled into the school parking lot. "We don't need word getting back to Childs that we regularly take you on cases."

I had some bad news for him. There was no way Childs didn't already know that. Adding to the trouble we were already facing was a mistake, however. "I'll try to refrain from telling everybody here that I'm a witch and you like cheating with my magic when it comes to doing your job," I supplied cheekily.

Chief Terry pinned me with a death glare. "When did you turn into Tillie? What happened to my little sweetheart?"

"A djinn tried to kill me, and I'm still mad. That's what happened to your little sweetheart."

He sighed. "I get that Margaret made a mistake, but you need to let it go."

Yeah, that wasn't going to happen. "Let's see what they've got," I suggested as I clutched my half-finished coffee.

Landon and Chief Terry walked shoulder to shoulder to the area that had been taped off by one of Terry's officers. Duncan Marks had been two years behind me in high school. He'd recently transferred from Hawthorne Hollow.

"Chief," Duncan said with a curt head bob that had me biting back a smile. "Agent Michaels." He was less effusive when greeting my husband. "Bay." His smile was wide when he aimed it at me. He'd always had a crush on me. I would've found his reaction irritating if I didn't know that it bothered Landon. One look at my husband told me that I could put up with it for a bit longer because it was worth the laughs.

"What do you have?" Chief Terry asked before Landon could respond.

"The deceased is Enid Walters," Duncan replied, turning to business. "She's the headmistress of the school, which opened about two years ago."

That wasn't right. "This school has been in operation longer than that. I did some research when I moved back to town. I guess it would've been about a year after I returned. It was in operation then and has been for some time."

"Different ownership," Duncan replied. "I asked the secretary. She identified the body for me. She's keeping the students away from the area."

"Wouldn't we have heard if the school changed ownership?" Chief Terry asked.

Duncan held out his hands. "All I know is what the secretary told me. The school used to be for troubled girls. It still is, to some extent, but it's no longer the sort of school where parents hide pregnant girls."

That was both a relief and a concern. "I can't believe that was still happening in this century," I muttered.

"I can see it," Chief Terry argued. "Teenage pregnancy is an epidemic in small towns. When students see other students proudly showing off what they've done, it exacerbates the problem."

What they've done? Was he kidding? "I'm disappointed you said that," I shot back. Now I didn't feel so bad knowing that my mother was likely going through his office hunting for Christmas presents. "I agree that teenage pregnancy is an epidemic in this area, but forcing girls to go to another school and wear their pregnancy like a scarlet letter is crap. The boys should have some culpability if that's how you're going to handle things. Instead, they get off without any repercussions. It's always the girls that have to carry the stigma."

"Oh, here we go," Chief Terry muttered. "I'm all for equality, young lady, but you can't pretend that this isn't a problem."

"Of course it's a problem," I shot back. "It's a small-town thing. Bored teens have nothing to do but drink and fornicate in a field. There are even fewer jobs for teens because adults are taking the jobs they used to get. Then there's a lack of sex education taught at home *and* at school.

"A school designed to augment the shame you believe they should feel doesn't solve anything," I continued. "Frankly, I'm disappointed in you. Would you have been a proponent of sending me to this school if I'd gotten pregnant in high school?"

Chief Terry's eyes widened. When he looked at Landon, there was terror on his face.

"Don't look at me," Landon admonished.

"I don't even understand how this happened," Chief Terry complained. "I'm done talking about this." He focused on the body. "You said she's the headmistress?"

I glared at his back a second longer, then joined him. The argument could be picked up later. The headmistress was tall, willowy, and had long dark hair starting to streak through with gray. I put her age at roughly fifty. She was still pretty, and her dark eyes were wide and unseeing.

"I think she's been here overnight," Landon said as he pulled on a pair of latex gloves. "She's wearing nylons. There's a run on the calf."

"That's probably from a bush," I volunteered. "Those are old-school nylons that my mother used to wear. They're designed to last three wears or so. Then they're trashed. One snag and they're done."

"Does your mom still wear nylons?" Landon asked.

"I don't know anyone under the age of sixty who still wears nylons."

"Well, Enid did," Chief Terry noted. The sound of high heels on asphalt drew his attention to the parking lot. A smartly dressed brunette was heading in our direction. She wore a pastel suit that came straight from Sears thirty years ago.

"That's the secretary," Duncan volunteered. "Bianca Golden."

The name wasn't familiar, but there was something about the face I swore I recognized. Rather than introduce myself, I hung back. This was Chief Terry's show.

"Bianca Golden?" he asked when the secretary arrived. He extended his hand. "Terry Davenport. I'm the chief of police."

Bianca nodded as if he'd told her a fact she already knew. "I'm well aware of who you are. I went to school in Hawthorne Hollow. I was on the cheerleading squad and saw you at games."

That's where I knew her from. She'd competed in cheer competitions against Clove. They hadn't been friendly rivals.

As if sensing my gaze, Bianca turned her attention to me. "How is your cousin?" she asked. There was a predatory smile on her face that she shuttered quickly.

"She's fine," I replied. "She's a mother now. She's married. She lives in a lighthouse." Why I felt the need to tack on the last part was beyond me. I loved the Dandridge. It only occurred to me after the information had escaped my mouth that perhaps not everybody would think it was a cool place to live.

"That sounds nice," Bianca replied.

"Do you live here?" I asked.

Bianca's forehead creased. "Oh, no. I live in Hawthorne Hollow still and commute. There's a night dormitory monitor who stays on the property, but she's the only adult who lives here. I can get you a list of all the employees if you need it," she said to Chief Terry.

"That will be helpful," he confirmed. "When was the last time anybody saw Mrs. Walters?"

"Ms.," Bianca corrected, as if by habit. "She wasn't married. I guess it was yesterday afternoon, at the end of the day. She would've walked out here to leave." She pointed to a nondescript SUV about four slots down. "That's her vehicle."

Chief Terry looked at the Ford Bronco and motioned for Duncan to go to it. "Would she have been the last to leave?"

"There's security," Bianca replied. "It's a service. They drive around the property once every two hours. They also respond if someone calls from one of the campus phones."

"Someone obviously called," Landon said as he ran his hands over the dead woman's throat. Perhaps Enid had a heart attack, a stroke, or had fallen and frozen to death.

"I called," Bianca replied. "I was the first one here this morning. It's the last day for office staff before the Christmas break. I had a lot of work to get through before my holiday vacation."

"Did you see her or her vehicle?" Landon asked.

"Her vehicle first. I was confused and checked it out. I looked through the window of the Bronco and then scanned the lot. That's when I saw her leg." Bianca swallowed hard. "I found her like this."

"Did you try to render aid?" Chief Terry asked.

"That was my first inclination, but I didn't touch her," Bianca explained. "It was obvious she was dead. There was frost on her body, as you see."

Chief Terry glanced back at the body before continuing his questioning. "Tell me about the students." He shot me a warning look—as if I was going to get on my soapbox and preach in front of Bianca. "How many students live on campus?"

"Thirty," Bianca replied. "They live in the dormitory there." She pointed to a pretty building that looked a bit dated. "Two girls to a room. There's also the dorm mother I mentioned.

"We also have a cook," she continued. "It's actually sisters who run a company. They serve three meals a day but don't live on the property. I believe they live in Shadow Hills."

Chief Terry nodded. "I'll need their contact information, too. Anybody else?"

"We contract a company for janitorial services. We usually have one person from their team of six who comes daily to clean the common areas of the dorm and the three classrooms."

"Six people switch off on those duties?" Landon pressed.

Bianca nodded. "The girls are responsible for cleaning their own dorm rooms."

"What about the students?" I asked. "Would any of them have a reason to want to kill the headmistress?"

Bianca looked appalled. "Of course not! They're troubled, not murderous."

"We still have to talk to them," Landon insisted. "We won't know exactly what we're dealing with until the medical examiner conducts an autopsy. It's possible this was a murder."

"It could have been an accident, the result of a fall, or natural causes," Bianca pointed out.

"It could," Landon agreed. "We still need to interview the students. It would be best if we got started on that right away, so if you need to secure permission from the parents, now's the time."

"That won't be necessary," Bianca replied stiffly. "We have the power to authorize interviews with the girls. The parents sign over that right when they enroll their daughters."

This school seemed weird, but I kept my opinion to myself.

"Then we would like to talk to them," Chief Terry pressed. "Maybe in that common room you mentioned."

"I'll make the arrangements," Bianca huffed. She turned on her heel and stalked away. "We'll be ready in thirty minutes. Here at Stonecrest, we pride ourselves on our punctuality."

"Thank you for your cooperation," Landon called to her back. His eyes were wide when they locked with mine. "She seems fun."

"I don't know her well," I said. "She was in cheer competitions against Clove. I remember her being a little high strung."

"That goes without saying," Chief Terry said. "That might be to our advantage." His eyes went back to Enid. "There's no obvious cause of death. It could've been natural causes."

"It doesn't feel like natural causes," I countered.

"It really doesn't."

4
FOUR

The medical examiner was in a bad mood because he'd been forced into the cold so early, but he promised to get a jump on Enid's autopsy.

"People wait to die or kill until after the holidays now," he explained as his staff loaded the body into the van. "It's sort of a lull."

"Lucky for us," I said.

Duncan closed in once he left. "I searched the Bronco," he said. "Nothing out of the ordinary. It was almost too clean. Most people I know don't keep their vehicles that clean."

"I've always thought that was a sign of a psychopath," I said.

"That's because your car is almost always dirty," Landon interjected. He was watching Duncan. "Why do you think we always take my vehicle? That's us—together," he said pointedly to Duncan. "You know, when we leave the house we share because we're married."

I shot him a dirty look, but it was impossible to miss the way Chief Terry ducked his head to hide his smile. Duncan, he was oblivious.

"I keep a messy vehicle too," he said to me.

Landon cleared his throat. "We should start interviewing the students."

"I can take Ms. Winchester home," Duncan offered. "She's probably bored and wants to head back to town."

"She's not bored," Landon countered. "And it's Winchester-Michaels."

He was making that up. I'd considered taking his last name when married, but he ultimately decided it was a bad idea. How we would name our children was still up in the air—and hopefully a decision far down the road—but my last name remained the same. Winchester elicited fear in our enemies. Landon wanted to leverage that fear.

"Really?" I drawled, arching an eyebrow.

Landon jabbed a finger in my direction while holding Duncan's gaze.

Duncan managed to maintain the stare-off for an impressive—and awkward—fifteen seconds. Then he lowered his gaze. "I guess I'll head back to town."

"Great," Chief Terry said. "Make sure you check the festival."

"Yes, especially the kissing booth," Landon agreed. "My wife and I have a date there later. You know ... my wife." He pointed at me yet again for good measure.

"Oh, geez," I muttered as I turned away from him. "Can you not be a pain?" I complained as Duncan trudged off dejectedly.

"Not when a guy is hitting on my witch," Landon replied.

"He wasn't hitting on me."

"He was flirting with you."

"He's had a crush on me since we were kids. It's not a big deal."

"He *has* always had a crush on her," Chief Terry confirmed. "He should've been focused on Thistle because they were the same age, but he much preferred Bay."

"That's probably because Thistle made his balls want to crawl back up inside of him and hide," Landon replied.

"Oh, gross." I elbowed his stomach, causing him to laugh. "You don't have to be weird. Duncan is harmless."

"He is," Chief Terry agreed. "You're being an ass."

"Fine." Landon's eyes flashed. "Let's head to the dorm. I want to get these interviews over as soon as possible. I'm guessing 'troubled teenage girls' won't be founts of useful information."

I hadn't considered that. "We're going to be dealing with a lot of attitude."

"Maybe that attitude is what killed their headmistress," Chief Terry said.

AS PROMISED, BIANCA HAD SET UP AN INTERVIEW station in the common room. She seemed surprised to see me with Landon and Chief Terry, but she pointed at two couches facing each other.

"I thought it might be more effective to interview the girls two at a time," she said. "They're likely to clam up if they don't have a peer sitting next to them. We can pick the two randomly."

Chief Terry darted a look toward Landon.

"That should be fine," Landon said. "Thank you."

Bianca practically purred as she sidled closer to him. "Don't mention it."

I glared at her back as she disappeared, and planted my hands on my hips to face Landon. "Why is it okay for women to flirt with you but not okay for anybody to flirt with me?" I demanded.

"My ego is more fragile than yours," he replied. "You're the smartest woman in the world. You know I could never love anybody but you, so it's a waste of time to be jealous of someone else."

He was obviously shining me on. "And you don't know the same thing about me?" I challenged.

"It's not about you with me, it's about my fragile ego," he replied. "You're stronger than I am, Bay."

He was full of it. "There will be no kissing until we come to a meeting of the minds on this," I warned as I heard the approaching footsteps on the marble floor.

Landon was all smiles as Bianca led two girls who looked about sixteen into the room. Both wore bland uniforms—skirts that covered their knees, white shirts, plaid ties—and their hair was pulled back in simple ponytails.

"This is Layla Dombrowski and Penelope Carter," Bianca volunteered. "Layla originates from Flint, and Penelope grew up in Hawthorne Hollow."

"It's nice to meet you, girls." Chief Terry was stoic as he gestured to one of the couches. Landon sat with him, and everybody got comfortable. "I'm guessing you've heard what happened."

"Everybody's talking about it," Layla confirmed. She had dark hair and eyes, and while some might've fallen for the doe-eyed looks she was shooting the men, it was impossible to miss the suspicious peeks directed my way. The girl was much more worldly than she was letting on. "Mrs. Walters is dead."

"She is," Chief Terry confirmed. "Can you tell me when you last saw her?"

I watched Layla and Penelope closely to see if they shared any secret glances or small touches. They didn't.

"I saw her at lunch yesterday," Layla replied. "She sometimes eats in the cafeteria with us—although mostly not. Yesterday she sat at the table closest to the window. That's the faculty table. She was with the other teachers but spent most of her time on her phone."

"She *always* spent most of her time on her phone," Penelope added. "She was addicted to it."

"Did we find a phone on the body?" Landon asked Chief Terry.

"I didn't see one, but they recovered a purse from the Bronco," Chief Terry said. "We'll check after the interviews." His smile remained kind when he aimed it at the teenagers. "What about you?" he asked Penelope. "When was the last time you saw her?"

"After school," Penelope said. "I was heading to afternoon detention with Mr. Soderquist and passed her in the hallway. She was on her phone, and she didn't look happy."

"Why did you have detention?" I asked, speaking before thinking. I'd been determined to let Landon and Chief Terry handle all the questioning when I sat down.

"I always have detention," Penelope replied. "It's become a challenge now. If I don't get it, the day feels wrong."

"She likes detention because it means she can get all her homework done in there and doesn't have to worry about it at night," Layla interjected. "She's weird about wanting to finish her homework as soon as possible."

"You're weird," Penelope fired back. "It's smart to get your homework done at a reasonable hour."

"Says you." Layla sniped. "She's definitely the weird one."

Their interaction, so seemingly normal, only filled me with more questions. "Why are you here?"

Landon shot me a warning look, but I ignored him.

"We were led to believe you were troubled," I pressed.

"Depends on who you ask," Layla replied. "My parents thought I was 'troubled' because I was hanging out with the wrong crowd." She used air quotes to match her feral smile. "They disliked the crowd I was hanging with because they're Black."

The comment, delivered with such calm geniality, was a shock.

Layla almost looked as if she pitied me. "You don't get it because you're insulated up here in a very vanilla world," she said. "Try visiting a city."

She was so matter of fact I could hardly question her on the subject. And, in truth, Hemlock Cove lacked diversity. It was the way it had always been. "What about you?" I asked Penelope.

"I refused to take that teenage pledge," Penelope replied. "My dad is a Baptist minister, and he wanted me to go to one of those purity things where you pledge yourself to your father until you get married—you get a ring and everything—but I refused. My mother decided I was likely to turn into a slut and wanted me sent away. This was their compromise."

I darted a look to Bianca but didn't ask any of the questions crowding my mind. "I don't decide who comes here," she said. "That's on the parents. They pay the tuition."

I looked to Landon for support and found he appeared as troubled as I felt.

"Let's just get through this," he said. "We'll talk about the other stuff later."

IT TOOK US THE BETTER PART OF TWO HOURS TO question all the girls. We spent about fifteen minutes with each duo, but none of them seemed to know anything of use.

Most of them had seen Enid during the afternoon the previous day. Almost all said that she'd been on her phone. None of them found that surprising, because apparently Enid was always on her phone. Nobody remembered seeing her after four o'clock in the afternoon, and yet I had to believe it had been later than that when Enid left the school because Bianca said she'd left at five, and Enid was still in her office at that time.

The last pair of girls was the most animated, which was saying something because all of the girls had been mouthy. Perhaps that was why they'd been deemed "troubled." If that had been the case when I'd been growing up, Thistle, Clove and I would've been sent off to become someone else's problem the moment we turned five.

"Headmistress Walters made me her pet project," Autumn Larson volunteered. She'd grown up in Traverse City and had been at Stonecrest a full year. "She said I have a bad attitude."

"Do you?" I asked.

Autumn's smile was mischievous. "Depends on who you ask. I think I'm a delight."

It was something Aunt Tillie would say. "What was the final straw that got you sent here?" I asked.

"I started dating a twenty-year-old with a motorcycle."

"And you didn't think your parents were right when they told you that was a bad idea?" Landon challenged.

"It didn't matter if it was a bad idea," Autumn shot back. "What matters is they're hypocrites who were both having affairs when they decided to judge my love life. Heck, my dad decided to have an affair with the girl who babysat me when I was ten. She was only a few years older than me. It was gross."

"That *is* gross," I agreed. "I'm guessing you made your opinion known."

"They ignored me. Do you know what they didn't ignore?"

"Dating a twenty-year-old with a motorcycle," I replied.

"Rather than deal with me, they sent me here." Autumn didn't look all that upset. "I kind of like it here."

"We all do," the teenager she'd been partnered with said. Her name was Violet Thomas. She had long purple hair—she was the only one I'd seen with a wild hairdo—and pretty blue eyes. She looked as if she was spoiling for a fight, yet she remained calm when answering questions.

"You're from Shadow Hills?" I asked.

"Yup." Violet leaned back on the couch. "My mother runs the laundromat. She has three other kids. None of us have the same father. She decided I was too much to handle. She got her boyfriend to send me here."

"Who is her boyfriend?" Landon asked.

"The man who runs the bank. He's married to the daughter of the man who used to run the bank, and when I started telling people about him dating my mom I was sent here." Violet rested her elbows on her knees and stared at me. "Convenient timing, huh?"

I couldn't disagree.

We questioned them for a few minutes longer, then sent them on their way.

"Nobody saw Enid in the run-up to her death," Chief Terry noted when it was just the four of us. "Does that seem odd?" he asked Bianca.

She shook her head. "Enid was a good headmistress, but she didn't engage with the girls that often. She left that to the staff she'd put in place. She often had other things on her mind."

"What sort of other things?"

Bianca hesitated, but only for a moment. "If I had to guess, I'd say she had a boyfriend. We weren't friendly enough for her to confide in me. We weren't enemies," she offered hurriedly. "She just kept what she did outside work to herself. I focused on the school."

"If she didn't live on campus, where did she live?" Landon asked.

"She has a cottage about a mile from here," Bianca replied. "One of those cookie-cutter places on the lake."

"Which lake?" I asked.

"Manistee Lake."

"Can you get us the address?" Chief Terry asked. "We'll be heading there next."

"Yes." Bianca left to gather the address.

I waited until I was certain she was out of earshot to speak. "Manistee Lake isn't big. She could've afforded a house there on a smaller salary."

"It's fairly isolated too," Landon added. "I'm kind of curious what she was doing on her phone all the time if she wasn't paying attention to the kids."

He wasn't the only one. "I'm guessing our goal is to figure that out next," I said.

"Unless you have a better suggestion," Landon said. "None of these kids seemed to care enough to kill her. Even the one who said she was a project didn't care."

"The 'care' has been whipped out of these kids," I said. "They've been told they're troublemakers, and sending them here reinforced the idea that they're somehow special for being in trouble. It will be a self-fulfilling prophecy with most of them."

"I think some of them will be fine," Landon countered.

"Sure, but what about those who won't?" I challenged. "They've been labeled, and some won't shake that label."

"The girls seem fine, Bay," Landon assured me. "These girls are survivors."

"We need to focus on Enid," Chief Terry said. "As much as we'd like to assume she died of natural causes, that seems unlikely."

5
FIVE

Chief Terry easily navigated to Enid's cottage. It was on the southwest side of the lake, just off Sands Park Road, surrounded by the type of houses that were being torn down on bigger lakes so new McMansions could be built. The trend hadn't quite reached this lake.

"These are old cottages," I noted as we exited Chief Terry's vehicle.

"They are," Landon agreed. His arms automatically wrapped around my waist as he gave me a hug and kiss. "Our new house will be updated."

Our house was a patch of land at a different lake. We'd bought the old campsite where we'd met as children—although we hadn't realized that until we were already together—and were planning to start constructing our dream house in the spring. We'd torn down the old cabins and cleaned the property before winter had arrived. At present, there was nothing we could do until the weather cleared. I was fine with that—there was nothing wrong with the guesthouse—but pretending I wasn't giddy about the idea of making decisions for our dream house was disingenuous.

"This isn't the sort of lake people flock to," Chief Terry volunteered. "It's not like Torch Lake, where all the houses are selling for seven figures and there's a sand bar bringing in tourists from other states. This lake is for fishing. People don't even swim in it."

"I've seen people swim here," I said.

"Not that many."

"I guess." I rolled my neck. "What do most of the houses here run?"

"They're all six figures because they're on the water," Chief Terry replied. "Most of them can't be worth more than five hundred grand, though. Most of them run between two hundred and three hundred thousand."

I did the math in my head. "The headmistress of a private school—one with only thirty students—can afford a house out here?"

"Good question." Chief Terry pulled out his phone and started typing. "Duncan isn't doing anything but mooning after Bay, so I'll have him run the property records."

Landon scowled. "You said that just to irritate me."

"Who? Me?" Chief Terry was the picture of innocence.

Landon started for the front door. "You know I don't like that guy."

"You didn't care either way until you learned he had a crush on Bay," Chief Terry countered. "He's harmless. When Bay was sixteen and he was just turning fourteen, he brought her flowers to one of the festivals. He asked her to dance in front of everybody. He was crushed when she turned him down."

Landon shot me an approving smile. "That's my good girl."

"Don't get too excited," Chief Terry said. "If I remember correctly, she turned him down because she had her heart set on dancing with Chad Benton, who was eighteen and spent all his time working out."

I smiled at the memory, even though it wasn't a particularly fond one. "He didn't own a shirt."

"Even at the winter festival?" Landon demanded.

"I didn't say it was the Winter Festival," Chief Terry replied. "It was the Fall Festival if I remember right. He wore a blazer with a tie but no shirt. He flexed next to the punch bowl the entire evening."

"Sounds like a douche," Landon complained.

I laughed at his downtrodden expression. "Oh, he was," I confirmed. "I still had a huge crush on him. He went home with Lila that night." Mentioning my high school nemesis, who was in prison for trying to kill me, made my stomach clench. "I guess it was for the best."

Landon pressed himself against my back as we crowded around Enid's front door. "It was definitely for the best. You ended up right where you were supposed to."

He planted a lavish kiss on my neck, ignoring the dirty look Chief Terry shot him. When Chief Terry forced the door open, we were feeling pretty relaxed. That changed the moment we crossed the threshold and saw what should have been a cozy living room.

"What in the hell?" Chief Terry's eyebrows practically popped off his forehead as he took in the far wall. It was completely covered with cork board and dry erase boards, each dedicated to stalking the same man.

"This is unbelievable," Landon noted as he abandoned me to move closer to the nearest dry erase board. "Does anybody know this guy?"

There was a file on the table nearest the cork boards, with a name neatly typed on the tab. I read it out loud. "Kevin Dean Dunne."

"KD Dunne," Chief Terry corrected. He'd paled since we walked into the cottage. "He's a big-time real estate guy in Traverse City."

I thought about the kids we'd interviewed all morning. There'd been a Dunne. "I wonder if he's related to Katie Dunne," I said.

Landon's shoulders jolted. "Wait a second." He pulled out his phone and started typing. It didn't take him long to come back with an answer. "He's Katie's father."

The odds of having a second Dunne take precedence in the investigation felt long. Still, the boards—where Enid had apparently stalked almost every move Kevin had made—were more than I could digest.

"Wow." I sank down on the couch and stared at the timeline she'd created.

"She was stalking him," Landon supplied as he brought the folder to the couch and sat with me.

"Clearly," Chief Terry agreed. "She has photos of him outside his office. They were taken on separate days because he's wearing different clothes in each."

I focused on the man in the center of the photos. "Is he considered a heartthrob in the area or something?" I wasn't familiar with him, other than I was reasonably certain I'd seen his photo on a few advertisements in store windows the last time I'd been to Traverse City.

"His ads are all over Traverse City," Landon replied. "He's one of the high-profile agents there. I met him once at the State of the City event two years ago. It was right around the time I was falling for you." He shot me a smile.

"So, basically the best time of your life," I teased.

"My whole life has been perfect since I met you," he assured me.

Chief Terry rolled his eyes. "Let's not be gross. You two act like teenagers sometimes. It makes me want to gag."

"Says the guy who was feeling up my mother outside the greenhouse three nights ago," I drawled.

Slowly—so slowly it was like a scene from a movie—Chief Terry tracked his gaze to me. "What?" His voice was strangled.

"We saw you," Landon volunteered. "We were in the pot field and saw you leaving."

"What were you doing in the pot field?" Chief Terry looked horrified. "You're a duly sworn officer of the law, Landon. You can't ... do that."

"You don't even know what we were doing," Landon argued.

"For the record, we were making out. Aunt Tillie has the field climate controlled now, so it's like a summer night in there." He turned momentarily wistful. "She has more than pot in there. There are tomatoes ... and corn ... and green beans." He sighed. "We keep a blanket there for picnics."

"It's winter!"

"Not in there." Landon's smile told me he didn't care in the least that he was freaking out Chief Terry. "I know this will drive you crazy, but it's romantic. It's like I'm a boy of sixteen again and I can feel up the girl I fancy."

Even I thought that was a step too far. "Who uses the word 'fancy' like that?" I demanded.

Landon merely shrugged. "I read it in a book. I fancy you."

"Aw." I patted his cheek, then poked at the book. "You need to stop before Chief Terry blows a gasket."

"Yes, you need to stop," Chief Terry agreed.

"We need to figure this out." I took the file from Landon. "It says here that Kevin is married."

"To one Joanie Dunne," Landon added. "I looked over the basics. Apparently, they were married straight out of college and have a few kids, including Katie."

I frowned. "He's cheating on his wife?"

"We don't know that he was having an affair with Enid," Chief Terry argued. "She was obviously infatuated with him, but we don't know that he was cheating with her."

That didn't feel right. "Why would a woman lose her head like that for no reason?"

"Maybe she was mentally ill," Landon suggested.

"Like that movie *Fatal Attraction*," Chief Terry said. "That woman went crazy and boiled bunnies."

"Bunny boiling aside, the male lead in that movie wasn't exactly blameless," I argued. "He had an affair with her and basically gaslighted her after the fact. She fell in love with the wrong man—

and trying to kill his wife was a bad move—but he deranged her and got off without having to pay for betraying his wife."

"I think having his bunny boiled and his family almost killed was more than enough payback," Chief Terry countered.

"Was it? He got to keep his family."

"I can't believe we're arguing about *Fatal Attraction* now," Chief Terry muttered.

"I'm just saying that the movie was a bit one-sided," I argued. "I don't understand why Enid would become obsessed with the father of one of her students for no good reason."

"It's called mental illness," Landon replied. He held up his hand to cut me off before I could argue. "I'm not saying that's what we're dealing with," he assured me. "But, I can see how someone unbalanced might have thought she saw something in a man she had one or two meetings with."

"How do you not trip over your tongue with all those mines you're stepping over when you speak?" I said. "You're suggesting Enid fell for this guy even though nothing happened."

"I'm saying it's a possibility," Landon countered. "We don't know. We have to talk to him."

"Obviously," I said dryly. I went back to flipping through the file. "If this was all in Enid's head, why did she end up dead?"

"Maybe she threatened Joanie and she did something about it," Chief Terry suggested.

"Ah, so now we're accusing Joanie." And I thought I was bothered before. "Why can't Kevin be the culprit?"

"Don't turn this into a men versus women thing," Chief Terry complained. "There's a legitimate reason I think it's unlikely to be Kevin. Actually, more than one reason."

"I'm all ears," I said.

My tone irritated him, but that didn't dissuade Chief Terry from laying it out for me. "He's a well-known face. You've never met him yet were convinced that you knew him."

"Because I visited Landon in Traverse City," I argued. "That wouldn't be true of other people."

"You visited me three or four times," Landon argued. "You hated going there when I had to work. That's why I spent most of my time traveling to you."

He made it sound like a hardship. "You said Hemlock Cove was the home you wanted."

"That doesn't change the fact that you recognized Kevin. I think—stress the word *think*—he might do some television commercials too. I'll bet you're not the only person who recognizes him."

"Which would put him at risk of discovery if he came and met with Enid in the parking lot," Chief Terry said.

"Maybe he didn't care," I replied. "Maybe it was a heat-of-the-moment thing."

"Anything is possible," Chief Terry said, "but there's another reason I don't think it was him. What you're describing—two people having a relationship and one person losing it while trying to end it—is a crime of passion. There were no marks on Enid's body. If Enid was killed, it was by means other than hands." Chief Terry mimed strangling an invisible person.

I hated—*absolutely hated*—that he had a point. "I didn't consider that," I admitted. "How did she die? She wasn't strangled. She wasn't stabbed. She wasn't shot. There was no head injury."

"We don't know that," Landon interjected. "There could've been a head injury. In this cold, she could've been hit in the back of the head and not bled out because of the frigid temps."

"I still think it could've been him," I said.

Chief Terry moved to the table by the window. There was another stack of files that we'd apparently missed. I hadn't noticed them until just now.

"What are those?" I asked, leaning forward. "More files on Kevin?"

"Files on the students." Chief Terry read the names aloud.

"Autumn Larson. Penelope Carter. Katie Dunne. Kasey Dutton. Kelly Cortez. Violet Thomas. Layla Dombrowski."

"How many are there?" Landon asked.

"Thirty-three," Chief Terry replied. "She had files on all her current students, Bianca, and two former students."

Landon left me on the couch and joined Chief Terry, who shrugged. "I think we're going to have to go through them all." His eyes moved to me. "And the file on Kevin Dunne, so don't get worked up."

I was over Kevin, at least for the time being. "What could she have on those girls? From what they told us, it sounds like they were sent to the school because their parents were jerks."

Landon pinned me with a stern look. "And you weren't predisposed to side with them?"

"Uh-oh," Chief Terry muttered when I sat straighter. "You kicked the hornet's nest now, son."

Landon ignored him. "Don't deny you went in there with an attitude, Bay," he said. "You were angry on behalf of those girls because you felt they were being punished just for being girls. It didn't matter to you whether they'd done anything or not."

"Maybe I think parents should be parents and not shirk their duties simply because they have a mouthy teenager," I shot back.

"Hey, I like my women mouthy." He held up his hands in surrender. "When we have kids, we won't give them up for anything. But not all parents can handle all problems. Perhaps you shouldn't judge the parents until you know what they were dealing with. Those girls might not have been telling the truth."

He had a point, of course. I wasn't entirely truthful as a teenager, but I wasn't in the mood to put up with any judgmental crap. "We don't know that they're guilty either," I said.

"For now, all we have are files and a potentially mentally ill woman. We need to keep digging," Landon said.

I flicked my eyes to the boards. "We'd better start digging fast."

"We'll take the folders back to Hemlock Cove," Chief Terry said. "We'll review them there."

"Fine," I said. "I guess I could eat a burger or something."

Chief Terry looked relieved. "Burgers will do us all good." He cast a heavy look to Landon. "After that, we'll start making decisions."

Something about the way they eyed one another told me I wasn't going to like those decisions.

6
SIX

Hemlock Cove bustled with activity as we parked downtown.

I took a deep breath upon exiting Chief Terry's vehicle and stared into the sky. The sun was struggling to make an appearance through the clouds, and the air was cold but not frigid. Winter was officially here, and while I liked a soft snow, the atmosphere was churning with an unexpected energy this early in the season.

"This is the last Christmas festival, right?" Landon asked as he arrived at my side. "I ask because I swear this is the third one since the Halloween Festival."

He wasn't technically wrong. The festival committee was smart in scheduling. "They're not all Christmas festivals," I replied.

"Um, I've seen Santa at all of them."

"Yes, well, Santa likes to festival hop." I gave him a cheeky grin. "They're given different names for a reason. One is a Transition Festival. That's the one at the beginning of the month, while we're transitioning from falling leaves to snow. Then there's the Holiday Festival. We're not supposed to call it the Christmas Festival even though Mrs. Little insists we do. It's supposed to be inclusive of Kwanzaa, Hanukkah, and Christmas. Keep in mind that Christmas is also the general theme of the Transition Festival.

"This festival is geared for the tourists, which is why it runs through Christmas and the new year," I continued. "It's the Yule Festival—this is a town of witches after all—and all the favorites are dusted off to make things easy because it's essentially a two-week festival."

"So, my kissing booth is safe, correct?" Landon queried.

I nodded. "The kissing booth is safe. It's one of the easiest booths. They just have to set it up and forget it."

"And the hot chocolate booth?"

"Also safe."

"What about the cupcake booth?" Landon rubbed his stomach. "I like those cupcakes with the witch legs poking out of them. They're delicious and adorable."

It took everything I had to keep from laughing. "The cupcake booth is safe too." I turned to face him. "Don't forget, this is the moms' favorite time to bake. They'll have all your favorite desserts at the inn too."

"This is why I don't mind living so close to your mother," he said. "Everybody at the office asks if I'm uncomfortable living on my mother-in-law's property. It's the baking that makes it okay. That and the bacon."

"And the pot roast," I said.

"That too." He gave me a soft kiss. "Are you okay? You look agitated."

"I'm thinking about Enid and her stalking. I'm guessing you're not taking me with you to interview Kevin?"

Landon looked chagrined. "That hasn't been decided yet." The way he averted his gaze told me that it had. He just didn't want to ruin our lunch.

I left him on the curb and moved to Chief Terry, who had been watching us. "What about you, big guy?" I asked. "Want to take me to meet Kevin Dunne?"

Chief Terry didn't like saying no to me. Unlike Landon, however, he wasn't afraid to tell me no when the situation warranted. "You can't go," he replied, matter-of-factly. "There's no way to explain your presence."

"Which is why you guys drove back to Hemlock Cove for lunch rather than to Traverse City," I surmised. "You wanted to drop me off." I couldn't decide if I was annoyed or resigned. "I hope they have pot pie in the diner," I said as I moved around him and to the restaurant's door.

"Bay," Chief Terry called to my back.

I ignored him and pushed inside, offering up a smile for Shirley Bevins—she'd retired from the diner years before but came back every Christmas because she enjoyed the season and made money in tips to cover her Christmas shopping—before heading toward our usual table. I heard Landon and Chief Terry murmuring to one another as they followed. I couldn't be certain, but I was almost positive I heard "stubborn pain in the ass." I pushed it out of my mind and grabbed the specials menu as soon as I sat.

"Beef pot pie," I read aloud, smiling. "Yum." I returned the menu to the table rack and shrugged out of my coat. When I looked up, Chief Terry and Landon were watching me. "What?" I demanded.

"If you're going to be a baby, I prefer you get it out of your system," Chief Terry replied somberly. "I hate when you hold back and then explode."

"I think you're confusing me with my mother," I said evenly.

"Don't say things like that," he complained as he sat across from me. "It makes for a weird picture in my head."

"Blah, blah, blah," I muttered. "They have beef pot pie," I said to Landon as he sat next to me.

"That sounds good," he replied. "I love beef and potatoes. I love you more, though," he crooned as he leaned to press his nose against my cheek.

I wasn't in the mood. "Don't." I nudged him back. "I'm annoyed with you."

"You can't be mad at me for doing my job, Bay," he said.

"It would look weird for us to take a reporter to interview a stalking victim," Chief Terry said. "You know that."

I smiled for his benefit, but it was more feral than friendly. Movement outside the window caught my attention, and I looked up to find Mrs. Little scurrying down the street, a plastic Santa trundling along not far behind. "Huh," I murmured.

Landon's eyes went so wide I thought they might pop out of his head. "Was that...?"

"The exact reason this whole plan of Tillie's is a bad idea," Chief Terry growled. His gaze was pointed when it landed on me. "You need to get her to reverse this."

I was nowhere close to agreeing to do that. "It's fine. Nobody noticed."

A chorus arose from outside: *"On the first day of Christmas, my true love sent to me, a partridge in a pear tree."*

At the table next to the window, a kid twisted in his chair to look out the window. The way he stiffened told me all I needed to know. Something creepy was on the sidewalk.

"On the second day of Christmas, my true love sent to me, two turtle doves, and a partridge in a pear tree."

I darted a look to Chief Terry.

"Do I even want to know what that is?" he asked.

"Probably not," I replied. I cracked my neck as I considered if I should do something. I decided I didn't want to stop the Christmas decorations from torturing Mrs. Little. It was too much fun. I pasted on my prettiest smile. "What are you going to ask Kevin when you sit down with him?"

"Don't look at me like that," Chief Terry moaned. "I hate when you look at me like that. I can't tell you no."

"We know how to question people, Bay," Landon said. His gaze was out the window as whoever was singing hit *"five golden rings"* at a screech. "Seriously, what is that?"

"I don't know." That was the truth. "Mrs. Little's Christmas decorations were pretty traditional: Santa, a snowman, and some manger stuff. She didn't have anything cool."

"Then where did that plastic Santa come from?"

"Maybe it was in her garage. Mrs. Little is cheap. She doesn't throw anything away. I bet she had decorations in her garage that we didn't know about."

"We can't have Christmas decorations running around singing at the top of their lungs," Chief Terry argued. "Brad Childs is essentially making himself a permanent visitor these days. How do you think he's going to react to this?"

"What can he do? Is he going to go to the local television stations, tell them the Christmas decorations in Hemlock Cove are singing? Even if he blames us, nobody will care. It's freaking Hemlock Cove."

"She has a point," Landon noted.

"I know she has a point," Chief Terry snapped. "That doesn't mean I have to like it. This is going to bite us in the ass."

"Ten lords a-leaping, nine ladies dancing, eight maids a-milking."

Chief Terry's head landed in his hands for numbers six and seven. Then the voice doubled in volume for the big line: *"Five golden rings!"*

I cringed at the accusatory look Chief Terry bored into me. "Bay," he said in a dark voice. "This isn't okay."

I didn't necessarily disagree with him. I wasn't going to do anything about it, though, so he would have to suck it up. "It's fine," I assured him before turning to Landon. "Make sure you dig into Kevin's personal life, because I maintain that he was having an affair with Enid no matter how bad the stalking looks."

"I've got it, Bay." Landon was firm, although there was a gentleness when he reached over and brushed my hair out of my face. "What are you going to do when we're in Traverse City?" He almost looked afraid to ask. He needn't have been; I had nothing diabolical on my agenda today.

"I don't know yet," I replied. "I'm going to stop in at the paper. The Christmas edition goes to print tomorrow."

"That's early." His forehead creased. "What will you do next week?"

"Nothing," I replied. "It's Christmas. Nobody cares. Once the new year rolls around, everybody will want a fresh edition with new coupons, but we'll be closed for the holidays. The tourists who come for Christmas have already finished their shopping. They're here for the festival and the inns."

"She's right," Chief Terry noted. "There aren't many who actually stay in town for Christmas, but we get a decent amount of tourists from the neighboring towns because they're in financial trouble and have had to cut back on the festivals."

Landon rubbed his chin. "That's good for Hemlock Cove."

"It is," Chief Terry agreed. "Of course, if the decorations are running through the town square like rabid dogs, things might get out of hand fairly quickly."

"It's fine," I assured him. "Stop being a kvetch."

His mouth dropped open. "Did you just 'kvetch' me?" he demanded.

I refused to shrink under his heavy glare. "If the kvetch fits."

"You're in trouble." Chief Terry extended a warning finger. "So much trouble."

"Well, you can think about my punishment when you're interviewing the stalking victim without me," I said. I had a huge smile on my face when Shirley appeared at the edge of our table. "I will have the beef pot pie and an iced tea, please."

Shirley bobbed her head. "How about you?" she asked Landon.

He ordered the same.

"And you?" Shirley prodded Chief Terry.

"Shepherd's pie and iced tea," Chief Terry replied morosely. "I'll also have a different daughter, because this one is annoying."

Shirley laughed as if he'd said the funniest thing in the world, but my heart clenched, and I had to look down at the table. He'd called me many things in my life, but daughter was never one of them. He'd taken on a parental role in my life, but he'd been careful not to usurp my father's territory.

"Oh, don't cry," Landon said as he slid his arm around my back.

"Why would she cry?" Chief Terry asked.

"She's crying because you called her your daughter," Landon replied. His hand rubbed up and down my back. "You're okay," he said to me. "How can you be surprised that he called you his daughter?"

"Oh, geez." Chief Terry looked pained. "You need to stop that, Bay. Of course you're my daughter. Don't ... do that." He waved his hand at me before averting his gaze. "This day sucks."

Landon was the only one who looked amused. "You're both so sentimental. It's creepy."

"You're creepy," I fired back as I swiped at my cheeks. I shouldn't be crying. It was making everyone uncomfortable. He'd taken me by surprise.

He did it again when he reached across the table and rested his hand on mine. "Bay, knock it off," Chief Terry ordered. "You shouldn't be surprised that I think of you as my daughter, but you still need to end this thing with the Christmas decorations."

I squeezed his hand before shaking my head. "I really do love you, but we're not stopping."

"Oh, man." Chief Terry used his free hand to rub the spot above his heart. "Now I kind of want to take her with us to question Kevin Dunne."

I perked up immediately. The feeling only lasted several seconds, because Landon started shaking his head. "No, we're going by the book on this one," he said. "Bay is staying here. Once we get a feel for Dunne we'll decide how to proceed."

"You're a total killjoy," I complained.

He kissed my cheek. "I love you too. Do we think this blizzard will really hit right before Christmas?"

"The atmosphere feels energetic," I replied. "When the snow is going to be light and fluffy, the atmosphere feels almost lazy. It's almost sparking."

"The weather forecasters always build this stuff up," Chief Terry said. "I'm sure it won't be that bad."

"It might be nice to be snowed in for Christmas," I said. "I mean if we manage to solve the mystery of what happened to Enid first."

"I could stand to be snowed in on Christmas with you," Landon agreed. "As long as your mother provides us with food. I don't want to be stuck eating box macaroni and cheese on Christmas."

"I can cook something other than macaroni and cheese," I shot back.

"Yes, you're becoming proficient with the charcuterie board too," he said. "I want real food for Christmas. Maybe we should be snowed in at the inn, so I don't risk starving over the holiday."

I gave him a withering look. "Maybe you should stay at the inn with my mother, and I'll stay at the guesthouse with my charcuterie."

"If you feel that's necessary, then I'll miss you." Landon refused to rise to the bait. "My bacon and I will miss you."

I glared at him. "This day is going to hell really fast."

7
SEVEN

The pot pie put me in a better mood. The blueberry pie that Shirley put in a box so I could have a snack later put me in an even better mood. The fact that she didn't provide Landon with a snack wasn't lost on him, but apparently, it was the last piece of blueberry pie, and Shirley wasn't sympathetic to his whining.

"Listen, you've obviously gotten by on your looks during your life," she said to him. "You're a handsome man. Sure, the hair makes you look as if you're channeling some of the teen shows from the nineties, but if that's your thing who am I to judge?"

Landon shot me a long-suffering look. Shirley was hardly the first person to make fun of his hair. I liked it—he'd been undercover in a motorcycle meth gang when we'd first met, and I'd been attracted to his rough-and-tumble look—but other people thought he would benefit from a haircut. Shirley was old school. To her, long hair signified he was a ruffian.

"You're judging me, so I didn't get any pie," Landon complained as we moved toward the exit. "Bay has long hair, and you gave her pie."

"Bay is a good girl," Shirley countered. "She's always been a good girl. She was crying earlier. Obviously, she needs pie."

I didn't have the heart to tell her I'd been crying because I was so touched by what Chief Terry had said, not because I was upset. I didn't want her to take back the pie. "I'm grateful for the pie," I promised, ignoring the dark look from Landon. "I'm sure it will ease the sting from their betrayal."

"Keep it up," Chief Terry warned as he held open the door. "I won't get you a Christmas gift."

"You've already given me my Christmas gift," I replied. "What you said was the best gift ever."

He didn't immediately respond, and when I looked up at him, his eyes were glassy.

"Oh, look at the two of you," Landon said. "You're schmaltzy schmaltzes. It must be the time of year." He took my shoulders and forced my attention to him. "I want gifts. Your love is great and everything, but I still want gifts."

"I want gifts too," I said. "From you at least." I gripped the bag with my pie. "I'm heading to my office to see how much work I can get done. When do you think you'll be back?"

"I don't know." He pushed my hair from my face and stared into my eyes. "I didn't realize I was punching a clock with my wife."

"You're not, but I need to figure out a ride home if you guys are too late," I replied. "I don't want to be stuck here all day when I could be cuddled up reading in front of the fireplace."

"No cuddling without me." He leaned in for a kiss. "As for a ride home, do whatever you need to do. Just text so I know if we need to pick you up."

"Make sure you ask the right questions of Kevin Dunne."

"I've got it, Bay." He hugged me tight. "I know how to interview a suspect."

"Okay, well ... have fun." Across the road, a lawn gnome popped into view. It was dancing behind one of the trash receptacles, singing a mixed-up rendition of the *12 Days of Christmas*.

"Did that come from Mrs. Little's yard?" Chief Terry demanded.

I had my doubts. "I think that's one of the gnomes that was tapped when we fought with Scout a few weeks ago."

Chief Terry hooked his thumbs into his gun belt. "It's singing."

"It may have picked that up from the other thing that was singing." Or perhaps I was just hoping that. "I'm sure it's fine."

"Oh, well, if you're sure." Chief Terry rolled his eyes. "This is your mess, Bay. You need to clean it up. You may be my daughter, and I might go gooey whenever you're around, but I'm standing firm on this." He leaned close and stared directly into my eyes. "If Childs sees singing gnomes, we'll all be in trouble. Get this situation under control."

I didn't like that he was worried. I especially didn't like that he thought I could suddenly fix this. "I'll figure out what's going on and get back to you."

He dropped a kiss on top of my head and walked to his vehicle. "I'm serious, Bay. We could all get in trouble for this."

"I said I would figure things out." That was the most I was willing to do. "We'll see what happens."

"This is going to blow up in our faces," Chief Terry complained to Landon. "It's going to be an absolute nightmare."

Landon nodded. "Sounds like a typical Christmas in Hemlock Cove."

"You would say that. You think everything she does is adorable."

"So do you." Landon gave me a quick kiss before pulling back, his FBI face in place. "Make sure you text, so I know you have a ride home."

"I should be able to figure something out," I assured him.

"Your mother is making pot roast tonight—with fresh rolls. You know how I feel about those rolls. I don't want to be late."

"You're a glutton," I muttered.

"There are worse things to be."

I stood on the sidewalk and watched them go, doing my best not to let bitterness about being cut out of the action swallow me.

Then I headed to the newspaper office, which was only a block away. I was lost in my own head for the walk, telling myself over and over again that they had no choice but to leave me out of things. They'd included me on their team when the prisoners escaped, and even though we'd gotten to the bottom of things, it had come back to bite us. They didn't want that to happen again, especially with Childs hanging around town. I had to accept it and move on.

I let myself in and immediately headed to my office. Viola, the newspaper ghost, was nowhere to be found when I called out to her. That was hardly surprising—some of the friends she'd made in life were still alive and she enjoyed spying on them.

When I'd originally fallen in love with the idea of being a reporter, I'd pictured myself chasing big stories in an urban area. I'd left Walkerville, the name of the town before it was rebranded as a witch town, and assumed I was going to have a grand life away in the big city.

I'd been wrong.

I missed home, and big city reporting was nowhere near as important as I thought. I occasionally got a meaty story to work on but found that I liked the fluff stories just as much. Owning my own newspaper had never been a dream until Landon made it a reality when the former owner threatened to take away everything I loved. Now I was in charge of everything ... and I liked it.

I hummed as I sent the list of stories to the page layout person. I double-checked that the accompanying photos were in the system, and then I turned off my computer and packed it up to take home. I didn't foresee being in the office much until after the first of the year. Anything that had to be done could be done from home.

I carried my computer bag to the lobby and put it on the desk before heading to the layout office with my list. When I finished there—and had left a Christmas bonus behind for both of my regular employees—I returned to the lobby. The plan was to go to Hypnotic and browbeat either Clove or Thistle into taking me home. That notion flew out of my head when I saw that Brad had entered the building without me realizing it.

"Warden," I said when I caught him looking inside my computer bag. My heart pounded, and I forced myself to take a calming breath. "I didn't realize you were here."

"I'm not a warden any longer, Ms. Winchester," Brad replied as he withdrew his hand from my bag. "I'm just an average citizen."

"I'm sorry about what happened," I said as I edged around the desk. I wasn't particularly worried about him hurting me—I had magic at my disposal and could protect myself in ways he couldn't imagine. He was hunting for dirt. There was plenty of that around if he looked hard enough. "I know you were diligent about your job, and it must feel as if you're being mistreated now that you've lost your position."

"I have ... issues ... about what went down," Brad confirmed as he leaned against the desk. He didn't leave any room for me to slide in front of him and collect the bag.

"I'm sure you do." I planted myself at the corner of the desk and stared him down. "I don't know what you think I can do for you."

"Who said I expected you to do anything for me?"

"The fact that you're hanging around my town and popping up at odd times seems to suggest it," I replied. "Perhaps I'm reading too much into the situation?"

"Or maybe not enough," Brad suggested. His gaze went to the painting on the wall. It used to be one of those starving artist landscapes you could find in any Holiday Inn Express. When I'd taken over the office, Aunt Tillie had decided to help with the decorating. The painting by twelve-year-old Thistle replaced it. It was supposed to be of a bubbling cauldron, but it looked abstract and menacing. Because there was no point in arguing with Aunt Tillie, I'd left the painting where she'd hung it. "What is this supposed to be?"

"I'm not sure," I lied. I didn't want to fuel Brad's interest in all things witchy. "My cousin Thistle painted it when we were kids. She was always much more talented when it came to stuff like that. My great-aunt decided to hang it here because she thought it was funny."

"Thistle is the one with candy cane hair?" Brad queried. He sounded like a police officer digging for information.

"She is," I confirmed.

"I've seen some of her work around that barn she lives in." Brad's tone was derogatory. "I've never seen anybody live in a barn. It's ... odd."

"Marcus—that's her boyfriend—converted the barn. He runs the petting zoo downtown and rents horses for trail rides in the spring, summer, and fall. Thistle has never been what I would call conventional. She likes living in the barn."

"She has sculptures on the petting zoo grounds," Brad noted. "They're ... interesting."

"As I said, she's very artistic."

"I've seen her art on display in her store, too," he noted. "The skull candles seem to be big sellers. Your other cousin, the one who lives in the lighthouse, isn't as crafty, I don't think. She has a baby to take care of, so that probably takes up most of her time."

He was telling me that he'd been tromping all over town to watch members of my family.

"You've been spending a lot of time in town," I said. "May I ask why?"

"You know why." His eyes darkened. "I know for a fact that what happened at my prison was not normal."

"I don't know what that means," I replied.

"You all came up with a convenient story about a prison break that covered all the bases ... unless you look too closely," he said. "I know that magic was involved."

"I didn't know you believed in magic." Because I needed something to do with my hands, I ceded my spot at the front of the room and moved behind the desk to start organizing the items there. "You should look around Hemlock Cove if you're a believer in magic. Someone is always hiring here."

"Yes, I'll get a job at the livery and tend horses for the rest of my life," he replied dryly. The bite to his tone made me straighten.

"What do you want from me?" I demanded. "I'm not the one who lost you your job. You had a guard sleeping with a prisoner. Other guards knew about it. Apparently, you had a regular underground trade system going on given all the cell phones that were confiscated when the big boys came in to take over the prison. How is any of that on me?"

"It's not," Brad replied. "I don't blame you for any of that. I do blame you for the fact that the truth of what happened hasn't come out yet. I know you used magic to catch as many prisoners as you did. I know your family is the only truly magical one in Hemlock Cove. What I don't know is what you're hiding."

"I'm not hiding anything," I lied. "I don't know what you want from me."

"I want you to fix what went wrong."

It was the first time he'd said it out loud, and I had to calm myself. "I have no idea what that means," I said. "What do you expect me to fix? How do you expect me to fix it?"

"You're a witch." Brad was matter of fact. "You can cast a spell. You can give me a do-over. I'll be better this time. I promise."

"I can't do what you think I can."

"Really?" Brad's expression was devoid of warmth and humor. "There are Christmas decorations running around town singing. They seem to be stalking that woman who runs the unicorn store. She's a real piece of work, by the way. She feuds with your great-aunt constantly. I know she cast the spell. If you can do that, you can fix what happened to me."

"I can't," I argued. "None of what you're saying makes sense."

"Then I guess I'll have to keep looking around town until you agree I deserve a do-over," he said. "One good thing about not having a job is that I have plenty of time to hang out and watch what's happening. I'll eventually see something you don't want me to—maybe even get it on camera." He flashed a bone-chilling smile.

I felt sick to my stomach. "Mr. Childs—"

He cut me off. "Ms. Winchester, don't bother denying it. Don't lie to me. I'm going to get my do-over. You're the one who has to come to terms with it."

"There's no such thing as a do-over," I shot back.

"You can make it happen. I'll be waiting." Now his smile was friendlier. "Have a nice Christmas."

I waited until he'd exited through the front door to swear under my breath.

8
EIGHT

Brad's visit unnerved me enough that I didn't complain when Aunt Tillie showed up downtown in her plow truck. The tune-up had gone well, because she was beaming from ear to ear as she watched a light-up reindeer run back and forth in front of Mrs. Little's window singing *O Little Town of Bethlehem*.

"How did you get it to stay lit up without being plugged in?" I asked as I hopped into her truck. She hadn't invited me to go with her for the ride home, but I was ready to leave for the day.

Aunt Tillie darted her eyes toward the reindeer. "Oh, you know."

Actually, I didn't. "You are still in control of the spell?" I asked.

"How dare you ask that?" she hissed. "There has never been a spell in the history of spells that I've lost control of. Only baby witches lose control of spells."

That was a gross lie. I remembered a million spells she'd lost control of when I was growing up. Recently, her pot field protection spell had grown out of hand and bit Landon. That's why we forced her to change things to give Landon a free pass.

"Aunt Tillie—"

"I said I've got it!" she barked. "Don't give me any grief."

Her adamance indicated she didn't have control. "You need to regain control before Chief Terry loses his mind."

Aunt Tillie was a terrible driver under normal circumstances. The fact that she was worse with the plow blade attached to her truck was straight out of a horror novel. She scraped against the curb as she pulled out, made a face when angling the blade, and then tried again. The odd sound the truck made gave me pause.

"What the hell was that?" I demanded.

"Just a little reminder that it's harder to drive in winter than it is in spring," she replied. "Don't worry about it."

I was worried. "Just get us home. Mom is making pot roast, and I need to talk to everybody. Warden Childs threatened me with exposure—like YouTube exposure—if I didn't 'fix' things so he has a do-over."

Aunt Tillie made a face. "Do-overs are so middle school. What does he expect you to do? It's not as if you can go back in time and make it so he's not a moron."

"I don't know what he expects." I drummed my fingers on the armrest as Aunt Tillie raced out of town like she'd suddenly joined NASCAR. "When was the last time they tested you to make sure you were safe behind the wheel?" I demanded.

"You want to be very careful about what you say next," she warned.

I let the truck descend into silence. The road to the inn was bumpy. I allowed my gaze to wander to Mrs. Little's yard as we passed. There were four new inflatable decorations. None of them were tethered.

"Where did those come from?" I snapped.

"Hmm?" Aunt Tillie frowned at the sight of the inflatables. "How should I know? Apparently, Margaret likes decorations."

"I'm pretty sure those are from somebody else's yard."

"Who cares? Maybe they wanted to take a walk. It's not a big deal. Mind your own business."

"This is my business. We helped set it in motion."

"You get more like your mother each and every day," Aunt Tillie complained. "Just ... don't worry about it. I have everything under control."

The more she talked, the more I realized she had nothing under control. "What should I do about Childs?"

"Kill him."

I froze. "You can't be serious."

"He's a threat. We eradicate threats."

"He's a human being, and I don't blame him for being suspicious," I argued. "Magic was definitely involved in what happened at the prison."

"He was still negligent. Two things can be true at the same time."

She was right, loath as I was to admit it. "I'm not killing him."

"You could cast a memory charm."

"I've never done a memory charm on someone who wasn't a direct physical or magical threat," I said. "That feels pretty invasive for a guy who hasn't technically done anything to us."

"You just said he was an exposure threat." Aunt Tillie didn't slow at all pulling into The Overlook's driveway. When she hit the brakes in front of the building, we careened into the snowbank.

I was furious when I looked up and found her casually unfastening her seatbelt. "Seriously, you shouldn't be allowed to drive."

"You whine like a teenager without a cell phone," she said. "I'm an excellent driver. In fact, I'm so good, NASCAR has called three times to see if I want my own car."

"Three times, huh?" I challenged.

"Yes, three times." She yanked the key out of the ignition of the ancient Ford. "I turned them down because none of their sponsors were acceptable and they wouldn't let me choose my own."

"At least you have standards." I paused when I got a good look at the decorations on the roof. Aunt Tillie had put them up two weeks earlier. The scenes had been changing, sometimes daily. Up until a few days ago, Santa Claus had been using his "stick" to threaten his reindeer and an elf that looked suspiciously like Mrs. Little. Aunt

Tillie swore it was a regular stick even though it looked like a different type. My mother and aunts had crawled up there to switch things while Aunt Tillie had been distracted at the previous festival. Now it appeared Aunt Tillie had decided to up her game.

"Is the Mrs. Little elf wearing ermine pasties for a reason?" I asked.

"She likes them," Aunt Tillie replied with a soft smile. "But that's not Margaret."

"It looks like her."

"Margaret would never look that good in pasties. Besides, if I admitted that was supposed to look like Margaret, I could be sued. As it is, Margaret would have to suggest she looks like that elf to get anywhere in court. Do you think Margaret will say anything about the elf?"

"I have no idea." That was the truth. "If someone tells her you have that elf looking like her while wearing a Santa stripper outfit, she might sue."

Aunt Tillie's lips curved. "Good luck with that." She dusted her hands as she started toward the front door. "As for the warden, you know what you have to do."

"I'm not killing him."

"Then you have to modify his memory."

"That seems unfair."

"Who said life was fair, Bay? Is the man a threat to this family? That's the only thing you have to ask yourself."

"The out-of-control Christmas decorations are a threat to this family," I pointed out. "Are you going to rein them in?"

"What did I say?" Aunt Tillie's eyes flashed with annoyance. "I've got the decorations handled. Stop being a kvetch."

I shook my head. "You'd better hope Chief Terry doesn't tell Mom about the decorations."

"Let me worry about Terry. I'm not afraid of him."

"You'd better get afraid. He's serious about the decorations."

"I've got it under control, Bay."

"Fine." I glanced back up at the scene on the roof. "Is she holding a whip?"

"Not if the police come. That's licorice."

I SPENT THE NEXT TWO HOURS READING ABOUT memory charms in the library. By the time Landon and Chief Terry arrived at the inn, I was exhausted and cranky.

"Nice face," Landon said as he joined me in the library. He didn't move to sit on the couch with me like he usually would, which only served to make me surlier. "Are you okay?"

I shoved the book I'd been reading back onto the shelf. "Brad Childs came to visit me this afternoon."

All traces of the mirth Landon had been harboring disappeared in an instant. "What did he want?"

"What do you think? He's convinced something magical happened. He's convinced I'm behind that magic. He threatened to expose me if I don't provide a do-over."

A muscle worked in Landon's jaw. "What did you say?"

"I told him do-overs don't happen and denied being magical. There was nothing else I could do."

Landon growled.

"That's the way I feel." I attempted a smile. "I hope he'll go away, but I'm not counting on it. I think we have to do something."

He looked suspicious. "What do you want to do?"

"I don't want to kill him, if that's what you're thinking."

"Of course you don't. Why would you want to kill him?"

"I don't," I assured him. "I thought maybe I could cast a memory spell, but the sort of work I need to do for him is extensive. I need to do more research."

"Okay, that sounds like a decent possibility."

I blew out a sigh. "How did your interview with Kevin Dunne go?"

"It went okay. We'll talk about that when we get home tonight. It's not proper dinner conversation."

"Does that mean he admitted to an affair with Enid?"

"It means we'll talk about it at home." Landon turned stern. "There are bigger fish to fry right now."

"I've never really understood that saying," I said.

"I never really used it until I moved to the country."

"Are you calling us hicks?"

"I'm calling you the love of my life." He pulled me in for a hug. He could tell I was agitated. "Just let it go for now," he whispered. "We'll figure out what to do with Childs. You were right about the Christmas decorations. He can't pin those on us yet, so we're okay. We have some room to navigate."

"He threw me off," I admitted. "He let himself into the newspaper lobby while I was working and caught me off guard. He's ... weird."

"He lost his job."

"Yeah, but he's freaking me out."

"I'll have a talk with him." Landon cupped my chin as he pulled back to stare into my eyes. "I'll pull the worried husband act and warn him off."

"Will he fall for that given everything he knows?"

"Everything he *thinks* he knows," Landon corrected. "He doesn't know anything."

I nodded. "Okay."

"Okay," he agreed, hugging me tight one more time before releasing me. "Come on. There's pot roast in the dining room, and Chief Terry is going to mention the Mrs. Little in the fur pasties on the roof to your mother. I don't want to miss either."

We followed the sound of raised voices into the dining room. Given the way Mom was facing off with Aunt Tillie, the stripper elf was already out of the bag.

"You're unbelievable!" Mom railed. "What did I say about the roof display? No sticks! No strippers! No horny reindeer!"

"Hey, you definitely misread that one," Aunt Tillie complained. "The wind blew those reindeer together. I was not thinking anything dirty when I put them so close. It's not my fault Prancer decided to mount Dancer."

I closed my eyes and willed myself to keep from laughing, which would only encourage Aunt Tillie and cause my mother to lose her mind.

"I want that roof display switched back," Mom snarled. "I mean it."

"Uh-oh," Thistle intoned as she walked into the room with Marcus and Clove on her heels. Clove had baby Calvin in her arms. "I take it Aunt Winnie knows about Mrs. Little's new job as an elf prostitute."

"Stripper!" Aunt Tillie barked. "She's a stripper. She could never be a prostitute. She's got cobwebs growing down there." She paused. "Not that the elf is Margaret. You're seeing things."

Thistle snorted. "Whatever." She turned to my mother. "We're here for the promised pot roast."

"I'm glad you came," Mom said. "It's nice that you are making more of an effort to be involved in family meals."

"Don't get too cocky," Thistle warned. "I just don't feel like cooking."

"Yes, Thistle has decided that charcuterie is cooking. I can't tell you how tired I am of cheese and salami bits," Marcus drawled.

"Bay took that cooking class too," Landon said to Marcus, grinning. "Bay doesn't even bother with the cheese half the time. Earlier this week, she dumped a bag of peanut M&Ms on it and called it dinner."

"Hey!" I jabbed a finger at him. "I offered to make soup and sandwiches."

"You offered to heat up Campbell's tomato soup and make grilled cheese sandwiches," he countered, "even though we had no cheese."

"Bread is good dunked in soup."

"You're lucky you're pretty," he teased, then kissed the top of my head before heading to the wine cart. "We need to drink enough to keep ourselves warm for the walk home, Bay."

"Fine, but I don't want to hear any complaints when you have a hangover tomorrow."

I turned my attention back to Mom, who refused to let Aunt Tillie out of the corner she'd backed her into.

"You're not eating until that display is back to the way it was," Mom threatened.

"That's elder abuse," Aunt Tillie argued. "You can't not feed an old lady. I'll die. Do you want me to die?"

"Is that question only for Winnie, or can any of us answer?" Thistle asked.

"Welcome back, Mouth," Aunt Tillie sneered. "This must be a new record, because you're already at the top of my list."

Thistle didn't look bothered in the least. "I do like being the best," she said. "Do I get a medal?"

"You're going to get my wand in your—"

Mom cut off Aunt Tillie by pounding her hands on the table. "What did I say?" she bellowed. "I want that stripper elf off the roof or no dinner!" Her words echoed throughout the room.

Aunt Tillie seemed to debate her options. When Calvin began to clap, all eyes turned in his direction. He was fixated on Mom and Aunt Tillie, appreciative of the show.

"Ah, a young dinner theater enthusiast," Landon said as he sat in his usual chair. "You gotta love a man who knows his place in the family and opts to be a spectator rather than a participant."

"Sam is on his way," Clove volunteered as she sat with the baby. Her eyebrows drew together as she scanned the room. "Do you guys have a highchair?"

"In the kitchen," Mom replied.

"I'll get it." Thistle looked eager to take a break from the anger roiling the room. "If you're looking for another subject to fight about while I'm gone, ask Aunt Tillie about the huge inflatable moose wearing jingle bells around its neck that's hitchhiking into town on M-88."

I froze as I reached for the glass of wine Landon had poured me. "Hitchhiking?" I asked.

Thistle nodded. "It's also wearing pasties."

"You're in so much trouble," Mom growled when Aunt Tillie tried to slide under her arm and make her escape. "Just ... so much trouble."

Thistle beamed at me as she headed for the kitchen. "I've really missed these meals."

"You won't miss being on my list," Aunt Tillie warned. "You'd better start running now."

"I was just about to say the same to you." Thistle saluted my mother. "Go get her, Aunt Winnie. Show her who's boss."

9
NINE

Dinner was loud, but that wasn't out of the ordinary. Threats were issued, retributions promised. Through it all, I sipped my wine and ate my pot roast.

When it was time to walk to the guesthouse, I was a bit tipsy.

"It's freezing, but I'm glad we're walking," I said as my shoulder bumped companionably against Landon's on the uneven walkway that led to our home. "I need to burn off the booze."

"You had two glasses more than you normally do," he said. "So did I."

The night air was brisk, and my cheeks were cold, but it didn't bother me because the first thing Landon would do when we got home was warm me up. He was a man who liked his routine, and there was nothing he liked more than cuddling in front of the fire. He even routinely used the word "cuddling" and didn't care who made fun of him because of it.

"Let's take a side journey in here," he suggested when we reached the pot field. "We can warm up, and then I can fill you in on Kevin Dunne while we look at the stars."

I'd almost forgotten about Kevin Dunne—how was that even

possible?—and was eager when turning back to him. "Did he admit to the affair?"

Landon chuckled as he steered me toward the pot field. The parcel was still warded—my friend Scout Randall and I had worked with Aunt Tillie for hours to get the wards just right—so if anybody at the inn were to see us they would think we'd disappeared behind a tree. Once beyond the wards, however, it was as if we emerged inside of a magical bubble.

Aunt Tillie was a powerful witch, and when she wanted to do something, more often than not she figured out a way to do it. The pot field was a shining example. It was climate controlled. There was no snow anywhere. When you stepped inside, you didn't see the outside world. You saw only what was in her bubble.

"Tell me about Kevin Dunne," I demanded the second we were inside the field.

"Just a second." Landon wrapped his arms around me and gave me a soft kiss before resting his cheek against mine. "You need to warm up first."

My eyes narrowed. "Was this a sly way to get me in here so we can roll around on our picnic blanket?" I pointed to the blanket we'd spread in the field weeks before. We were regular visitors, so we'd taken to leaving it.

"I always want that," Landon said on a laugh, kissing me again before releasing me. He was full of life and laughter when he spun me out. "But that's not my plan tonight." He tilted his head as he studied me. "You look like an angel under the moonlight," he noted. "Has anybody ever told you that?"

"And this isn't you seducing me?" I challenged.

"Nope. I'm waiting to seduce you in front of the fire."

"Good plan. Now tell me about Kevin Dunne."

"I will. I just need to hear more about Childs first." Landon was deadly serious when I darted a look over my shoulder at him. "Did he put his hands on you, Bay?"

It was only then that I realized why he was so agitated. And also why he'd waited until now to bring up his true concern. He hadn't wanted to lose it in front of my family. "He didn't get close enough to touch me. I was careful. Besides that, I don't think he wants to physically hurt me. He has some unrealistic expectations regarding what a witch is capable of."

"Did he use the word 'witch?'"

I shook my head. "No, but he used the word magic. He knows we're different, Landon." All the playfulness I'd been convinced we were about to embrace fled. "He feels something very important was taken from him," I explained. "He believes that I had a part in taking it from him."

"I don't understand how he can believe that." Landon's hands landed on his narrow waist. "He's the one who had guards sleeping with prisoners. The other guards knew about it. He also had an illegal contraband pipeline into the prison."

"Television and movies have taught me that's always a thing," I offered. "*Orange is the New Black* showed people smuggling telephones up their hoo-has is the norm."

Landon's lips twitched. "Did you just use the word 'hoo-ha' with a straight face?"

"Yup."

"Is it any wonder that I fell in love with you the moment I met you?" The intent in his eyes was obvious as he took a step toward me.

I stopped him with a pointed finger. "First off, you didn't fall in love with me at first sight," I countered. "You fell in lust. We both did ... although I wouldn't have admitted that under threat of death back then."

"Come over here and kiss me," he ordered.

I pretended I hadn't heard him. "Secondly, I didn't tell you about Childs to get you worked up. I don't want you beating your chest and going King Kong on the man. He's a problem, and we need to deal with him, but we have to be smart about it."

"Fine." Landon threw his hands in the air. "Now come over here and kiss me." He made a playful grab for me, but I easily sidestepped him.

"Tell me about Kevin Dunne," I ordered.

"Will you come over here and kiss me if I do?"

"I thought you wanted to save the romance for in front of the fire?"

"I can do both."

"And that's why I fell in lust with you so fast," I teased. "You're always up for doing it everywhere." I giggled as I escaped his grasping hands yet again. "If you don't tell me about Dunne, I'll melt down," I warned. "Then neither of us will get any romance tonight."

On a groan, Landon rocked back on his heels. "He seemed surprised by our visit." He turned to business seamlessly. "When he heard Hemlock Cove's police chief was coming to visit, he looked genuinely thrown. I know there are good actors out there, but he looked shocked ... and confused."

"Did he think it was about Katie?"

"He did." Landon bobbed his head. "That was his first assumption right away. Then we mentioned Enid, and he ushered us into his office."

"That's weird," I mused. "Were you in the bigger office area before then?"

"We were, but I don't think it's all that weird. He's the top agent in that office. It's his business, and he has other agents working under his banner. When he thought his daughter might have been hurt, he could think of nothing else but that. When he heard we were there about something else, practicality prevailed, and he pulled us away from potential customers."

"Yes, it all sounds very pragmatic," I drawled. "Tell me the rest."

"You're a cynical soul, Bay." He tapped the end of my nose. "We explained what happened, that we'd discovered Enid's body on the school grounds. We were careful to say it was near the office building but left the rest of it vague in case we can use that information later."

I nodded. That was smart.

"Then we explained that it was likely she died between the end of business yesterday and early this morning. We avoided a cause of death."

"You don't have a cause of death," I reminded him.

"Hopefully, we'll have that tomorrow. We explained that we went to Enid's house and found some concerning items. I showed him the photos of the boards but didn't mention the file."

"That would freak me out," I said. "Was he freaked out?"

"He seemed ... stunned. He must have looked over the photos a dozen times. He just kept saying 'I don't understand' over and over."

"I don't understand either," I admitted. "If he wasn't involved with her, why would she be so fixated on him?"

"That happens, Bay. People assign emotions to individuals who don't reciprocate. You've seen it yourself. People lose their minds over one-sided romances."'

"Is there more?" I asked.

"Not really. He looked at the photos, denied ever having a relationship with her, and claimed the only interaction they ever had was when they discussed Katie."

"Do you believe him?"

"I have no reason not to. He didn't show any signs or tells of a guy who had murdered a mistress."

"That doesn't necessarily mean anything," I argued.

"It doesn't, but I like to think I'm a relatively good judge of character. I knew you were the one for me right away."

That wasn't exactly the way I remembered it. "You dumped me and went off to think about things when you found out I was a witch."

"Hey!" He poked my side. "I don't want to hear about that ever again. I was confused."

I didn't hold that against him. He didn't know magic was real before me and was thrown by what happened when he witnessed a magical takedown. He wasn't gone long in the grand scheme of things, and once he returned, he was devoted to the point of distraction.

"I'm actually glad you took the time to think things through," I admitted. "Now I don't have to worry about you changing your mind and leaving."

"Oh, I'm never leaving." Landon was serene. "Your mother keeps me in food, and you're my favorite person in the world. What more could a guy ask for?"

I had questions about what he was going to do when our house was finished and he didn't have access to my mother's cooking on a daily basis, but this was not the time to go begging for trouble. "Anything else about Dunne I should know?" I asked.

He shook his head. "He seemed shocked. If he was having an affair with Enid, he missed his calling and should've been an actor, because I believed his denials."

"Would I have believed him?"

"No," Landon answered without hesitation. "You would've assumed he was lying. That's the way you're built. You already feel bad for Enid, so you'd believe her over anyone else right now."

That was a bit of a stretch. I'd been as thrown by what I saw in her house as anybody else. I didn't believe that an affair was a legitimate reason to stalk someone. "Let's head home." I held out my hand for his.

"I thought we were going to roll around on our blanket," Landon whined when he realized I was leading him out of the field.

"We can roll around on the floor in front of the fireplace," I countered. "I want to get home." In truth, I had some things I wanted to think about. If Landon stretched the romance out between two locations, I wouldn't get any thinking time until the following day.

I opened my mouth to flirt him back to happiness, but the second we emerged from the pot field, a wave of wasted magic hit me. It wasn't strong enough to be a weapon, but it was impossible to ignore.

"What the...?" I caught a tendril of magic and lifted it to get a better look. Under the limited moonlight, it was dull green.

"What is that?" Landon demanded as he stared at my finger. He'd shown more than once that he was in tune with the magical world.

"Someone tried to throw a spell," I replied as I glanced around. A shiver ran up my spine. I felt someone watching me, but there was no indication from which direction.

"What sort of spell?" Landon was breathless.

"I don't know." I poked at the green mist, but it dissipated before I could get a good look at it. "Come on." I started down the walkway toward the guesthouse. We were too exposed. The guesthouse was covered by wards that could kill someone if they used magic against them with bad intentions. I wanted to get behind those wards.

Landon followed me. There was no need to glance over my shoulder to know that he was fixated on the trees as we passed.

"We're okay," I assured him as the guesthouse came into view. "We're fine."

"Are you trying to convince me or yourself?" he asked.

"Both."

That answer elicited a wan smile. "Let's get inside." He pulled out his key and unlocked the door, ushering me in before following. All the while, he kept scanning the trees surrounding the guest cottage.

Once the door was shut, he let out a pent-up breath. He didn't turn on the interior lights. Instead, he positioned himself near the front window and stared into the darkness. "What do you think?" he asked.

"I don't know." I kicked off my boots and removed my coat. I actually hung my coat in the closet before going after Landon's coat. He let me take it from him without a word. When I returned to him, he was still watching for signs of an enemy.

"I think—"

A barrage of magic hit our wards. It ricocheted back, causing Landon to shelter me with his body. I pushed him off.

"We're under attack," he hissed.

"Whoever it is tested the wards. They didn't get past them."

"Is that what you think happened at the pot field?"

"Probably."

Magic sparked against the wards again. The faint sound of giggling peeled through the darkness.

"Oh, well, *that's* creepy," Landon complained as he leaned over to stare out the window again. "Are we under attack from magical kids?"

Something occurred to me. "Or magical students at a private school for misbehaving youth."

Landon snapped his eyes in my direction. "The Stonecrest students?" The way he worked his jaw back and forth told me he was having trouble with that suggestion. "Why?"

"Maybe one of them killed their headmistress," I replied. "We questioned them today. Enid had files on all of them."

"I forgot all about that. We haven't gone through the files yet."

"We might want to. I'm curious what Enid had on them. Why would she keep separate files at home when I'm certain she had official files in her office?"

Landon's hand landed on my back. "What should we do about our guests?"

There wasn't much we could do. "I don't think they're a threat. They're testing my magic, but theirs isn't strong enough to get through the wards. We could go looking for them, but they might try to lure us over the wards and attack."

"I don't want to risk that."

He wasn't the only one. "Let's wait it out." I leaned into him, his warmth suffusing me. "They'll give up soon and retreat to plot things out. We're safe here."

"I love you, Bay, but I don't want to be trapped in this place for Christmas. There are cookies out there that need to be eaten, gifts that need to be opened, and Aunt Tillie always makes special Christmas wine."

"Don't forget the Christmas whiskey." I grinned at him, then sobered as I looked out the window again. "We're fine waiting here."

"That *is* the mature thing to do," Landon agreed. "When did you turn mature?"

"About the same time you did."

"Funny how that happened when we were together."

"We're not totally mature. You're hiding candy in the nightstand—and not sharing. There's nothing mature about that."

"If you're a good girl, I'll show you my candy," he said in a husky voice.

"Yeah, let's go to bed. I'll be able to ascertain what happened out there better in the morning."

10
TEN

I wasn't certain I'd be able to sleep, but after the events of what felt like a really long day, I was out within minutes. When I roused the next morning, Landon was working on his phone.

"Anything good?" I murmured as I shifted to rest my head on his chest.

He adjusted to make room for me and pressed his cheek to my forehead. "That depends on what you consider good."

"I think this moment is good."

"You have amazing taste." He kissed the top of my head and went back to typing on his phone. "I woke up to a text from the boss."

I stiffened. "This isn't going to be good, is it?"

"I guess it depends on how you look at things." Landon lowered the phone. His boss Steve Newton was a nice guy who seemed to understand that magic was part of our everyday lives. He just didn't want to know the specifics.

"Just tell me," I instructed. "You make it worse when you drag things out."

"That's not what you said the night I brought the vodka whipped cream to bed."

I glared at him. "Do you want me to praise your sexual expertise or deal with the actual problems of the day?"

"Both."

"You're a god among men in the sack," I replied automatically. "What does Steve want?"

"He said Childs has been sniffing around with the state police, asking questions about you and your family. He wants to know how many unexplained incidents you've been attached to. And he wants to make sure I'm not tipped off that he's searching."

"Crap." I slapped my hand to my forehead as I rolled to my back. "He's turning into a problem."

"There's not much we can do about it."

"I could alter his memory."

"And now that he's poked his nose in and asked questions of the state police, what do you think will happen if he suddenly loses his memory?" Landon challenged.

"Double crap," I muttered.

Landon rolled to his side and cuddled me. "We'll be fine," he assured me. "We'll figure things out."

That was easy for him to say. He wasn't being followed by a vengeful warden. "What if he catches me on camera doing weird things?" I asked. "What if he sells the footage to CNN or something?"

"Do you think CNN will be interested in what could potentially be ridiculous—and faked—footage showing a hoax in northern Lower Michigan?"

"It depends on how slow the news day is," I replied. "I can see someone on a news desk being interested in what looks like magic being thrown around a witch town. That's the sort of cutesy story they'd wedge between disaster reports or reserve for weekend coverage. Either way, it could mean bad things for us."

Landon pursed his lips. "I'll talk to him, Bay. Don't get worked up about this."

"What if he doesn't listen?"

"He's a reasonable man."

The man who had let himself into my newspaper office and tried to blackmail me with exposure didn't seem all that reasonable. There was nothing I could do to fix this, however, so I decided to let Landon give it a try.

"Fine." I flicked my eyes to the clock on the nightstand. It was old, reminding me of my teenage years, and I'd yet to throw it away even though it was no longer practical given the fact that everybody used their phones as alarm clocks. "We should probably shower and head up to the inn. I want to check for signs that somebody was watching us last night."

"What signs?"

"I don't know. It sounded like we were dealing with a pack of teenage girls last night. The giggling was eerie. It was only a few months ago that we dealt with another pack of teenage girls. If we have to face off with another group, I'm going to start debating the trustworthiness of teenagers."

Landon chuckled. "That's what you're most worried about?"

"Aren't you?"

"Not so much." He pulled me tight for a hug, stared into my eyes, then nodded. "Let's get ready. Maybe we'll get lucky and wrap up whatever is going on with Enid today."

WE SPENT THIRTY MINUTES GETTING ready. I had no choice but to blow-dry my hair because of the cold.

A quick scan with my magic suggested we weren't in any danger. That allowed us to wander into the woods and look around. There were footprints, but it was hard to tell if they belonged to multiple people or just one wandering back and forth.

"What do you think?" Landon asked as he hunkered down to look at the prints.

"It could be one person or several. It could be teenagers or someone who wants us to believe it's teenagers. Whoever it was, they couldn't get past the wards."

"They were on the property. They couldn't get past the wards at the guesthouse and the field. You told me those wards are stronger than your average wards."

That was both true and false. "Actually, the wards on the rest of the property are dormant. They're there but drawn so they only ignite if we tell them to or they sense a life-or-death menace."

Landon frowned. "Is that supposed to make sense?"

"It just means that the protection wards are triggered by intention as much as magic. If they blocked every magical being Scout and Stormy wouldn't be able to visit. And not all magical beings are evil. Some are just fine."

"Were those taunting us last night just fine?"

"Probably not, but I only say that because it's impossible to come up with a scenario that involves giggling in the woods while spying that isn't nefarious."

"Oh, listen to that vocabulary." Landon gave me a smacking kiss. "I love when you call things nefarious. I fell for your vocabulary as much as your cute little butt."

I glared at him. "You are so schmaltzy these days. What's up with that? I mean, I like a bit of schmaltz with my toast, but you're the king of the schmaltz these days."

"I am," Landon agreed. "Christmas brings it out in me. I'm looking forward to our first big Christmas together."

"We were together last Christmas," I argued.

"Yes, but we weren't married."

"So, the fact that we're married makes this a special Christmas."

"Sweetie, the fact that we're together makes everything special," he replied. "I can't help it I have a soft spot for Christmas. Halloween is your favorite holiday, but I love Christmas. I want it to be the best Christmas ever every year."

I went warm all over. "That's really sweet." I kissed his cheek. "But the more pressure you put on the situation, the more likely it is to fall short. Let's just have a happy holiday and not try to make it the best ever."

He cocked his head, considering, then shook it. "No. I want the best Christmas ever. I won't back down."

"Fine." I went back to staring at the footprints. "I don't know what we're dealing with. We need to get to the inn. They need to know we had company last night so they can be prepared if visitors show up again today."

"Do you think someone will go after the entire family, or is this a targeted attack on you?"

The way he phrased the question told me he was worried. I didn't have a response that would satisfy him. "I don't know, but I guess we'll find out."

WE ENTERED THE INN THROUGH THE FAMILY living quarters. Aunt Tillie wasn't in her usual spot on the couch yelling at the morning newscasters. When we entered the kitchen, it was empty too.

"If there's no bacon, we're going into town for breakfast," Landon warned.

I pushed through the swinging doors that led to the dining room. That's where we found my mother and aunts serving breakfast.

"You're late," Mom chided.

"Oh, thank the Goddess," Landon said when he caught sight of the platter of bacon. "You're my favorite this morning," he teased my mother with a kiss on the cheek before he practically skipped to his usual chair.

"Punctuality isn't the worst habit," Mom said to me.

I rolled my eyes. "We were in the woods. We had an ... *incident* ... last night." The words were barely out of my mouth when I heard footsteps and looked up to see Chief Terry joining us. "You're late," I said.

"I was already here and then had to take a call." He pointed in the direction he'd come from. "You're in big trouble, young lady."

"What did I do?"

"You let this one run wild, and now there are Christmas decorations running all over town." He jerked a thumb at Aunt Tillie.

"I told you," I hissed at her. "There's no way all those decorations I saw yesterday were from her yard. On top of that, there's a gnome hanging out by The Whistler. He's no longer singing *Who Let the Dogs Out*—which I'm grateful for—but he's joining in on the Christmas carols."

Aunt Tillie wasn't one to admit when she'd made a mistake. Ever. The year she decided that the singer Pink looked cool because her hair was pink and then dyed her hair accordingly? Even when she stripped her hair twice and half of it fell out, she didn't admit she was wrong.

"I have no idea what you're talking about," Aunt Tillie replied in blasé fashion. "If there are Christmas decorations running amok, it has nothing to do with me. Frankly, I'm hurt that you would assume I'm behind something like that. I'm just a sweet old lady trying to enjoy Christmas." She sent Chief Terry a pointed look. "It might be my last Christmas, after all. Given my age."

I choked on the water I was sipping, and Landon thumped me on the back. He looked amused despite the glares Chief Terry lobbed around the table. While I felt sorry for him, the decorations running roughshod all over Hemlock Cove wasn't the worst thing I'd ever witnessed. It was actually kind of funny.

Chief Terry's expression told me he believed the opposite. "Last night, when she was trying to close her shop, Margaret Little was surrounded by three lawn inflatables, four light-up reindeer, three huge lawn ornaments that apparently rolled themselves downtown, and one baby Jesus that was missing a leg."

I turned and buried my face in Landon's shoulder so Chief Terry wouldn't see that I was fighting laughter. Landon's hand immediately went up to cover the back of my head. The news wasn't enough to get him to stop eating. "What happened to baby Jesus's leg?" he asked.

"According to Helen Dutton—it's her baby Jesus, but it started out as a Cabbage Patch Kid apparently—one of the neighborhood dogs has been humping her manger characters all season. The humping got a little overzealous with the baby in the manger, and he lost a leg."

I kept telling myself it wasn't funny, but when I pictured the dog and the baby, laughter kept bubbling up.

"Helen Dutton lives three miles from Margaret," Mom said pointedly to Aunt Tillie. "I thought only Margaret's decorations were supposed to be taking on a life of their own."

"Well, obviously I'm not to blame for this situation," Aunt Tillie replied. "If I were to have had a hand in it—which I didn't—but if I were, I would say perhaps there was some sort of miscommunication in casting the spell."

"So is this the end of it?" Mom asked.

"I don't have a clue." The look Aunt Tillie darted in my direction told me we were nowhere near done. "It's possible the spell might keep growing."

"Oh, crap," Mom moaned.

"Again, I have no personal knowledge of what's happening," Aunt Tillie stressed. "If I did, I might think that's how things were going to play out."

"End the spell now," Chief Terry ordered, his eyes blazing. "The Bunton family on the south end of town have an entire army of lighted polar bears. I do not want those things running around the downtown area and freaking everybody out."

The polar bears weren't my immediate worry. I was much more interested in what could happen if the angels at St. Joseph's Catholic Church decided to take their light show airborne.

"Now let's talk about you," Chief Terry said as he sat next to me. "I heard you guys talking when you came in. Why were you running around in the woods?"

Landon filled him in. When he finished, Chief Terry swore under his breath.

"Nice mouth you've got there, Grinch," Aunt Tillie said. "That's not a very good representation of the Christmas spirit."

"I'm done talking to you." Chief Terry shook a finger in her face before focusing on me. "Are you okay?"

"I'm fine," I assured him. "Whoever it was didn't have the magic necessary to bypass our wards."

"That doesn't change the fact that they were out there," Chief Terry argued. "Do you think it was the kids from Stonecrest?"

"It makes the most sense," I replied. "The thing is, how would those kids know where to find us? Aren't they forced to stay on the campus? If they followed us, why didn't we see them until last night? I was downtown for the better part of the afternoon and was alone part of that time."

"Maybe it's an open campus," Landon suggested.

"That sort of defeats the purpose of a correctional school, doesn't it?"

He leaned back in his chair and munched his bacon. "Maybe we should go back there and question the kids."

"If we do that, the girls will shut down."

"Especially if you take 'The Man' with you," Aunt Tillie added. "They're afraid of law enforcement, whether they did anything or not."

"I don't believe that," Landon said. "If they're innocent, why would they be afraid?"

"It goes with being a teenager," I replied. "I remember the summer I graduated, when Chief Terry caught us skinny-dipping at the lake and accused us of breaking the law."

"You were breaking the law," Chief Terry grumbled. "You lied and said your clothes had become invisible—and that you weren't making out with that Hudson boy—but I knew better."

"Perhaps in that instance I wasn't actually innocent," I said. "Aunt Tillie is right. They won't talk to police officers, especially men."

"Does that mean they'll talk to you?" Landon queried.

"They're more likely to talk to me than you."

"I prefer you weren't around potential magical threats alone." Landon was serious. "I'd feel better if you had backup. Maybe you can tap Scout."

Scout Randall was dealing with her own problems. She'd recently met her parents for the first time and was hunting a former member of her team who had betrayed them.

"Or you could take me," Aunt Tillie suggested. "I'm excellent with teenagers."

"Since when?" Landon shot back. "Teenagers hate you."

"I've always been good with teenagers," Aunt Tillie argued. "At one time, I considered becoming the Dr. Phil of teenagers. I was going to be Counselor Tillie. I was so good, they wanted me to do it professionally. But that made the other counselors jealous, so it never came to fruition."

"Obviously, that's not true," Landon pointed out.

"Of course it isn't. Teenagers suck. But I can help Bay with these girls."

I thought about turning her down. She was a pain in the ass, but kids fell into two camps. They were either enthralled with her or terrified. Either could work for us.

"I'll take Aunt Tillie," I announced. "We'll be fine even if we find out they've got some weird coven there. Trust me."

Landon didn't look convinced, but he nodded. "Okay, but keep in touch."

11
ELEVEN

Landon caught me outside the inn as I exited to warm up my car. Aunt Tillie was bundling up for a day of mischief—she also had to feed her pet pig Peg, or my mother would melt down—and I knew she'd whine if my car was too cold.

"Hey, hold up." Landon scurried to catch up with me. He took my keys before I could start the car. "You know, maybe we should start looking for a new vehicle for you." He cast my old Ford Focus some serious side-eye.

"Why?" I asked.

"Because your car is a million years old."

"It's eight years old."

"In car life, it's Aunt Tillie's age."

"You'd better hope she doesn't hear you," I warned. "She will make you allergic to bacon."

Landon puffed out his chest, but I saw the way his eyes darted around. "She wouldn't really make me allergic to bacon, would she?"

"Oh, you're cute." I patted my gloved hand against his cheek. "Do you need something specific?"

Landon looked wounded when I pulled my hand back. "Where is the love, Bay?"

"I'm just asking. I want to start my day."

"You want to mess with those kids to see if one of them is a diabolical witch," he said.

I shrugged. "Seriously, what's on your mind?"

"I want you to remember that I love you, and it would be best you didn't die. You'll ruin every Christmas going forward if you die on me."

"I won't die," I promised. Something occurred to me, and I stilled. "If I died and you remarried, would you still let my death ruin future Christmases?"

"I reject every part of that question," Landon replied. "You're never dying on me. There will be no second wife. Christmas will never be ruined."

"It's purely hypothetical."

"No." His eyes flashed with annoyance. "You're never leaving me."

I waited until he calmed down. "If the wrong person heard you say that they would assume you were a crazy stalker or something. You might want to take it down a notch."

"I'm fine at this notch." He was firm. "What's the plan, Bay? What are you going to do if you find a girl exhibiting witchy signs?"

"I have no idea." That was the truth. "Right now, I'm just trying to see if I come across a hint of magic. After that, I'll see how I feel."

"Okay. Be careful." He gave me a kiss. "Also, if I were you, I would seriously consider getting Aunt Tillie to reverse that Christmas decoration spell. Terry won't be happy if he keeps getting calls about manger creatures with one leg."

"Yeah, that's the stuff of nightmares," I agreed. "I'll talk to her." Even I didn't believe myself.

"You think it's funny," he accused.

I *did* think it was funny. "They're Christmas decorations," I pointed out. "All they do is sing. How can that be bad?"

"I really wish you hadn't asked that," Landon replied. "Whenever you say something like that, things go off the rails."

I had news for him: Things were already off the rails. I didn't want to ruin his day so I opened my arms and pulled him in for a hug. "It will be fine," I assured him. "Trust me."

"I love you," he replied. "That's enough."

"Does that mean you don't trust me? I'm hurt."

"That question feels like a trap. Ask me again in ten hours."

"It's going to be a perfect day. You'll see."

AUNT TILLIE'S NEW WINTER COAT WAS camouflage. It matched her combat helmet. During the summer, she often dressed Peg in a matching camouflage tutu. The teacup pig wasn't acclimated to cold weather, so she'd wisely left her home today.

"Are you still getting Landon a dog for Christmas?" Aunt Tillie asked as I pulled onto the highway that led to the school.

"I am," I confirmed. "He needs something to love."

"Isn't that what he has you for?"

"Fine. He needs something to mother."

"A dog isn't a temporary part of the family, Bay," Aunt Tillie replied in her most serious voice. Thistle had taken to calling it her "Tilliesplain" voice. "You can't just lock up the dog at the guesthouse when you and Landon are working all day. That's not fair."

"I have no intention of locking the dog in the guesthouse," I replied. "I already talked to Mom. She's willing to take the dog during the afternoons several days a week. She thinks the dog will be a good playmate for Peg. On other days, I'll take the dog to work with me."

Aunt Tillie made a face. "Why didn't I know that?"

"Perhaps because you didn't ask. Or perhaps because unless the conversation is about you, you don't listen. As for taking him with me, it makes sense. If something comes up while I'm downtown, he can go to the petting zoo. I already talked to Marcus. I have everything covered."

"Huh." Aunt Tillie looked momentarily perplexed. Then she smiled. "I think a dog will do you guys some good."

I waited for her to get a backhanded dig in. "That's all you have to say?"

"It is," she confirmed. "Well, other than you should let me name it because you'll come up with a stupid name. But as far as ideas go, I don't mind this one. You guys aren't ready for a baby, although Landon thinks he is. A few days with a puppy will show him it's best to wait. Your mother will spoil the dog like a real grandchild. It's really the best of both worlds."

It was something I hadn't considered. "You never had children," I said as I pulled into the school parking lot. "Why?"

"I didn't want them when I was younger. Then, when I got older, it was too late."

"You could've adopted."

"I had your mother and aunts. They were close enough to mine. Then, much later, I had the three of you. That was more than enough."

"Oh, that's so sweet." I poked her cheek. "Why don't you just say that you loved us more than you could've loved your own kids?"

"Because I don't believe in lying to children." Aunt Tillie turned her attention to the school grounds. "This was a Catholic school when I was a kid."

I nodded. "Obviously, you didn't go here. Did you know any of the kids who did?"

"Not really. My mother wasn't big on religious schools. She wasn't a fan of witch schools either, for that matter. The kids who went to the Catholic school didn't particularly like us because they thought we were squirrelly."

"Not you," I teased.

"Yes, well, there wasn't a lot of crossover. It closed years ago.

There was a charter school, and another religious school. Then there was the school where they shoved the pregnant girls."

I made a face. "I can't believe nobody stepped in and did anything when they were locking pregnant teenagers up here."

"I hate to break it to you, Bay, but that was one of the nicer things they did with pregnant teenagers back in my day. Heck, back in your mother's day they were still sending pregnant girls off to Europe—they were really on a long-forgotten family member's Iowa farm—and when the girl got back from her 'trip' she would magically have an infant brother or sister."

"Yeah, I've heard about that," I said as I pocketed my keys and pushed open the driver's door. "It seems so alien."

"People will tell you that back in their day, things like that didn't happen, but they did," Aunt Tillie said as she joined me in the parking lot. "It happened just as much—maybe more. Everybody knew what was going on. They kept it to themselves.

"There were no DNA tests to trap philandering husbands," she continued. "You couldn't prove that someone was the father, so the girls carried all the stigma on their shoulders. The truth is, some people liked it that way."

"I take it you didn't." I watched her profile closely. "That doesn't seem like something you would like."

"It wasn't," she agreed. "I used to dole out my own justice back then ... and I made it known too."

"What did you do?"

Her smile told me it was something truly evil. "Let's just say I put a little something in the water."

I was almost afraid to ask. "Meaning?"

"Meaning that any man who didn't take responsibility for the child he created not only saw his fortunes take a turn for the worse, his penis took a turn too. It essentially became a turtle without a shell. It shrank and went into hiding whenever anybody got near it."

There were times I thought she was a total pain and I needed a break from her. There were other times she was my hero. "That's pretty cool."

She shrugged. For once, she wasn't looking to pat herself on the back. "There's right and wrong, Bay. What happened back then—and it happened a lot—wasn't okay. The men got away with it and the women were shamed and treated like crap by the very same women who were hiding their own daughters' secrets. In that sense, the world today is much better."

"What way isn't it better?" I was honestly curious to hear her answer.

"Places like this still exist, don't they?" she asked as she waved her hand at the campus.

I inclined my head toward the administration building. "Come on. Let's check in with Bianca—she's the administrative assistant—and then we'll feel things out. She might not let us hang out with the girls if we don't give her a convincing reason."

"I'll handle that."

I slowed my pace. "What are you going to do?"

"Just let me handle it. This is not my first private school adventure. I've got this."

"Fine, but try not to do anything weird."

"No promises."

AUNT TILLIE SCHMOOZED BIANCA IN A way I didn't see coming. The administrative assistant looked harried when we approached her desk. Aunt Tillie announced we were there to spy on the girls and make sure they weren't involved in Enid's death. I froze, but instead of sending us on our way, Bianca gave us a free pass to roam wherever we wanted.

"Okay," I said as we got comfortable in the common room. The bell signaling a change of classes clanged, and I expected to see a student or two from our vantage point. "Just feel them out. Don't be weird with them. We're just trying to get an idea who might've been outside the guesthouse last night."

"This isn't my first spy mission at a private school for bad girls," Aunt Tillie replied dryly.

"Oh, yeah? How many missions have you been on at private schools for bad girls?"

"You might be surprised." Aunt Tillie narrowed her eyes as the girls started to spin into the room. I remembered most of them by face but few of them by name. There were a few standouts, however, including Autumn Larson. She was the self-avowed bad girl who had gotten too much attention from Enid.

"She's a witch." Aunt Tillie jabbed a finger at Autumn.

I frowned when Autumn lifted her chin and stared at us. She was too far away to have heard, but the look she shot us was just short of triumphant.

"How can you be sure?" I demanded. I was coming into my own as a witch—and a very powerful necromancer—but some of the nuances of my trade remained a mystery.

"She has a wart on her nose," Aunt Tillie replied simply.

I made a face and looked again at Autumn. She was still staring at us. "I'm pretty sure that's a diamond stud in her nose," I replied.

"She's still a witch."

"Until you have more definitive proof, I'm going to move along." I inclined my head toward the blonde who bounced into the room. Her skirt was a good two inches shorter than most of the other girls. "What's the point of shortening your skirt at an all-girls school?" I asked.

"Maybe she likes girls."

It was such a simple answer I felt like an idiot for not getting it myself. "Duh." I slapped my forehead. I felt like a moron. "That's Katie Dunne. She's the daughter of the real estate agent the headmistress was stalking."

"Yeah, that's weird." Aunt Tillie leaned back and, to my surprise, undid the button on her pants.

"What are you doing?" I hissed, horrified.

"I had way too many sausage links for breakfast," Aunt Tillie replied. "I think your mother has been shrinking my pants as payback."

"Or you've been gaining weight."

"Don't be ridiculous," she snapped. "I've worn the same size pants since I was in middle school. The girl in the slutty skirt is a witch too."

I was only mildly irritated the first time she declared one of the students a witch. Now I was agitated. "You haven't even talked to her," I argued.

"That doesn't mean she's not a witch."

"Coming from the woman who thinks Mom is shrinking her clothes, I think I'm going to need more than that." Most of the girls didn't look in our direction, so it was easy to spy on them. Only three, Autumn, Katie and Violet, paid us any attention.

"That one too." Aunt Tillie jabbed her finger at Violet before rocking to a standing position.

I glared at her. "Where do you think you're going?"

"Back to talk to the secretary."

"Why? Also, I think you're supposed to call them administrative assistants now. 'Secretary' is demeaning."

"Says who?" Aunt Tillie wrinkled her nose. "I'm sure she would be fine with me calling her a secretary."

"If you say so."

"I'll prove it." Aunt Tillie started out of the common room, leaving me no choice but to chase her.

"Hey, don't you think you should button up your pants?" I asked.

Aunt Tillie looked offended. "No. I've got it."

"You still haven't told me what you plan to do."

"I want to see the files on those three girls."

"You think Bianca is just going to hand them over to you?"

"Yes."

"She won't. There are laws."

"You let me worry about those so-called laws."

I trailed behind. "Just once I wish you'd realize you're not in charge of everybody's life. Just once."

"Keep wishing."

TWENTY MINUTES LATER AUNT TILLIE WAS still sulking in my car.

"I can't believe she said no," she complained, throwing her hands into the air for good measure. "Who tells me no?"

"To be fair, she didn't tell you no," I countered. "She just pointed out that the law doesn't allow her to share private files on students."

"Well, the law is stupid."

"It is," I agreed, even though I didn't particularly feel that way. Placating her in the moment seemed like a good idea. "Don't worry about it. Enid had files on all the students. Landon confiscated them, but if I flirt with him enough later tonight, he'll let me look at them."

"You shouldn't have to flirt with your husband to get what you want," Aunt Tillie huffed. "He should do what you say because he loves you."

"Yeah, it doesn't really work like that in our relationship. We compromise." I tapped my fingers on the steering wheel as I considered our next move. "How do you feel about a trip to Traverse City?"

"That depends. Can we eat lunch at that really good Chinese place?"

"Sure." I bobbed my head. As much as I loved Hemlock Cove, the food options were limited. "That sounds good."

"Okay, we can go to Traverse City. What's there?"

"The guy Enid was stalking."

"Ah, the father of the girl in the slutty skirt." Aunt Tillie nodded. "Let's pay him a visit." She reached for her seatbelt. Her pants were still unbuttoned.

"You can't call her slutty," I argued. "Her skirt was shorter, but that doesn't make her slutty."

"I can call her whatever I want. When you reach a certain age, you can be as mean as you want, and there's nothing anyone can do about it. Do you want to know why?" She didn't wait for me to respond. "I'll tell you why. People are afraid to offend you when you're old. You can say whatever you want and nobody comments. In fact, most people laugh because they need to believe it's a joke."

"Is that why you say the things you do?"

"I do what I want regardless. I'm just stating a fact."

We'd barely started the day, and I was already tired. "Let's talk to Kevin Dunne. Landon told me not to, but you're old, and I can't argue with you when you say you want to meet him, can I?"

Aunt Tillie's brow wrinkled. "Who are you calling old?"

"You just said you were old."

"I did not. You're imagining things."

"You make me really tired," I lamented.

"Yup. You're definitely old."

12
TWELVE

I shouldn't have felt guilty about visiting a real estate agent in another town in the middle of the day. I did, though, because I knew Landon would be agitated when he found out how I'd spent my time with Aunt Tillie. Despite that, I didn't turn back when we arrived at Kevin Dunne's office.

"Okay, here's the plan," I started, turning to Aunt Tillie.

She stopped me. "No, we're not playing *that* game today," she said. "You're terrible at coming up with explanations for why you want to dig for information. You come up with lame excuses. It's time to accept your inheritance from me. You're a gifted storyteller. Use that ability."

My forehead creased. "You're a terrible storyteller," I argued "Please don't tell me I'm as bad as you."

"Excuse me?" Aunt Tillie's eyebrows shot up her forehead. "I am the best storyteller you've ever met."

"No, you're not. Scout is actually the best storyteller I've ever met. I don't even know when she's lying or telling the truth when telling hilarious stories about her past."

Aunt Tillie looked wounded. "She's an amateur."

"No, she's good. You're bad. We need to make sure we have a good plan in place before we go in. I was thinking we would tell him that you're eccentric and losing your mind, and we want to find a place for you at one of those assisted living properties that allows old people to feel a sense of independence."

If looks could kill, I would be dead. Aunt Tillie was practically vibrating with fury. "Did you just call me old?"

"What's your idea?" I challenged rather than answer the question. Much like Aunt Tillie, I was a bad liar when it came to family, and she would know I was making it up if I denied thinking she was old.

"I thought we would go in and tell him I want to start an animal rescue for raccoons, and it has to be on a big stretch of property but away from The Overlook property because my nieces don't like raccoons."

Now it was my turn to frown. "Why raccoons?"

"Why not raccoons?"

"It's so random. Why wouldn't you start a rescue for animals other than raccoons? That's too specific."

"Raccoons are great," Aunt Tillie argued. "In fact, you know how I've been searching for a second sidekick?"

I nodded. Her current sidekick was Evan, the day-walking vampire. She'd brought Evan out of his shell when our witchy friend Scout had healed his soul and given him back the essence of himself ... with a few enhanced abilities to make his return all the more entertaining. Aunt Tillie had taken it upon herself to engage Evan, and to my surprise, they made an interesting twosome. Evan's personality was suddenly as loud as Aunt Tillie's, which was not necessarily a bad thing.

Then, a week ago, she decided she needed a second sidekick and had approached our witchy friend Stormy about adding Easton, Stormy's gnome shifter familiar who used to be a cat and now looked like a hot man, to her cadre of colorful companions. She already had Peg, who she liked to dress in custom-made tutus and combat helmets. Easton had balked about being the second sidekick, wrangling for first position. They'd been locked in contentious negotiations since.

Aunt Tillie's new interest in raccoons was a whole other problem.

"Mom will not let you bring raccoons into the inn," I said. "She won't stand for it."

"Um ... I don't have to ask your mother for permission to do anything," Aunt Tillie argued. "I'm an adult. I'm allowed to do whatever I want. On top of that, I own fifty percent of the inn ... and the property. I'll do what I want."

She paused a beat. "Who said anything about raccoons?" she added. "Nobody mentioned raccoons. I had better not hear the word 'raccoon' come out of your mouth in front of your mother."

That was all I needed to hear to know she had a plan for domesticating raccoons. "They belong in the wild," I insisted. "Plus, you have Peg. If something were to happen to you, Mom would already have to take on the pig. It's not okay to saddle her with another animal."

Aunt Tillie looked appalled. "What's going to happen to me?"

"I'm not saying anything is going to happen to you," I hedged, suddenly uncomfortable. "It's just ... you have Evan *and* Easton. Their names even sound like they could belong in a boyband. Like ... Tillie and the Es. Why do you need raccoons too?"

"I wasn't thinking of them for the inn, nosy," Aunt Tillie shot back. "I was thinking of them as trained sentries for my field. They could keep people from getting too close, and they could attack if high school kids decide they're looking for a tasty treat to steal. And I'm not talking about tomatoes."

I knew exactly what sort of treats she meant. Aunt Tillie's pot field was legendary in high school circles. All the kids seemed to know it existed, but none could find it. It had become something akin to an epic adventure, and Aunt Tillie enjoyed playing the game.

"No." I shook my head, firm. "You cannot bring in raccoons to go after high school students. Raccoons have diseases ... and rabies. Do you want some poor unsuspecting high school kid to get rabies?"

"First off, my raccoons wouldn't get rabies because I would magically protect them," Aunt Tillie replied. "They would have the absolute best lives. Second, if a kid comes sniffing around with the express desire to steal my pot, I won't feel bad about them getting rabies."

"Oh, geez." I pinched the bridge of my nose before pushing open the driver's side door. "Let me do the talking."

Aunt Tillie huffed, but I was quicker and made it to the front door before she could catch up. I was all smiles for the secretary behind the desk. "Hi. I'm hoping to talk with Kevin Dunne. I'm trying to find some property for my great-aunt—"

"To house raccoons!" Aunt Tillie blurted breathlessly as she caught up to me.

"For my great-aunt to live out her final days with a nice view and peace," I countered. "She has dementia."

"I'm going to need a whole other list for how much you're on my list," Aunt Tillie threatened.

I ignored her. "We have cash if we find the right property," I said to entice the secretary.

She beamed at us. "Right this way."

It was as easy as that. Within three minutes we'd been ushered into Kevin Dunne's office. The secretary explained he was in the conference room giving a pep talk to his employees and would join us shortly. He walked through the door before I could argue further with an annoyed Aunt Tillie.

I vaguely remembered his photos from the benches, and yet I was surprised by the man who walked through the door. His smile was friendly enough, but the photos suggested that Kevin was chiseled and put together. The guy who stood in front of me now was schlubby and a bit bloated.

"Um, hi. I'm Bay Winchester." I extended my hand. "My great-aunt has dementia, and we're trying to find property close to the family property we already have so we can build her a house and hire a nurse to care for her."

"I'm going to train raccoons to serve as my personal army," Aunt Tillie explained. "They're going to attack anyone I don't like, including this one." She jerked her thumb at me. "Do you have anything that will work?"

If Kevin was thrown by what we wanted, he didn't show it. His smile didn't diminish as he sat in his desk chair. "First, I need to know where you reside," he started. "I'm Kevin Dunne, by the way." He turned to me, and for the first time since he'd walked into the office, I caught a trace of the charm that Enid must've felt when she decided to stalk him.

"Hemlock Cove," I replied. "My understanding is that your network extends to that area."

"It does." His smile widened. "Hemlock Cove is an up-and-coming area. You're smart to buy now. When your aunt is no longer ... with us ... you'll make a killing moving the property a second time."

"Where am I going?" Aunt Tillie asked blankly.

"I just meant that when you make the ultimate trip," Kevin explained.

"You mean to Orlando?"

Kevin looked distinctly uncomfortable. "I..."

"He means when you die," I blurted. "You're not going to live forever, after all."

"I'm barely middle aged." Aunt Tillie sounded wounded. "What is the matter with you?"

I pretended she hadn't spoken. "You look familiar for a different reason," I prodded. "I think ... I think I met your daughter yesterday."

"Is that so?" Kevin straightened on his chair. Now a hint of wariness took over his features. "Where would you have seen Katie?"

I decided that concocting too big a lie wouldn't behoove me under the current circumstances. If Kevin found out I was lying, it would come back to bite me. I opted to tell the truth ... at least partially. "My husband is an FBI agent. I was with him yesterday when he received a call about a body being discovered at Stonecrest

Academy. Because he didn't have time to drop me at home, I went with him to check it out."

"I see." Kevin's expression now turned decidedly neutral. "I heard about what happened at the school. A sad situation."

"It is," I agreed. "I consult with my husband occasionally—I'm kind of a secretary of sorts and record information for him—so I was there when they interviewed the kids. Katie seems like a lovely girl."

"She has a lot of energy," Kevin said. "So, tell me where you're looking in Hemlock Cove."

"As close to The Overlook as possible," I replied.

Now Kevin registered true surprise. "You're *those* Winchesters?" He looked tickled. "I've been trying to get a meeting with your family for months. I want to talk to you about selling some of your land. You're in a prime position to take advantage of what's coming down the pipeline given your location."

"I'm not in any position to sell family land," I replied. "I don't own any of it."

"I do," Aunt Tillie volunteered. "I'm not selling any of it to an opportunist like you."

I shot her a quelling look. "Ignore her. She's ... senile."

"It's okay." Kevin clucked his tongue sympathetically. "I understand it's challenging to control people of a certain age. They become like children and blurt out whatever comes to mind."

I darted a worried look to Aunt Tillie—that was not the sort of sentiment she would enjoy—and found her glaring at Kevin as if he was the fly and she was the swatter. "My mother, Winnie Winchester, would be the one you need to talk to about that," I explained, internally cringing when I pictured Kevin showing up to float the idea of selling family land. He would become a display on the roof if he wasn't careful. Those reindeer would be mounting something else by the time my mother finished with him. "My husband and I own property by the lake—the old campground out there—and we plan to build, but that process won't start until spring."

"You bought the old campground?" Kevin looked impressed. "That property sat vacant for years. Nobody was interested. Then you and your husband swooped in and got it for a song right before Hemlock Cove's real estate market caught fire. A very smart move."

"Yes, well, I like being smart."

"It so rarely happens for her," Aunt Tillie drawled. "Now, tell me about properties where I can keep raccoons and train them as guards."

Kevin smiled at Aunt Tillie—he was good at never breaking character—but it was obvious he didn't know how to take her. "Sure."

I acted as if I was taking pity on him when I changed the subject back to Stonecrest. "Did you know the headmistress?" I asked feigning bland curiosity. "The one who died?"

"Vaguely." Kevin's fingers were deft as he typed on the keyboard. "I knew her through Katie, of course—she's been a bit of a wild child of late, so I felt it best to get her into the most structured environment available—and I met Ms. Walters when I was touring the school."

He'd admitted Katie had issues. His vagueness about Enid was something else, however. "It's horrible how she died."

Kevin straightened. "I was under the impression they didn't have a cause of death yet."

Crap. He was right. Landon was expecting autopsy results today. "Well, the way she was found in the parking lot, they're assuming she was either attacked or took a nasty fall." That wasn't exactly a lie. "It must be traumatizing for your daughter."

"Very little traumatizes Katie." Kevin made a face. "She's a bit of a monster right now. I keep telling myself that's the case for most teenagers, but now I understand why so many of them can't be diagnosed with personality disorders until they're adults. They all read as sociopaths."

That was an interesting take on his own daughter. "Um..." I darted a look to Aunt Tillie, but she didn't seem bothered by the statement.

"Raccoons would make great sentries," she insisted. "You can train them, and they're cute, so people don't naturally assume they're going to do anything bad."

I nodded and patted her knee. "Yes. Bring it up with Mom. I'm sure she'll have an opinion on the subject."

I turned back to Kevin. "You didn't know Ms. Walters?"

"Not really," Kevin replied. Even though he was focused on his computer, I saw the muscle that jumped in his jaw. "I did talk to her when I brokered the deal for the school. It belonged to another entity before she took it over. I got her a great price. In return, she gave me a break on tuition for Katie. It was a good deal for both of us."

"That's all?"

"Should I have known her a different way?" Kevin asked. He looked confused.

"No," I answered a little too quickly. "Of course not. I was just ... shocked ... when I saw the body yesterday. I hate when someone dies so close to Christmas."

"Yes, that's always a tragedy," he agreed. "Okay, I have some properties for you to consider. This is what I have to start with. I should be able to come up with a secondary list as soon as tomorrow."

"Awesome." I forced a smile I didn't feel. "We'll take the list and go over it at lunch. We look forward to seeing what else you have."

"I think this is going to be a fruitful partnership for both of us."

He was dreaming if he thought I could manipulate my mother into selling him property. "Yes, I love fruitful partnerships."

ONCE WE WERE BACK IN THE PARKING LOT WITH the printouts Kevin had presented—fact sheets on various properties—I turned my attention to Aunt Tillie.

"He thinks you're nuts. You know that, right?"

Aunt Tillie waved off my concern. "I'm fine with it. What I'm not fine with is how weird he was about his kid attending that school. He almost seemed disinterested."

I nodded. "I felt the exact same way."

"I can tell you right now, if one of my girls had been attending a school where a body appeared in the parking lot, I wouldn't be ignoring the situation."

I was right there with her. "I can't decide if he was lying about knowing Enid. Part of me thinks he was covering—he would have to be a good liar to do what he does as well as he does—but something felt off."

"I didn't like him," Aunt Tillie muttered. "He called me old and said I was going to die."

I didn't point out I'd been in on that. Instead, I focused my attention on a sporty red car pulling into the lot. A woman with shoulder-length strawberry blonde curls was in the driver's seat. Her attention was fixed on the front door.

After a few seconds, Kevin exited the building and headed straight for her car.

Even from our vantage spot in the far corner of the lot, it was impossible to miss the way he leaned in for a kiss. The driver seemed all too eager to return the gesture.

"Is that his wife?" Aunt Tillie asked.

I shrugged. "I haven't seen a photo of her. He doesn't feel like the sort of guy who would marry someone who shows up to make out with him in the parking lot outside of work, does he?"

"No." Aunt Tillie shook her head.

I took a screenshot of the woman's license plate before she zipped out of the parking lot. "Maybe I can convince Landon to run this for me. We'll have to forego Chinese and go back to Hemlock Cove to eat lunch."

Aunt Tillie didn't look thrilled at the prospect. "What's in it for me?"

"Irritating Landon and Chief Terry with your plan to corner the market on soldier raccoons."

Aunt Tillie perked up. "I can go without Chinese for that."

Somehow, I wasn't surprised. "I knew you would."

"I'm nothing if not predictable," Aunt Tillie agreed. "Should I order combat helmets for my raccoons?"

"They wouldn't be proper sentries without them."

"I'll start shopping online right now."

13
THIRTEEN

I was lost in my head—numerous possibilities regarding the woman's identity flitting through my mind—and wasn't immediately cognizant of what was happening when we returned to Hemlock Cove. It wasn't until I parked in front of the diner and saw the huge inflatable Christmas tree bulbs bouncing down the sidewalk that I knew we were in trouble.

"Aunt Tillie!"

"This is not my fault," she maintained. "I have no idea who is responsible, but I didn't do this. No way. No how. It wasn't me." She folded her arms across her chest as she stared at the ornaments. "You don't think they would flatten a small child?" She sounded genuinely concerned.

"Unbelievable," I muttered as I climbed out of the car. "You're just ... unbelievable."

Apparently, I wasn't the only one who found Aunt Tillie unbelievable, because Mrs. Little picked that moment to exit her store and extend a threatening finger at Aunt Tillie.

"You," she hissed.

"No, you," Aunt Tillie shot back.

"You."

"You."

They reminded me of three-year-olds hurling insults in a sandbox. "Is that all you're going to say to one another?" I asked.

Aunt Tillie shot me a quelling look. "I don't need you sticking your nose in my business. This is my show."

"By all means." I made a sweeping motion with my hand before leaning against my car and folding my arms over my chest. "Have at it."

Aunt Tillie's eyes narrowed suspiciously, but she was apparently game because she took a decisive step forward. "What do you want, *Margaret*?" She said Mrs. Little's first name as if she was uttering the C-word ... and the F-word ... and maybe even a few other words that would infuriate my mother.

"I want you to stop ... whatever this is." Mrs. Little sounded desperate as she motioned to the small park that separated the police station from the festival grounds. There, a huge abominable snowman inflatable appeared to be chatting with someone's Santa. The Santa decoration had clearly been attached to something else at some point because he had no legs—or pants, for that matter—and had somehow fashioned his legs from decorative yard candy canes.

"Oh, that's freaky," I grimaced.

"Do you think?" Mrs. Little looked beside herself. "People are starting to talk, Tillie."

"I don't care." Aunt Tillie was not the type to back down. No matter what. "That's not my problem."

"How is it not your problem?" Mrs. Little seethed. "You caused this."

"Prove it." Aunt Tillie was the picture of innocence. "Prove that this is my fault. I'll wait here." She shot me a triumphant look. "I've got her now."

I smiled, but not because I believed she'd won. It simply seemed the thing to do. Then I saw Landon and Chief Terry exiting the police station. I watched—partially-fascinated and partially-terrified—as they slowed their pace and took in the weird Santa on the side of the building. They looked at each other, said something, and then slowly looked to me as if they sensed I was watching them.

"Crap on a cracker," I complained when I snagged gazes with Landon. He wasn't happy.

Aunt Tillie looked to see who had caught my attention. She didn't appear bothered in the least when she saw who it was.

"It's fine," she assured me. "Don't be you and start kvetching. I've got everything under control."

"Aunt Tillie..." I didn't know what to say, so instead I buried my face in my hands.

It didn't take long for Landon and Chief Terry to reach us.

"Can I talk to you?" Chief Terry asked. It wasn't a request.

"I'm good," I replied without looking up. "Just ignore me. I'm going to stand here for a bit and make my Christmas wish early."

"Your Christmas wish?" Landon snorted out a laugh.

"When she was little, she used to wait for the first star on Christmas Eve," Chief Terry replied. "She'd sit outside and wait, no matter how long it took. Then she made a wish."

"And it would always come true," I volunteered. I refused to look up. "I know what I'm going to wish this time."

"The only reason those wishes came true is because you said them in front of Terry," Aunt Tillie barked. "You were a simple kid and only wished for things he could provide. You can't be daft enough to think those things magically appeared under the Christmas tree. Terry made them appear."

I stilled. My first thought was that she was trying to be difficult—she was Aunt Tillie, after all. When I thought about it, though, I realized she was right.

I lowered my hands and stared at the man in question. "You did all of that for me?"

Chief Terry's expression didn't change. "I have no idea what you're talking about."

I glared at Aunt Tillie.

"Don't be a ninny," she chided. "He's only saying that because he doesn't want you to think you weren't magical."

"She *is* magical," Chief Terry shot back.

"She's evil is what she is," Mrs. Little argued. "Both of them. Tillie is training her to follow in her footsteps."

"Shut up," Landon and Chief Terry barked in unison.

"This wouldn't be happening if you weren't the worst person in the world," Landon growled. "Don't you take any responsibility for this?"

"Are you seriously insinuating that I'm responsible for the town being overrun by Christmas decorations?" Mrs. Little demanded. "I didn't cause this, they did."

"You might not be responsible for the actual act, but it was your insistence on trying to hurt them that caused this. It's all on you."

"Yes, let's never make Tillie face repercussions for her actions," Mrs. Little said dryly. "That's a fabulous idea. She's the reason my life is a constant struggle. She's the reason I cry myself to sleep at night."

That statement was meant to draw sympathy, but we all burst out laughing.

"Nobody's buying that," Chief Terry said when we'd finished giggling at Mrs. Little's expense. "You helped cause this. You and Tillie need to come to a compromise to end it." He was grave when he focused on my great-aunt. "You're up for that, right?"

Rather than immediately respond, Aunt Tillie flicked her eyes to me. "This feels like a trick."

"Give it a try," I replied, weary. "We'll get a table. What do you want me to order for you?"

"A chicken wrap and fries," Aunt Tillie replied. She planted her hands on her hips as she glared at Mrs. Little. "I won't be long, because I guarantee she doesn't really want to compromise."

I had no doubt she was right, but it was a start. "Have fun." I waved as I started toward the diner with Landon and Chief Terry. "I have some news."

"So do we," Landon replied as he held open the door. "Did you get anywhere with the kids at the school?"

"I guess that depends on your definition of 'getting anywhere.'" I used air quotes. "Aunt Tillie pegged three of the kids as witches without speaking to them—including Katie Dunne. But I'm not sure I believe her. She was bored and didn't particularly like the school."

Landon nodded as he placed his hand on the small of my back to prod me toward our usual table. "Is that all you did?"

He knew me too well. "Why don't you tell me your news first?" I suggested as I sat next to him. My voice was bright and chirpy, a dead giveaway.

"You did something bad." Landon jabbed a finger at me. "Tell me what right now."

Rather than respond—I wasn't in the mood for a fight—I turned to Chief Terry. "Did you really make my Christmas wishes come true? Are you the reason I got the bear that year?"

Chief Terry shrugged. "Does it matter?"

It did to me, but probably not for the reasons he assumed. "I still think those wishes were magical," I assured him. "Maybe even more so now. I just can't believe I didn't figure it out. I feel like such an idiot."

"I didn't just make your wishes come true," Chief Terry replied. "I did it for Clove and Thistle, too."

That was hardly surprising. "Thanks." I meant it. "That makes what I have to tell you next all the more difficult. Here I am finding out that you went out of your way to be the best father ever, but now you're probably going to be angry when you hear how I spent my morning."

"I already figured that." Chief Terry winked at me. "Tell me anyway."

I filled them in, and when I got to the part about lying to Dunne to get information, they both looked furious.

"What did I say about questioning him?" Chief Terry demanded.

I shrugged. I hated when he was angry with me. "Aren't you

interested in the fact that Aunt Tillie wants to train raccoons to protect her pot field? That's the better part of the story."

Chief Terry folded his arms across his chest.

I had to hope for help from Landon. "This really isn't my fault," I said. "Seriously, I was just minding my own business and trying to solve a murder."

"How do you even know it's a murder?" Landon demanded. "For all you know, she could've died of an aneurysm."

"Did she?"

"No. She was poisoned."

Poisoned? Well, that was interesting. "How would poison drop her outside like that?" I wasn't expecting an answer. I was merely asking it as part of my process. "If you were feeling sick from poison, wouldn't you curl up on your office couch?"

"Her house was only a mile away," Chief Terry countered. "If I was really sick, I might brave the drive so I could have privacy."

Shirley, who was on shift again today, picked that moment to take our orders. She was tickled when she heard Aunt Tillie would be joining us. "Is she outside handling the giant gingerbread men?" she asked.

I jerked my eyes to the window and frowned when I saw the gingerbread men. They had to be six feet tall and were standing in the middle of the street impeding traffic.

"Bay, I don't want to pick," Chief Terry started.

"Then don't," I shot back. "Aunt Tillie has it under control." I risked a glance at Landon and found him frowning. "She does," I insisted.

"She does not," Landon countered. "It's obvious that she has no control over what's happening."

"She's Aunt Tillie. She'll fix it."

"Bay, there's a Santa with candy canes for legs running around," Chief Terry said sternly.

I waited for Shirley to double-check our order. When she was gone, I had my argument ready. "I'm assuming that Santa was in a sleigh of some sort but couldn't operate the sleigh and was forced to fashion his own legs from candy canes."

"I don't need an explanation, Bay," Chief Terry warned. "This is unbelievable."

"I'll talk to her." It was the best I could do. "Now, what sort of poison are we talking about?"

"We don't know," Landon replied. "We only know it was lethal and in a large enough dose that she probably was on her feet only a few minutes after ingesting it."

"Then she would've felt sick right away," I mused.

"Probably."

"That suggests one of the students gave it to her," I surmised. "They would've been the only ones near enough."

"Unless it was something she had in a thermos, or something she brought with her and kept in the refrigerator."

"I didn't consider that. But you're saying it can't be Kevin."

Landon held out his hands. "We can't completely rule him out, but it seems unlikely."

I tapped my fingers on the table. There was no reason to run the license plate of Kevin's lunch date if he wasn't the culprit. Still... "Could you check on a license plate for me anyway?"

Landon was immediately suspicious. "Why?"

"Kevin left his office with the driver right before we came here. I want to know who she is."

"Maybe she's a client."

"Maybe." I smiled.

"But you don't think so," he surmised.

"There was something off about her," I replied. "Can we just leave it at that? I mean ... they immediately started making out when he got in the car. That suggests she wasn't his wife."

"Don't you want to make out with me every time you see me?" Landon asked.

"I do, actually," I countered. "But we're newlyweds. Kevin has been married to his wife how long?"

"Point taken."

"No, I really want to know how long," I prodded.

Landon let loose an exasperated sigh, a sound of defeat. "Sixteen years."

I did the math in my head. "So the wife was pregnant with Katie when they got married."

"Why does that matter?" Landon asked.

"Kevin didn't seem all that ... *fatherly* ... when it came to talking about Katie," I replied. "I mentioned that I'd met her. He essentially called her a monster."

"Is that so?" Now I had Landon's full attention. "He left that part out with us."

I was hardly surprised. "He didn't seem all that worried about his daughter being at a school where a potential murder happened."

"Maybe we should pay him another visit," Landon suggested to Chief Terry.

"It couldn't hurt," Chief Terry agreed. "Run the license plate for her. Now I'm kind of curious."

I showed Landon the screenshot I'd taken. It didn't take him long to run it through the database. "Georgie Hamilton," he read aloud. "She works at a bank in Shadow Hills. She lives there."

"So, not Kevin Dunne's wife." I didn't want to crow—no, really—but I knew something had been off about their interaction.

"Not Kevin Dunne's wife," Landon agreed. "His wife's name is Joanie."

"You already mentioned that. What can you tell me about Georgie?"

"She's married," Landon replied. "Her husband's name is Andrew. He works in construction, and he and Georgie married right after high school, about thirteen years ago."

"No divorce documents filed?" Chief Terry asked.

Landon shook his head. "No. They appear to still be living together."

"Hmm." I shot him a pointed look. He didn't take it well.

"I'm not congratulating you on this find, Bay," Landon said sternly. "I'm still angry you went there after I told you not to."

"He doesn't know why we were there," I argued. "We told him we were looking for a piece of property for Aunt Tillie to raise attack raccoons. He thinks she's senile."

"He may be right."

"Why don't you say that to Aunt Tillie's face?"

"I just might." Landon blanched when he looked to the window.

When I followed his gaze, I thought my stomach was going to drop straight through the floor. There was a huge—I mean absolutely massive—Rudolph inflatable on the other side of the window. It was so tall I could only see the bottom of its face.

"Forget Grandma, the whole town will be run over by that reindeer," Chief Terry moaned.

"Is it just me, or do they just keep getting bigger?" Landon asked.

"It's not just you," Chief Terry said. "You'd better get a handle on this, Bay. I haven't seen Childs around town today, but he'll appear eventually. What do you think he's going to do when he sees the Santa with no legs?"

I lifted one shoulder in a lazy shrug. "Offer to get him some crutches?"

"Your wit astounds me." Chief Terry's glare was sharp. "This could lead to big trouble, Bay. You have to do something."

"I'll talk to Aunt Tillie, but I can't make any promises."

"You need to do better than that," Chief Terry insisted. "What happens if one of the Christmas decorations kills someone?"

"I guarantee they weren't programmed for that."

"It doesn't matter. What if someone sees the big-ass reindeer and drives into a wall or something?"

He was right. "I said I'll talk to her."

"Get rid of the decorations, Bay. It's best for everyone."

Including Mrs. Little. That's the part that bothered me. "Are you guys going back to the school this afternoon?" I asked.

"We have multiple visits to multiple players in our future," Landon replied. "What about you?"

"I haven't decided yet. I'm sure I'll find a way to keep myself busy."

"I'm sure you will."

14
FOURTEEN

Aunt Tillie wasn't opposed to reining in the spell, which told me even she was worried about how out of control it had become. She would never admit that, of course, but the worry was written all over her face.

"We'll dial it back just a smidge," she suggested. "I think it was the mandrake. I might've accidentally doubled it when making the potion to dump on Margaret's lawn. I thought maybe that was the case, but then I couldn't remember."

That was likely a lie. She'd probably doubled the mandrake because she thought it would be funny and never envisioned things getting this out of hand. "I don't want Mrs. Little to win," I said, "but we have to do something. The Santa with the candy cane legs will give kids nightmares."

"Yeah, that was interesting, huh?" Aunt Tillie looked more intrigued than worried. "I'm not sure how he managed it, but that shows the propensity for actual thought. Maybe I'm so powerful I'm turning inanimate objects into soulful beings."

"Or the spell is taking on a life of its own," I countered.

"Yeah, there's that too."

I sat on the bench in front of the police station as Aunt Tillie worked her magic. Thistle found me there when she closed up Hypnotic early.

"Aren't you worried you'll miss business?" I asked her as she sat with me.

"It's been dead all day," she replied. "Most people have already finished their Christmas shopping. We had a good holiday shopping season. We still have the last event tomorrow, but it's fine."

"Where's Clove?"

"She went home early. Sam has some family coming in. They're staying at the Dandridge. His mother wants to make sure everything is clean."

"In other words, she's freaking out about being the best hostess ever," I surmised.

"Pretty much."

I let the conversation lapse into amiable silence.

"What's Aunt Tillie doing?" Thistle asked as she watched our great-aunt work.

"Chief Terry is close to a meltdown—did you know he was the one who used to grant our last-minute Christmas wishes?—and Aunt Tillie agreed that some of the decorations were getting out of control. She agreed to pull back on the spell a smidge."

"Just a smidge?" Thistle's grin was at the ready. "When was the last time Aunt Tillie admitted she was wrong on a spell?"

"I don't believe that's ever happened, and she's not admitting it now. She just thinks it's okay to dial it back a bit."

Thistle chuckled. "As for Chief Terry, I'm not exactly surprised. I haven't thought about those wishes in a long time, but looking back, it makes sense."

"I can't believe he did it," I admitted.

"You. He did it for you."

I balked. "He loved all of us."

"I would never say otherwise, but you were the one who stole his heart. Don't bother denying it," she chided when I opened my mouth to argue. "You were always his favorite."

"He loves us all. That's who he is."

"Fine, but he loved you best. It's okay. Some people bond. I don't take it personally."

"It feels like I'm taking something from you if I agree that he liked me best," I argued.

She smirked. "You want to admit it because it makes you the special one, but your heart is too soft to say it. I get it."

I pursed my lips as I watched Aunt Tillie finish. "We're going to Shadow Hills to spy on the mistress of a man who was being stalked by a dead headmistress. Want to come?"

"Absolutely." Thistle answered without hesitation. "Who doesn't love a good mistress stalking? I'm bored anyway. Marcus is home more because the petting zoo is closed for the holidays and he's a bit of a pain. He's constantly asking, 'What are you doing' and following me around. I mean ... I love him, but if I wanted constant supervision I'd still live at the inn."

I laughed, as I was certain she'd intended. "It will probably be a boring afternoon, but we might luck out."

"I'm not sure I'm up to date on this one," Thistle added. "Now is as good of a time as any to catch up."

"We can get some of that yummy Christmas fudge they have."

"That is the best idea you've had all day."

"I even surprise myself with how smart I am occasionally."

"You're humble, too. You must get that from Aunt Tillie."

"Don't push me," I warned. "I can only take so much in a day."

ADDING THISTLE TO THE MIX FOR OUR trip to Shadow Hills was both a blessing and a curse. On one hand, I had someone to talk to other than Aunt Tillie. I was getting tired of her raving regarding her potential raccoon army. On the other, nobody irritated Aunt Tillie like Thistle. Worse, Thistle not only knew she irritated her, she fed off it.

"I don't understand why you would pick raccoons," Thistle insisted from the front seat. She'd forced Aunt Tillie into the back. "Raccoons aren't very intimidating. Well, unless they're rabid, but you can't very well have rabid raccoons running around."

"Why not?" Aunt Tillie demanded.

"Because rabies has like a hundred percent mortality rate. The only hope of surviving is getting an aggressive treatment before the infection sets in," Thistle replied. "Do you want Calvin to toddle out to the pot field and get bit by one of your rabid raccoons?"

A quick glance at Aunt Tillie's face in the rearview mirror indicated she hadn't gotten that far. "They would look awesome in little combat helmets though."

"I agree." Thistle sounded utterly reasonable. "But raccoons should never become pets unless there's no other choice. Unless you stumble across one that's been separated from its mother and is young enough to socialize, you need to stay away from them."

"Then what should I get to protect my pot field?" Aunt Tillie sounded frustrated. "You know darned well people will keep looking for it. I need appropriate guards."

"Why not use Peg?"

"Peg is soft," she replied. "That's like asking an indoor cat to fight an outdoor cat. I should've made her tougher when she was younger. If I try to keep her outside to train her now, it won't go well."

I tried to picture Landon's face when he found out Peg was now an outdoor pig. "No, you can't do that," I agreed. I pulled into the lot of the bank where Georgie worked. There was an area designated for employee parking. Unfortunately, there was no sign of Georgie's car. "She's not here."

"The bank is closing early," Thistle replied, pointing at the sign on the door. "They're shutting down for the holidays."

"There are still days left until Christmas," I complained.

"This isn't the big city. People feel banking can be done early enough to give the employees a nice break. I don't disagree with that."

I didn't either. I was still annoyed. "Then we need to figure out where she lives. I didn't ask Landon to get me an address because I didn't think we'd need it." I wanted to kick myself.

"It's Shadow Hills," Thistle reminded me. "How hard can it be to figure out where someone lives? Watch this." She lowered her window and smiled as a woman—one who looked vaguely familiar—walked past. "Excuse me," she called out. "I don't suppose you can tell us where Georgie Hamilton lives?"

"Why?" the woman asked snidely. "Let me guess, did she sleep with your husband? Get in line. She's slept with half of the husbands in town."

It was only then that I recognized the woman. Phoebe Green. She was one of the women constantly giving my friend Stormy a hard time.

"We just want to know where she lives," Thistle replied. "We don't need the running commentary."

"She lives on State Street," Phoebe replied. If she was bothered about providing us with the sort of information that could be used to stalk or hurt somebody, she didn't show it. "She lives about three houses down from the first corner. Her house is orange brick. You can't miss it."

"Thank you," Thistle called out to her. "You've been a big help."

"I enjoy watching people beat the crap out of each other," Phoebe replied. Her eyes moved to me and there was a ripple of recognition. "Good luck."

"Thanks," Thistle replied. She was obviously oblivious to my reaction to Phoebe.

It only took us five minutes to find Georgie's house. Once we were on State Street, it was a simple matter of looking for her vehicle, which we found in front of an orange brick house as Phoebe promised.

"Do you want to just spy, or try to talk to her?" Thistle asked.

My original plan had been to spy on her. That was when I thought she was working. Now I wasn't as certain. "Um..."

Aunt Tillie was out of the backseat before I could decide how I wanted to answer. By the time Thistle and I caught up with her—both of us hissing her name and threatening great bodily harm—she'd already knocked on the door. I had a good grip on the hood of her coat when the door opened.

"I'd assume you're selling Tupperware, but you don't have the hair for it," Georgie said to Thistle. "That leads me to assume you're selling for Avon, but none of you know how to put on makeup. That means you're here for a different reason, and I can't say I care enough to guess what it is." She moved to shut the door in our faces, but Aunt Tillie stopped her with a foot in the opening.

"Listen, I can tell by your attitude that you're going to be a pain," Aunt Tillie started. "It's written all over your face ... and in that bra you're wearing to pretend your boobs are twice as big as they really are. It's only mildly noticeable, by the way."

My cheeks caught fire. I was dumbfounded.

"We're not here to sell anything, and if you want us gone, all you have to do is suck it up and answer our questions," Aunt Tillie continued. "Then we'll be gone quicker than you can say 'I'm screwing a married man behind my husband's back.'"

Georgie straightened. Aunt Tillie's direct approach only worked on a specific sort of person. Georgie happened to be one of those people.

"Who are you?" Georgie demanded, her gaze moving between us. This time, there was no mirth on her features. "What do you want?"

"Information on you and Kevin Dunne," Aunt Tillie replied. She'd completely taken control of the conversation. "How long have you been an item?"

"Why does that matter?" Georgie demanded. "Also, you can't prove we're an item. It's not true." She looked haughty, as if she'd somehow won the argument.

"We were in Kevin's parking lot just before noon today," I volunteered. "We saw you pick him up."

Georgie's smile fell. "In that case, fine, we're an item." She paused, as if something had occurred to her. "Are you private investigators? Did Joanie hire you?"

I jolted at mention of Kevin's wife. "Do you think she hired us?" I asked dumbly.

"I've sort of been expecting it." Georgie's eyes twinkled. "In truth, I've been hoping for it. What's the plan here? How soon does she plan to leave him?" Georgie shot up a hand before we could respond. "Scratch that. It's none of my business what timetable she's working on. If she requires something specific to make things work faster, I'm more than happy to give her whatever she needs."

I stood in front of Georgie for a very long time, debating how I was supposed to respond. I looked to Thistle for direction.

"It's very rare that I have nothing to say," she volunteered. "For once, I'm speechless."

"Well, I'm not." Aunt Tillie scowled at Georgie. "Are you seriously trying to bully your way to ownership of another woman's husband?"

"Oh, don't look at me that way," Georgie snapped. "I don't need the judgment. Kevin and I are in love. It was love at first sight actually."

"Does your husband know that?" I demanded. I couldn't believe the direction this conversation was taking.

"Actually, he does." Georgie was blasé. "He knows I want a divorce. Unfortunately, the housing market being what it is, we can't afford to live separately until we unload this place. Everything is revoltingly civilized despite the circumstances right now."

"Wow!" It was all I could say.

"Right?" Georgie's smile was sunny. "So, what does Joanie need to get the ball rolling to leave Kevin? I was hoping it would come to this. He wouldn't just come right out and tell her the truth—he's too much of a weakling—but I knew if I was brazen enough, she would eventually find out."

"We're not here about Joanie," I replied, although part of me felt guilty for saying that. "We're here about Enid Walters."

All of the color—and bravado—fled Georgie's features. "Are you kidding?" she demanded. "What does that whore want?"

"Um..." Yup. I was at a loss again.

"That whore is dead," Aunt Tillie replied. "We're here to see if you did it."

"No way." She vehemently shook her head. "Don't be a moron. Why would I kill Enid?"

"Because she was sleeping with your boyfriend," I replied.

"She so was not." Georgie wrinkled her nose to signify disgust. "She wasn't sleeping with him. She wanted to sleep with him. In fact, she stalked him."

"How do you know that?"

"He told me. He said she was infatuated with him, to the point he was uncomfortable and didn't know what to do about it. Why would he lie?"

I could think of a few reasons. Thistle was the one to volunteer the most obvious one.

"I suppose the answer 'to get into your pants' never crossed your mind," my mouthy cousin drawled. "That was the reason. He wanted to nail both of you without consequences."

"That's not true." Georgie was having none of it. "We're in love. We have the sort of connection that can't be replicated. We are ... two sides of the same soul coin."

I couldn't decide if I wanted to laugh or throw up. "What about his wife?" I demanded. "I get that you're willing to throw your husband away for this idiot, but how does his wife fit into this?"

"Listen, I don't know her, but she's standing in the way of my happiness," Georgie replied, matter-of-factly. "She seems perfectly nice. Everything I've heard about her suggests she really is. That doesn't change the fact that she's standing in the way of my happily ever after. She has to go."

"What about Enid?" I prodded. "Was she standing in the way of your happiness?"

"Why would she?" Georgie challenged. "Even if what you say is true—it's not, but let's pretend it is—Kevin will have to leave his wife before either of us has a chance at happiness. Wouldn't it make more sense for me to go after Joanie instead of Enid?"

I hated that she had a point. "I hadn't considered that," I hedged. "I guess it sort of makes sense."

"It does," she agreed. "I wouldn't go after Enid even if she was my primary rival. She simply didn't have the same things to offer."

She started to tick off her list on her fingers. "I'm younger. I'm more successful. I have a better personality. I'm not a crazy stalker. Why would I care about Enid?"

"She kind of has a point," Thistle said.

"So, there it is," Georgie said when it became apparent we weren't going to keep pushing her. "I didn't kill Enid. If you're not here to handle the Joanie situation for me, I have nothing else to say. I need to cook dinner for my kids and my soon-to-be-ex-husband. So, if that's all..." She left it hanging.

"That's all," I said. "Sorry to have bothered you."

"No problem. If you see Joanie and want to drop the bomb on her, you could still be of use to me. If not, don't bother coming back. There's only so much time in the day, and I don't want to waste any on you."

With that, she closed the door in our faces, leaving us with more questions.

15
FIFTEEN

I was at a loss for what to do next, so I headed downtown. Shadow Hills had a festival going, though it looked a little depressing considering what we were used to. Still, I needed time to think, and the festival made for great cover.

"Oh, this is just sad," Thistle said as we headed for the hot chocolate booth. "They have like three things to amuse people ... and one of them is a beer tent."

"What's wrong with a beer tent?" Aunt Tillie demanded. "A beer tent is a great idea. In fact, I pitched one to our festival committee. Guess what the response was."

"No," Thistle and I answered in unison.

Aunt Tillie made a face. "How did you know?"

"Mrs. Little heads the committee," Thistle replied as I stepped up to order three hot chocolates. "There's no way she would allow you to participate in a festival ... especially if alcohol is involved."

Aunt Tillie looked flummoxed. "I'll have you know that I'm an excellent festival planner."

"Yes, I'm sure you could do it professionally."

We took our hot chocolate to a table and sat. It was cold, but the warmers that had been placed around the town square cut back on the bitterness.

"Why don't we use warmers?" Thistle asked. "They're nice."

"They break constantly and are a pain to keep up," I replied. "We had some, but they cost more than they're worth. Now we just make people suck it up."

"That's a little depressing."

I sipped my hot chocolate. It was good, but not as good as we were used to. Apparently, I'd become a festival snob without realizing it. "We need to talk about Georgie." I took another sip. "Do we believe her? Do you think she had a motive to kill Enid?"

"I think she was trying to bolster herself as much as us regarding the undying love she and Kevin supposedly share," Thistle replied. "I don't think she's nearly as convinced that she and Kevin are forever as she pretends, but I'm not sure she was worried about Enid."

"The wife," I surmised. I'd been thinking about that too. "She wasn't afraid of Enid because even if Kevin was lying and had been seeing her, she wasn't the true hurdle. If she'd been good enough, at least in Georgie's mind, then Kevin would've left his wife for her. It's the wife who is the real wild card."

"Pretty much," Thistle agreed. "What do you know about her?"

I shook my head. "I haven't really thought about her. My first assumption was that we should be looking at Kevin."

"Because he would kill to keep the affair quiet?"

I was sheepish. "In hindsight, that seems pretty stupid."

"Obviously, there's more going on than we realized," Thistle said. "Do you think Landon and Chief Terry will chase Georgie?"

That was a very good question. "They'll wait to see what I volunteer about her. Landon knew I was going to track her down. He'll want to hear what happened and then make his decision."

"What about the wife?" Thistle pressed.

"We'll have to wait and see." The sound of familiar laughter had me raising my head, and I found Stormy heading in our direction. She had her best friend Sebastian with her.

She pulled up short when she saw us. "What are you doing here?" she demanded. With Christmas right around the corner, she probably thought she wouldn't be seeing us until after the big day.

I lifted my cup of hot chocolate. "Taking a break. What about you?"

"We just came from checking in on Maggie Gibson," Sebastian replied. "We took her a care package."

I knew the name, but only because Stormy had mentioned it a few days earlier. "That's the missing woman," I surmised.

"She's been found," Sebastian replied. He had a gregarious personality—he was loud like Aunt Tillie—and he amused me a great deal. "She's back with her husband and daughter. We wanted to deliver some food because she's supposed to rest. The doctor said she was dehydrated and needed rest."

Apparently, I was behind. I sent a questioning look to Stormy. "I guess I'm lagging."

"Don't worry about it." Stormy sat with us and sent a pretty smile to Sebastian. "Will you get our hot chocolate and give me a minute?"

Sebastian looked annoyed but nodded. "Fine, but don't forget you owe me quality time." He was stern. "I won't be ignored."

"Got it," Stormy promised him. "The entire afternoon is for just us. I promise."

Sebastian grumbled as he turned to disappear. Stormy was serious as she focused on us. "We have some catching up to do, but it's best to wait until after Christmas," she explained. "I've been neglecting Sebastian. I owe him time."

"It's fine." I waved off the apology in her voice. "We've been dealing with our own stuff too."

"I heard." Stormy bobbed her head. "All the Christmas decorations are coming to life. It's freaky. I had to spank a pair of frisky tinsel reindeer behind the restaurant this morning. They were getting it on."

My mouth dropped open. "The decorations have migrated here?"

"You didn't know?" Stormy looked amused.

"Well, crap." I glared at Aunt Tillie. "You'd better get this under control before the entire state is overrun."

Aunt Tillie was blasé. "What did I say? I've got this. Don't be a moron."

I growled but managed a smile for Stormy's benefit. There was no reason to ruin her Christmas. "I don't suppose you're familiar with Kevin Dunne?"

"The real estate agent?" She leaned back in her chair and smiled at Sebastian as he returned with their hot chocolate. There was no question the two of them were going to sit with us—at least for a bit—and gossip. "He's been seen here a time or two. People think he's up to something."

"He's at the center of a case we're working on. He's trying to help people get their hands on Hemlock Cove property to flip it in a few years because he thinks he's going to make a killing," I explained. "I figured maybe he was doing the same here."

I caught her up on what we were dealing with. She looked appalled.

"They actually have a private school for misbehaving girls in this day and age?" She made a clucking sound with her tongue and shook her head. "That is just all kinds of wrong."

"It's unfortunate," I agreed.

"And Kevin Dunne's daughter is one of the students?" Sebastian pressed. "That's horrible. I wouldn't have guessed that. Although, now that you mention it, we rarely see Katie."

Now I was thrown. "You know her?"

"They live here," Sebastian replied.

"I can't say I knew that," Stormy admitted. "I've only been back in town a few months, but I've never waited on him. I only know him from the commercials and bench advertisements. I heard a hint of gossip about him being seen with various women around town."

"Those benches seem like they should be a total waste of time given the technology now available," Sebastian said. "He's definitely local. He bought the house on the hill."

"What hill?" I asked. I was familiar with the layout of Shadow Hills—all of the small towns in the area were something of a curiosity when I was a teenager—but I wasn't aware of a specific hill.

"Out on the highway," Sebastian replied. "The highway to Alden."

Now things began to clear. "I never take that route because it's quicker to get to Traverse City from Hemlock Cove than to cut through Shadow Hills. It sort of makes sense that he would live here, doesn't it? Traverse City real estate is expensive."

"Yes, and he helped create the real estate problem in Traverse City," Sebastian agreed. "He spent three years touting the real estate boom on television, in ads. Eventually, it actually happened. He wasn't the only one. There were a few other agents who joined with him."

Now *that* was interesting. Was it germane to what we were working on, though? "He mentioned Hemlock Cove's real estate values are going to go through the roof," I said. "I wonder if he's trying to manufacture that."

"I wouldn't put it past him," Stormy said. "What does that have to do with your headmistress getting poisoned?"

"Probably nothing. I can't see someone poisoning someone else over real estate."

"Poison is an intimate murder weapon," Thistle said. "It's mostly used by women."

"Which brings us back to the wife," I said. "Maybe she knew her husband was screwing around with Enid."

"Joanie?" Sebastian asked. "Trust me, she's not the murdering type."

"You know her?" I perked up.

"She's a regular at the festivals," Sebastian replied. "She volunteers for the festival committees." He pointed to a pretty woman with curly auburn hair tucked under a blue ski cap working at the burger booth.

I stilled. Was he suggesting that was Kevin Dunne's wife? "That's Joanie Dunne?" I asked dumbly.

Sebastian snickered. "I told you they're local."

The woman was laughing and chatting with the other people in the booth as if she didn't have a care in the world. "She has kids, right?"

Sebastian nodded. "That's KJ." He pointed to a tall blond boy standing next to the Christmas tree. He was posturing with several other friends, having a great time. "That's short for Kevin Junior. I think he's almost thirteen now."

I'd already done the math. "We figure Joanie got pregnant with Katie and that hurried the marriage between her and Kevin. Then the other two kids came along."

"I don't know Kevin well—I've talked to him a few times, and he's interested in buying the funeral home—but he strikes me as the sort of guy who would still like to sow his wild oats," Sebastian said. "But he is a good father. I see him with his kids way more than I see him with his wife."

This just kept getting more interesting. "They have three, including Katie?"

"Yeah. The other is Sara." Sebastian pointed again, this time to a girl about ten playing a running game with a bunch of other kids her age. She was laughing and having a good time. "I see her with Kevin a lot. He takes her to the coffee shop constantly. Apparently, she's a big fan of drinks with whipped cream and cookies."

"So he's a good father," I realized. "He's a crappy husband, but a good father."

"We don't have proof Kevin was cheating on his wife with the dead woman," Thistle reminded me. "Your gut tells you Enid was stalking him for a reason. Maybe she wasn't. Maybe she just wanted what Joanie had, and he didn't participate in the delusion."

I didn't want to believe it—not even a little—but it was definitely a possibility. "What if Enid approached Joanie and told her she was having an affair with her husband? Or maybe told her she thought Kevin belonged with her, not with his family. What would Joanie do?"

Sebastian followed my gaze to the woman working in the burger booth. On the surface, she didn't appear to have a care in the world. The surface could be deceiving, though. "Are you asking if Joanie would go on a murder spree to keep her husband from being stolen?" Sebastian asked.

As if she'd heard the question, Joanie looked up and caught my gaze. I held it rather than dart my eyes away. I smiled, because it seemed the thing to do, and then turned back to Sebastian. "I'm curious what you think she would do," I confirmed.

"She's a nice woman," Sebastian insisted. "A really nice woman. She wouldn't purposely hurt anybody."

"Not even to protect her children?" I pressed.

Sebastian balked. "You're not talking about protecting her children. You're talking about protecting a philanderer, and I have trouble believing that Joanie would do that. I mean ... she and Kevin don't spend a lot of time together."

"You just said Kevin is a good father," I reminded him.

"He is. I see him with KJ and Sara all the time. I saw him with Katie before she switched schools, which I hadn't realized she'd done until you told me. I guess I should've realized that being a good father doesn't naturally equate to being a good husband."

I nodded. "What if Joanie equates Kevin being caught cheating with her children's happiness? Would she kill someone then?"

Sebastian looked exasperated. "All I can tell you is that Joanie doesn't come across as a killer. Of course, a lot of people who kill don't come across that way."

I blew out a sigh and finished off my hot chocolate. My gaze automatically drifted back to Joanie. I almost came out of my skin when I realized she was watching me. Why would she be watching me? Was it because she thought I was watching her?

"What about Georgie Hamilton?" I asked. "What can you tell me about her?"

"Well, news has begun to spread that she and Andrew are separating," Sebastian replied. "They have to share the same roof until they figure out their finances. Ten years ago, that would've been scandalous, but it happens more and more frequently now so people aren't really talking about that."

"Are they talking about Georgie being in a relationship with Kevin?"

Sebastian didn't hesitate before he started shaking his head. "Definitely not. If that was a thing, we would've heard. They're not together."

"Georgie assumed I was a private investigator and proudly volunteered the information," I argued. "She wants Joanie to find out. She just doesn't want to be the one to tell her. She sees Joanie as a hurdle to her happiness."

"Maybe she killed Enid," Stormy volunteered.

"Except she didn't believe Kevin and Enid were involved."

"We don't have proof that they were involved," Thistle interjected. "Enid was definitely infatuated with Kevin—she stalked him—but there's no proof that Kevin felt the same about her."

"That's all true," I concurred, "but I feel in my gut there was something going on between them. Maybe it was something that happened in the past, and Enid couldn't let it go. There was something there. Georgie didn't believe that, so I have trouble ascertaining a motive for her. Why go after Enid when she believes Joanie is her true enemy?"

"Maybe if she kills Joanie, Kevin will assume she did it, and that will be the end of their relationship," Sebastian volunteered.

That wasn't as ridiculous an idea as it might seem.

"What are you going to do?" Stormy asked.

I turned my attention to Joanie again. She was still watching me. The smile was long gone.

"I don't know," I replied after a few seconds. "I just ... don't know."

"You could try talking to her," Stormy suggested. "It can't hurt to at least feel her out."

I didn't see that I had much choice, though. It sounded easy enough. "Yeah. I'll go talk to her."

16

SIXTEEN

I decided to approach Joanie alone. The others weren't as invested because I was convinced that Enid was killed due to an affair. Also, Sebastian and Stormy didn't want to be drawn into it because this was their town, and it might come back to bite them.

I waited until Joanie took a break to make my move, leaving Stormy and Sebastian to entertain Thistle and Aunt Tillie.

I slid past the burger booth when Joanie disappeared in that direction. I followed her to a stand of trees that provided a natural barrier. Maybe she was a closet smoker, I told myself. Maybe she'd gone beyond the trees so her kids wouldn't see her.

When I emerged in the small clearing beyond the trees, all I saw were two empty benches and several sets of footprints in the snow.

I stood, rooted to my spot, for several seconds. Then I let out a sigh and turned, only to find Joanie had snuck in behind me, hands on hips, scowl on lips.

"Hey!" I made an attempt at being smooth. Just the sight of Joanie was enough to get my blood pumping. I was incredibly nervous. "I was just looking to see what was over here. I thought maybe there was a part of the festival I missed."

Joanie didn't immediately respond, which only served to jangle my nerves further.

"Turns out that's not the case," I said. "I guess I'll head back." I was anxious to get away from her—I was no longer gung-ho about feeling her out regarding the possibility of her husband having an affair. All I could think about was escape. Unfortunately, that wasn't in the cards.

I made it a grand total of two steps before Joanie made her move.

Now, I grew up with two cousins who were more like sisters. We scrapped with the best of them. There was often dirt involved ... and sometimes tree branches ... and because Aunt Tillie was something of a weapons enthusiast, Thistle had once hit me with a rifle. She didn't shoot me, she used it to beat me because she thought I liked the same guy she did.

When Joanie grabbed a handful of my hair and tugged, I wasn't prepared.

"Hey!" I shoved at Joanie's hand, but that only increased the pain as she had no intention of letting go. "Let me go!"

Rather than listen, or embrace reason, Joanie yanked even harder. "Don't think I don't know who you are," she hissed. She spit on the side of my face she was so close. I redoubled my efforts to escape.

I used a bit of magic to buck Joanie off. She would never detect it —at least I hoped that was the case—and she tried to take my hair with her when she was tossed aside.

As she geared up for a second attack, she looked murderous. Thankfully, Stormy's boyfriend—a Shadow Hills police officer —intervened.

"Don't!" Hunter Ryan yelled, extending a finger toward Joanie as she prepared to throw herself at me. The look on his face reflected pure bewilderment. "Does somebody want to tell me what's going on here?"

Joanie shot him an incredulous look. "Are you kidding?"

"Not so much," Hunter replied. "What's going on?" He darted a desperate look in my direction, but I wasn't certain how to respond. I kind of wanted to hear what Joanie had to say.

"She's stalking me," Joanie announced.

"I'm really not," I said to Hunter.

"She is," Joanie insisted. "She's been at the festival for an hour, watching me the entire time. I even saw her asking questions about my family. Sebastian and Stormy pointed out my kids to her."

Uh-oh. I sensed my troubles increasing tenfold with that little announcement.

"Is that true?" Hunter asked.

"No," I insisted. "I am not stalking her."

"Did you have Stormy and Sebastian point out her kids?" Hunter demanded.

"Of course not." I forced myself to remain calm. "Why would I do that?"

Hunter flicked his eyes to Joanie. "Why would she do that?"

"She's having an affair with Kevin."

Holy cannoli. In hindsight, I should've considered that as a potential problem. I assumed Joanie had no idea about her husband's infidelities. Perhaps I'd been looking at things all wrong.

"Come on," I whined when Hunter gave me an inscrutable look. "Do you really think I'm here banging a real estate agent? I've got a husband. I can barely keep up with him."

"Ha!" Joanie drew herself straight. "She knows Kevin. Isn't that proof enough for you?"

"Not really," Hunter replied. His attention was drawn to the space behind me, to the trees, at the sound of footsteps. I didn't have to look to know who was joining us. "Do you want to tell me want's going on?" he asked.

"We were having hot chocolate," Stormy replied. "Bay went to stretch her legs. I ... have no knowledge of what went down here."

"That's true," I said to Hunter when he made a face. "They were having a good time when I left. She has no idea what's going on." The last thing I wanted was to get Stormy into trouble.

"She's sleeping with my husband," Joanie exploded. "I already told you what's going on. Why are you doubting me?"

"Because I know this woman," Hunter replied.

"You know me," Joanie shot back. "Have you ever known me to lie to law enforcement?"

"No." Hunter looked as if he was sweating underneath his heavy coat. "The thing is, she's married to a member of law enforcement. An FBI agent."

I held up my ring finger as a form of proof. "Happily married," I stressed.

"She was spying on me," Joanie insisted, although the smallest smidgen of doubt had invaded her eyes. "If you think I don't know what spying looks like—my husband likes to stick his wick into every candle on this side of the state—then you're dreaming. She came here to scope me and my children out because she thinks she'll somehow break up my marriage."

Hunter was clearly dumbfounded. I couldn't blame him. I was confused too.

"Let's take this from the beginning," Hunter started.

"No!" Joanie shouted. "We are not taking this from the beginning. I want her arrested."

"On what charges?" Hunter challenged. "I was walking down the sidewalk when this little ... *scuffle* ... started. You attacked her."

"Because she's stalking and threatening my children."

Stormy cleared her throat, drawing Hunter's attention. "I can't speak to what happened on this side of the trees," she volunteered. "Bay has only been gone for three minutes or so, though, and on the other side of the trees there was no stalking of children."

"I saw her!" Joanie threw her hands in the air. "You pointed out my children to her."

"I most certainly did not." Stormy looked appalled. "I wouldn't do that." It was only then that reality set in and she realized that she sort of had. "Oh, wait."

"I asked them about Kevin Dunne," I said. "He's involved in a case tied to the death of a headmistress at a private school in Hemlock Cove. He's making noise about helping people buy up property in Hemlock Cove to flip it, but that's another matter entirely."

"See!" Joanie made a move for me again, but Hunter extended his arm to stop her. "She's stalking me."

"I'm not stalking you," I shot back. "I merely asked about Kevin's family because I was trying to get a feel for him."

"Because you're sleeping with him," Joanie snapped. "Don't bother denying it. This isn't my first rodeo. I know darned well that you're one of Kevin's girls. You have the look ... and you're here stalking my family. You're hardly the first."

Hunter held up his hand to quiet her. "Are you saying Kevin sleeps around?"

The look Joanie shot him could've peeled paint. "Kevin sleeps with anything that moves. You're not special, honey," she said to me. "He'll never leave me for you, because if he does, he'll lose half of his money, and if there's one thing Kevin cares about more than anything else, it's money."

That made me inexplicably sad. "How many mistresses would you say Kevin has had?"

Rather than be offended by the question, Joanie shot me a pitying look. "You're not a mistress, honey. None of you are. The word 'mistress' suggests Kevin has actual feelings for you. He's just a sex fiend. He doesn't care about you. He'll keep you around until you start making too many demands. Then he'll dump you and pretend it's because he's trying to do the magnanimous thing and not lead you on."

She pressed her hand to her heart and adopted an apologetic look. "I'm so sorry I can't give you what you want," she said in a shaky voice, mimicking her husband. "I want to be with you—

clearly, we've connected on a level that's never happened to me before—but I can't hurt my children that way. I can't leave my wife. She'll take everything and ruin my family. I can't do that to my children. I care about you, but I can't be with you. I'm sorry."

She dropped her hand and glared at me. "If you fall for that, you're a moron. He never had any intention of leaving me. He bangs randos for a few weeks, and then he moves on. He will never love you, no matter what he says."

When I was a kid, I had a nervous habit of tugging on my ear when my mother and aunts started arguing. I realized I was doing that now and forced myself to stop.

"Okay, let's take a breath," Hunter suggested. He gently nudged Joanie. "Let's take a walk. I want to hear your side of things from the beginning."

He also wanted her to calm down.

"What about her?" Joanie demanded. "She could run away."

"She could," Hunter readily agreed, "but I know where she lives."

"Maybe she'll run away from her home."

"I sincerely doubt that since her family owns several businesses in Hemlock Cove. She owns a business too. On top of that, as I said, her husband is an FBI agent. She's not going anywhere."

Joanie didn't look convinced. "You're not going to arrest her for stalking me?"

"I want to talk to you," Hunter replied. "Let's see if we can get a few breaths in and go from there."

I watched them leave, my stomach constricting. When I was certain they were out of earshot, I finally spoke. "Well, that answers *that* question."

"It certainly does," Stormy agreed. "Obviously, Joanie knows about her husband's wandering eye."

"And he's obviously nailed way more women than we thought," Thistle added. "I'm guessing he's left a trail of broken-hearted women in his wake."

I didn't disagree. "Including Enid."

Thistle considered it for a moment before nodding. "Yeah, including Enid. I don't think there's much of a doubt that he was nailing her too."

"Do you think he knows that his wife is aware of his extracurricular activities?"

"I don't know him well enough to give an opinion either way," Stormy said. She glanced at Sebastian, who shook his head. "We can ask around. Maybe someone has information about the two of them."

I was reluctant to push Joanie any further than she'd already been pushed. "I don't want to make things any worse than they are for her."

"I can ask around," Stormy said. "What are you going to do?"

That was a very good question. "I'm not going to bother Joanie again." I was firm on that. "She has enough to worry about. I very much doubt she killed Enid."

"Really? Because the first thing she tried to do when she thought you were sleeping with her husband was attack you," Thistle noted. "Do you think you're the only one she's reacted that way with?"

"Probably not." I was reluctant to admit it, but Thistle had a point. "I just don't know what to do. I'm positive that the voices we heard last night were female."

"The giggles," Thistle said. "What does that matter?"

"I have to think the killer was responsible for stalking Landon and me."

"Maybe those aren't connected," Thistle suggested. "Maybe you crossed paths with an intrigued magical student who came to the property out of curiosity. It might have nothing to do with Enid's death."

"That feels too far-fetched," I said.

"We live in a town where Christmas decorations are coming to life and taking over," Thistle reminded me.

I pressed my lips together, debating, then held out my hands. "I need to think. It feels as if there's an answer close."

Thistle managed a smile that didn't touch her eyes. "You'd better figure it out soon. I have a feeling things are going to get worse before they get better ... and maybe on multiple fronts."

17
SEVENTEEN

I was tired by the time I got back to Hemlock Cove. Even though I offered to take Aunt Tillie back to the inn, she assured me she was in control of her own transportation and disappeared in the direction of the festival grounds.

"That's probably not good," Thistle noted as she stared in the wake of Aunt Tillie's disappearance.

"What was your first clue?" I asked dryly.

"I've met her." Thistle managed a wan smile. "When you figure out what to do about your dead headmistress, let me know. I'll help."

"But you're done for now," I surmised.

"I don't know what to do for you, Bay." Thistle shrugged. "I would help if I knew how."

I blew out a sigh. "I don't know what to do either."

"Are you going to tell Landon about what happened in Shadow Hills?"

"Why wouldn't I?"

"I don't know. I thought maybe you'd keep it quiet since he didn't give you the okay to go digging on the wife."

"First, I don't need Landon's permission to do anything," I

started. I felt silly even saying it, because I knew Landon would be angry ... and I *would* care about him being angry. "Second, Landon is not the boss of me."

Thistle snickered.

"He's not," I insisted.

"I didn't say he was." She held up her hands in supplication. "I'm just saying that he's going to be mad."

"Yeah, well, it will be fine."

"Okay." This time the smile Thistle flashed was genuine. "We have a couch if you need a place to sleep."

I glared at her. "There's nothing to worry about. He won't be mad." I internally cringed when the lie rolled off my tongue. That didn't stop me from continuing forward. "It will be fine. Although ... have you got any candy on you?"

Thistle's expression was blank. "Candy?"

"Landon likes candy, and I might need some to distract him."

Thistle broke out in a wide grin. "I don't, but I bet you can pick some up at the festival."

"Good idea. Then I'll drag him into the kissing booth and feed him candy until he forgets to ask what I did with my day."

I WENT TO THE HOMEMADE CANDY BOOTH first. There were a lot of items from which to choose, and I filled an entire box. It was good timing, because I barely made it three steps after paying before Landon intercepted me.

"Is that my Christmas present?" He leaned close to peer at the box.

"Do you want it to be your present?"

"That depends on what's inside." He gave me a quick kiss, chaste by his standards. That had me wondering if he'd already figured out that I'd found trouble during the day.

"What do you think is inside?" I asked as I maintained my smile.

"I'm guessing it's candy." His fingers brushed my hair from my forehead. He was a tactile man, and he liked doling out little touches. I was suspicious today, however. "Since you spent the day with Aunt Tillie, for all I know it could be Brussels sprouts or something."

"You think I got you Brussels sprouts?" Even though I was leery, he made me laugh. That's what he always did.

"You never know." He cocked his head. "Anything you want to tell me?"

And there it was: he knew, but he wanted me to volunteer the information.

"I'm going to curse the crap out of Hunter the next time I see him," I muttered, shaking my head. "He's got a big mouth."

Rather than feign ignorance, Landon shrugged. "I think he's a good guy."

"You would. He called you to tattle."

"Actually, he didn't. He called Terry to get the rundown on what we're working on." Landon's hand was back to brush my hair again. It was as if he needed something to do with his hands. "Are you hurt?"

I shook my head. "No, but you might have to massage my head later. She pulled my hair pretty hard."

"Do you think you deserve a head massage?"

That felt like a trick question. "If you're angry, just say so. I don't want to play games. You're my husband, not my keeper."

Landon's eyes narrowed. He pulled his hand back and looked around the festival.

"I don't want the entire night to be ruined," I insisted. "If you have something to say, say it so we can fight about it and then take the candy to the kissing booth."

"So it is candy." Landon pursed his lips, seemingly debating, then closed his eyes. "I can't decide if I'm angry."

"Seriously?"

"Seriously." He bobbed his head and made a reach for the candy. I had my wits about me enough to sidestep him.

"Just a second." I held up a finger on my free hand. "I want to fight if we're going to fight."

"I don't want to fight."

"But you haven't ruled it out," I said.

"I'm still thinking about it."

"Well, track me down when you've made up your mind." I headed to the coffee booth. I wanted a hot chocolate to take to the kissing booth. Now that I knew I had the upper hand—hot chocolate, candy, the kissing booth, and a conflicted husband—I was desperate to put this behind us.

"You're trying to push me to make a decision before I'm ready," Landon complained as he followed me. "That's not fair."

I glanced over my shoulder at him. "I'm not trying to push you into anything. I've been on my feet most of the day, and I want to rest. I'm going to do it in the kissing booth."

"With my candy."

"I didn't say this was your candy."

"You insinuated it."

"Or you assumed, and I didn't correct you."

He was quiet, but when he sighed, I knew he was resigned to letting me get away with today's adventure. "Fine. I'm not angry."

I let him sulk, and even decided to pay for the hot chocolate. After a few minutes of eyeing each other, I knew he wasn't quite as over it as he pretended.

"I just want to say that I wish you hadn't gone to Shadow Hills to spy on the wife without telling me," he started as we walked away from the candy booth. "Actually, I wish you hadn't interrogated Dunne, but it's done."

"I had no intention of approaching the wife," I explained. "I didn't even know she was going to be at the festival until Sebastian pointed her out. We were just there for hot chocolate and to talk."

"You went to a festival without me?" Landon sounded wounded. "That is just ... so wrong."

"It's a Shadow Hills festival. It's nothing like a Hemlock Cove festival."

"You still cheated on me."

I didn't like the way he phrased it. "Don't even."

Apparently, my response was enough to earn a smile. "I'll get the hot chocolate. You claim our spots in the kissing booth. I'll meet you there in five minutes."

"Okay." I reached out and grabbed his hand before he could move too far away. "I love you, Landon ... even when you're a pain."

He cupped my face in his hands and gave me a lavish kiss. "Right back at you."

True to his word, he met me in the kissing booth. He was all smiles when he flopped down next to me on the couch and pressed his lips to my cheek.

"I take it you want to get right down to business," I drawled.

He handed me my hot chocolate. "Actually, that's just an appetizer," he replied. "I want to talk about serious issues before we get to the main event."

I froze with the hot chocolate halfway to my lips. This would be my second sugar rush of the day, and I had to be careful because my eating habits were going to come back to bite me now that I was thirty. "I thought you agreed not to be angry." I hoped I didn't sound too whiny.

"I didn't say we were going to fight." He tucked me in at his side. "I said we were going to talk."

"See, that could go either way. I don't want to talk if it leads to an argument."

"Hand me the candy."

I slid the box into his hands and watched as he opened it. The delight that washed over his face was almost enough to make me forget that I was expecting things to get ugly between us.

Almost.

"This is the prettiest candy I've ever seen." He popped a chocolate reindeer into his mouth and turned to me. "Hunter said Dunne's wife lost her mind and attacked you because she thought you were stalking her." He was all business now.

"I'm not sure she really thought that," I hedged. I thought back to the way she'd watched me once when she caught me looking at her. "There's a distinct possibility Kevin's other female companions have approached Joanie."

"To what end?" Landon sipped his hot chocolate and studied me. He really didn't look angry, which I took as a win.

"Georgie—she was a bit of a nightmare—thought we were private investigators hired by Joanie. She wanted the truth to come out, and even suggested she'd pay us to do it ... as long as nobody could pin it on her."

"Because she assumed that Joanie didn't know about the affair," Landon surmised. "But Joanie does know, to the point we should believe he had several affairs."

"I'm willing to bet there were a lot of them," I agreed.

"I wonder why she stayed," Landon mused.

"They have three children. Sebastian said they have a nice house. She has the sort of life she probably always dreamed of ... other than one little thing."

"Her husband is a complete and total tool," Landon said. "Just out of curiosity, what would you do under similar circumstances?"

"You would've been castrated after the first incident," I replied automatically.

He chuckled as if it was the funniest thing I'd ever said, and then shifted his crotch away from me. "I would never cheat on you." He paused a beat. "Wait ... you don't think I ever would?"

"Of course not. You're not the cheating type. I know that."

"It's not just that, Bay. I love you to the point of distraction. I don't want anybody else."

"But Kevin Dunne does," I replied. "He isn't content in his marriage. I'm willing to bet that he never goes home at night and crawls into bed with Joanie and a bag of dill pickle potato chips with the express goal to do nothing but play footsie and eat chips."

Landon's smile was soft. "I like when we do that."

"I do too. I get the feeling that Kevin was sucked into a marriage he didn't want. Sebastian said he's a good father—you always see him with his children—but you never see him with his wife."

"Because he's a crappy husband," Landon said.

"I don't understand how he could love the kids and treat their mother so poorly," I admitted.

"I don't understand that either. I look at you and know I'll love whatever comes out of you. When that kid is grown and out of the house, though, I'll be equally as thrilled, because then it will just be you and me again."

"Aw." I leaned my cheek against his shoulder and smiled up at him. "That's unbelievably sweet."

"It's the truth. You're it for me. Obviously, Joanie is not it for Kevin."

"But I don't think Georgie is it for him either. She just doesn't realize it."

"What about Enid?"

"Maybe she figured out she wasn't it for him but couldn't let it go. I don't know if Kevin is responsible for Enid's death. I don't know that I believe he killed her, because Joanie knows about his affairs. Why would he kill Enid to keep it secret? Joanie isn't going to divorce him. That much became glaringly obvious today."

"Maybe he doesn't realize that Joanie knows about his affairs," Landon suggested.

"Maybe. I don't know what makes sense yet."

"I can give you time to think about it."

"And we're not going to fight?" I was still dubious.

"Nope. We're going to get dinner here and then go home to eat more candy in bed."

"That sounds like a good night to me."

"I was hoping you would like it." He dropped a kiss on top of my head before readjusting. "I'm not massaging your scalp as punishment for you sticking your nose into this case when I told you to take a step back, though. That's my passive-aggressive way of giving you grief."

The fact that he was so open and honest about it made me grin. "I can live with that."

WE STAYED IN THE KISSING BOOTH long enough to finish our hot chocolate. Then we headed out to pick up something for dinner. Our warm and fuzzy feelings died when we saw the Rudolph inflatable from earlier—the one that was two freaking stories tall—staring down a dog dressed as an elf on the sidewalk on the east side of the town square. They looked ready to come to blows.

"Crap." I threw up my hands in frustration.

"That's what I was about to say," Landon replied. He clutched the candy box against his chest, as if he would fight to the death to protect it. "This is not good, Bay."

"What was your first clue?" a familiar voice demanded from behind us. Chief Terry was closing in. "I told you to fix this, Bay!"

I shrank from him in surprise. He had the grace to look angry at himself for blowing up at me, but he didn't back down. "I'm sorry, but this is unacceptable. You need to get Tillie down here to fix this."

As if drawn by the sound of her name, Aunt Tillie appeared on the other side of Landon. Her attention was on the inflatables. I wasn't even certain she realized who she was standing next to.

"Can you fix this?" I demanded of her.

She was sheepish as she turned to look at me. "I guess that depends on your meaning of the word 'fix,'" she replied.

"Can you make it stop?" I growled.

On a sigh, she shook her head. "I may—*may*—have built a time element into the spell in case Winnie tried to reverse it if she went soft in the face of Margaret's wrath," Aunt Tillie replied.

"What sort of time element?" Landon asked.

"The spell ends at midnight on New Year's Eve."

Landon and Chief Terry groaned in unison. I was hardly

surprised. "I was afraid it was something like that," I admitted. "How could you possibly cast a spell like this and not give us an out?"

"This wasn't supposed to happen." Aunt Tillie gestured to the giant reindeer. "It was just supposed to be a few decorations chasing Margaret around. I certainly didn't ask for this."

"And yet we're stuck with it," Chief Terry snapped. "We're stuck with it, and that man is trying to bring us down." He gestured to the right, where Brad Childs stood next to the hot chocolate booth taking in the show. He looked thrilled ... and maybe a bit feral. "How do you suggest we deal with this, Tillie?" Chief Terry was beside himself.

"I'll figure something out," Aunt Tillie replied. It was as close as she would come to an apology. "Don't freak out. I've still got this."

As if on cue—and to prove she didn't have it—the two inflatables started singing different Christmas carols, screaming the lyrics at one another as they stared each other down.

"How do we at least mitigate this until it's over?" Chief Terry asked.

I didn't have an answer for him. "I don't know," I replied, "but we should probably do something, though."

"Oh, do you think?" Chief Terry never stayed angry with me for more than a few minutes. His glare told me this time was different. "You'd better get to it, Bay. I want this problem handled. Now."

"I'll see what I can come up with," I promised.

"You'd better come up with something fast, young lady. You're in trouble."

18
EIGHTEEN

I wanted to go home—more than anything—but Landon was determined to talk with Childs before we took the candy to its final resting place and ate it in bed.

"Here." He handed me the candy box. "It will make me look less official if I'm carrying around reindeer candy."

I took the box from him, pressed my lips together, and did my best not to burst out laughing.

Childs seemed to be expecting us, because he was sitting on a bench watching the inflatables wander down Main Street when we caught up to him. "Now there's something you don't see every day," he said without looking up.

Unease squirmed through my stomach.

"Definitely," Landon replied. "I'm a huge fan of Hemlock Cove's gusto when it comes to festivals. They're fully committed to selling the uniqueness of the town."

"The uniqueness of the town, huh?" Childs snorted. "If you say so." His eyes moved to me. "Is that why your family has called this area home so long? Is it the uniqueness that calls to you?"

The question felt pointed, as if he was trying to trap me. "My family has been here a really long time. I believe we originally moved here because they were giving away homesteads for a buck to populate the area. My family took three adjoining homesteads, and that property was eventually united into one parcel."

Childs blinked twice. "I ... um ... is that true?" He looked confused.

"That's the story I was told," I replied.

"I thought maybe you were here because things were somehow more magical. Like ... your property was magical or something."

Our property was magical. The bluff was a nexus, but a teeny-tiny one, especially in comparison to Hawthorne Hollow. But we provided the magic to this land, we didn't draw magic from it.

Childs didn't need to know that.

"You've been spending a lot of time here," Landon said, dragging the conversation back on topic. "You're here two or three times a week now."

"That's what happens when you don't have a job," Childs replied. "I have nowhere to go in the middle of the day, so I come here. You shouldn't have a problem with that. There's nothing to hide in Hemlock Cove, right?" He sounded haughty.

Landon flashed a tight smile. "If you want to hang around Hemlock Cove, knock yourself out. There's always a festival, and they're magnificent."

"They *are* magnificent." Childs was all smug charm now, to the point I wanted to smack the smirk off his face.

"What's not okay is you letting yourself into my wife's office when she's alone and lying in wait to frighten her," Landon continued. His tone was blasé, but there was a sharpness to his eyes. "My wife deserves to feel safe in her office. Don't you agree?"

Childs looked thrown. "I did not enter your wife's office to terrorize her. That's a business building."

"And yet she's the only one who ever goes in there. All the ads are placed at the bakery once a week. Bay goes there for coffee. All the business owners know to find her there. Nobody ever goes in that office except her ... and then she found you loitering in the shadows when she was packing up for the holidays."

"I wasn't doing anything nefarious," Childs protested.

"No? You made demands of my wife while physically backing her into a corner."

It was only then that I realized what Landon was doing. He was going on the offensive, and in a way that warned Childs we were done messing around. If Childs kept after me, Landon would take it to a higher level, and he was explaining exactly how things would look to a judge if we were forced to go that route.

"That's not what I was doing," Childs insisted. "I was simply explaining to your wife that ... I..." He floundered.

"What?" Landon challenged. "What exactly were you trying to force my wife to do? She was alone in her office—too isolated to call for help—and you wanted what exactly?"

Childs swallowed hard. "I know what you're doing," he said in a low voice.

"Well, that makes one of us, because I have no idea what you're doing," Landon fired back. "I understand that losing your job was a blow, but it's not okay to terrorize my wife. If she tells me you infringed on her personal space again, we're going to have issues."

Childs narrowed his eyes to dangerous slits. "You can't force me to back down. I know what's right."

"So do I," Landon said. "It's not right to terrorize my wife." He slid his arm around my back. "Let's go, sweetie. You need your rest. It's been a trying few days, what with this man trying to frighten you in your own office."

Landon was playing it up big. This was the best way we had to get Childs to back off until we got the Christmas decorations under control. I had my doubts about whether or not the former warden would do as Landon hoped, but it was worth a try.

"I promise I won't go anywhere near your wife's office again," Childs bit out. "Is that good enough for you?"

"Not even close," Landon replied. "You want to be very careful about your next move." He leaned close and whispered the next part. "You might think you have nothing to lose—and you'd be right about being a dangerous man—but I'll do whatever it takes to protect my wife. Don't ever threaten her again."

Childs looked momentarily flummoxed. Then he nodded. "I have no intention of threatening your wife, but I *will* get what I want."

"No, you won't." Landon prodded me away from Childs. "You're asking for the impossible. I'll show you exactly what I'm capable of if you move on my wife again."

"I get it." Childs jutted out his chin. "Have a nice night."

I DIDN'T CONGRATULATE LANDON ON A JOB well done during the drive home. I honestly wasn't certain he'd made the right move. I ran it through my head several times and wasn't any clearer when we arrived at the guesthouse.

"Tell me what you're thinking," Landon instructed as he killed the engine of his Explorer.

"I don't know what I'm thinking."

He made a face of doubt.

"I don't," I insisted. "I get why you did what you did—it was actually a shrewd move—but I don't know that it's going to be enough to get Childs to back off."

"Neither do I, but I needed to do something overt." Landon was matter of fact as he held my gaze. "If you weren't magical and he accused you of these things, I would step in."

"But I am magical."

"He has no actual proof of that. And if he loses his mind and attacks you—let's say with a knife or a gun—we're going to need to have some of this on the record."

I balked. "You don't think he would attack me that way, do you?"

Landon hesitated, then held out his hands. "If you'd asked me how I felt on the subject two weeks ago, I would've laughed at the notion. He seems pretty intent, though. He's almost obsessed. I need to make sure that you're as safe as possible from his obsession."

I nodded, and not just to placate him. "I wish there was a way to help him, but I've been over it a hundred times in my head. I just don't think there is."

"I don't think so either," he said. "I need to have stated the warning, because if he comes at you again, I'm filing an official complaint."

My shoulders jolted. "And what happens if that goes to court?"

"What do you mean?"

"What's to stop him from outing us in front of a judge?" I demanded.

"Um ... we'll want the complaint to go to court. Do you have any idea what a judge is going to think if Childs stands up and tells everyone that he was chasing you because you're a witch and he's demanding that you give him a do-over on his job because he's convinced you have magical powers?"

"Huh."

"Yes, 'Huh.'" Landon lightly tapped the end of my nose. "We need to be careful how we play this, because if he comes after you and you're forced to protect yourself..." He broke off, agitated at the possibility.

"I'm not killing him," I warned Landon. "It's not happening."

"Never say never, Bay."

"Never. He's done nothing to earn killing."

"Not yet," Landon said. "What happens if he comes after you with a gun and threatens to shoot you in the head if you don't cast a spell that gives him what he wants?"

"It won't come to that." Perhaps it was wishful thinking, but I was determined to stand by that assertion.

"I truly hope so, Bay, but I'm going to be prepared. You're my heart. I'm going to protect my heart." With that simple but heartfelt declaration, he gave me a kiss and then took the box of candy from me. "First one in bed gets the most candy." He was out of the Explorer like a shot, heading toward the door.

"What the hell." I pushed open the passenger door and hopped out. The driveway was a mess, and I slid on the ice. I regained my footing but didn't make it far before a wall of magic exploded around me and sent me careening back toward the Explorer. I hit it with enough force that my back ached as my hands were pinned to the front of the grill on either side of me.

"Bay?" All traces of mirth fled Landon's eyes as he turned to see what was happening. He hadn't been thrown back, but when he realized there was a glowing trap of sorts holding me against his vehicle, his first instinct was to race to me.

I opened my mouth to tell him to stay back—I wasn't certain what was happening—but it was already too late. Landon's long legs slowed in his attempt to get to me, and after two steps he froze in place.

"Hey!" Landon struggled against the invisible force holding him, but he couldn't move. One of his feet was firmly planted in front of the other, as if his boots were glued to the ground. "Bay?" The fear when he lifted his eyes to mine made me sick.

"Hold on." I tried to push myself away from the Explorer—my only thought was to get to him—but the magic pinned me back. "Crap." I wanted to use a much stronger expletive, but now wasn't the time to test out my curses. At least not those types of curses. "Crappity, crap, crap."

"Bay, I'm coming." Landon's determination was fierce, but there was no way to escape whatever was happening. Even if he could, then what? He didn't have magic at his disposal to free me. "Bay!" Landon's frustration was palpable.

"Eat some candy," I ordered. His arms seemed to be fine, but his legs were frozen. "I'll figure a way out of this."

To my surprise, Landon opened the box of candy and shoved a piece of chocolate into his mouth. Then he proceeded to methodically chew. He didn't look happy—the chocolate had been blessing him with bliss an hour before—but it seemed to calm him.

"You really are a slave to food," I muttered as I focused on the spell that had incapacitated me. "Okay, then." I tested my muscles by trying to physically pull away from the vehicle. I wasn't expecting it to work and wasn't surprised when it didn't. I glared at the darkness to my left. "Goddess, you guys think you're so funny."

Giggles erupted from the trees. Landon jerked his eyes in that direction, fear etched across his features, but nobody stepped out from the shadows to threaten us. That told me all I needed to know.

"Hey." I wanted to snap to get Landon's attention because he was fixated on the woods, but I couldn't move my arms. "Landon, look at me," I ordered.

He slowly dragged his eyes to me. The giggles echoing from the woods again had him frowning. "It's creepy," he complained.

"It could be worse," I said. "It could be dolls ... or clowns."

Landon's mouth dropped open. "Why would you even say something like that?"

"I don't know. I wish I hadn't." I forced myself to remain calm. "I'm about to do something that might freak you out, but I need you to remain calm. I can't get free without a bit of help."

"What does that mean?" Landon demanded.

"It means you should keep eating your candy and take a deep breath."

Landon growled.

I couldn't focus on his fear. My greatest strength was my necromancer power, so I called upon it. "*Come*," I intoned, engaging with my magic.

It only took seconds for several ghosts to appear. I recognized one of them. Viola looked as if she would rather be anywhere else but helping me.

"Now what?" she complained. "I was having a grand time listening to Margaret plot against you guys. She's completely off her rocker. She's trying to figure out a way to drop you in a volcano."

"I'll deal with Mrs. Little later," I replied. "Right now, I need you to break apart the spell holding me here. I can't even see it, so I'm not sure how to approach it."

Viola narrowed her eyes as she floated closer. She knew that arguing with me was a waste of effort. My necromancer powers were through the roof these days. She couldn't stop me from ordering her to carry out what I needed. She no longer bothered trying to talk me out of a plan.

"Hold on," she said after looking me over from top to bottom—twice. She grunted when fighting the spell, which seemed like overkill because she was a ghost and couldn't get winded, but after a few seconds, she seemed to find the right spot—like a button only she could see—and I pitched forward in my haste to escape the trap.

"Done." Viola's smile was wide as she pretended to dust off her ghostly hands. "Is that all?"

"Sure." I flicked my eyes to the other ghosts. There was nothing familiar about them. "Newbies? Where did they come from?"

"How should I know?" Viola made a face. "I'm not the one in charge of the ghosts. If you want to know where they came from, that's on you."

Neither ghost looked particularly young—or traumatized—so I opted to wave them off. "Thanks for the assist."

"It's not like I had much of a choice." With that, Viola was gone.

I studied the tree line. I didn't see anybody moving out there. The giggles returned in small waves.

"Are you just going to let me stand here and suffer?" Landon demanded when I didn't start in his direction.

I shook myself from my search and went toward him. "Sorry." Once I was at his side, it was easy to find the source of the spell that had locked him in place. I turned it back in an instant, and the magic that had been expelled to cast the spell disintegrated in a green mist.

Landon let loose a breath when he could move again. "What the hell was that, Bay?" he asked.

"Someone who wants to mess with us," I replied. "Whoever it is has magic ... but not much. These are coordinated attacks, but there's very little strength behind them."

"You needed ghosts to free you." His tone was accusatory. "That indicates we were in danger."

How could I explain to him in a way that would allow him to breathe? "It's fine," I assured him. "I could've gotten out by myself. I just didn't want to risk exerting too much magic and hurting you in the process."

"Oh, well, as long as you're sure that it's not a big deal." He shoved another piece of candy into his mouth and pouted.

Because there was nothing else to do, I pointed him toward the house. "Come on. We can eat the rest of the candy in bed and play your favorite game."

Landon looked appalled. "Maybe I'm not in the mood to play that game."

"When aren't you in the mood?" I asked reasonably.

He considered it a moment, then shrugged. "Fine. We can play the game. If I hear giggles, though, all bets are off."

"My giggles or their giggles?" I was going for levity, but the attempt fell flat, and Landon openly glared at me. I kept my smile in place. "Come on. If you let it go, I'll scrub your back in the tub."

"I don't like the creepy giggles, Bay," he complained as he pulled his keys out. "I'm over them."

He wasn't the only one. Unfortunately, I couldn't decide what we were dealing with here. I didn't have a single clue, and that worried me. I kept my opinion to myself, though.

"We'll figure it out tomorrow," I promised.

Landon didn't look convinced. "And if it takes longer?"

"Then we'll handle that disappointment too. I'm doing the best I can here."

"You're definitely scrubbing my back in the tub."

"I wouldn't have it any other way."

19
NINETEEN

I slept surprisingly hard despite our adventure. When I woke the next morning, I was rested and ready to greet the day. Landon, however, was still surly.

"I'm mad," he announced as I finished straightening my hair.

"I told you I didn't mean to eat the last reindeer in the box," I replied. "There are still snowmen ... and bells. There are plenty of bells."

"Nobody likes the bells," Landon shot back. "That's not what I'm mad about."

"The bells taste exactly the same as the reindeer."

"You can claim that all you want, but they don't. The reindeer are better. I seriously don't want to talk about that."

"Fine. What do you want to talk about?"

"We're being terrorized by creepy giggles, Bay." He was deadly serious. "I can't stand it. I need it to stop. The giggles are giving me nightmares."

He did have circles under his eyes. "You didn't sleep?" I traced the shadows dogging his handsome face. "I didn't realize."

"That's because you were dead to the world. There was snoring, drooling, and those little murmurs you make when you're having a dirty dream."

I shot him a withering look. "Don't go overboard."

"You murmur my name constantly."

"Please." I gave my reflection one more look and then moved away from the bathroom vanity. "If I was murmuring anybody's name in a dirty dream it would be Colin Farrell's."

"Hey!" Landon's eyebrows hopped up his forehead. "Don't push me, missy. I can only take so much."

I laughed, as I'm sure he'd intended, and started into the living room. "Come on. We need to get to the inn. Aunt Tillie needs to know what happened last night."

"Why?" Landon helped me into my coat. "Her decorations aren't haunting us. Unless ... are they?" His eyes opened so wide at the possibility I was worried they might pop out of his head. "Is Rudolph sticking his red nose into our business in an attempt to frighten us to death?"

He sounded so outraged I couldn't stop myself from grinning. "It's not the decorations," I assured him. I wasn't certain of a lot right now, but I was certain of that. "I'm pretty sure it's the girls from the school. Aunt Tillie picked three of them out as witches right away."

"Aunt Tillie once told me that the rabbits that were breaking into her greenhouse were descendants of the rabbit from *Monty Python and the Holy Grail*, and she was dead serious."

That was hardly shocking. "Yes, but I'm fairly certain she was serious about this situation."

Landon didn't look convinced. "Bay—"

I shook my head to cut him off. "We're going to figure it out. I need you not to panic."

That had him narrowing his eyes. "I don't panic."

"No, not you." I tried to keep my tone light and teasing.

"I don't," he insisted. "I was the calm one last night."

That wasn't exactly how I remembered it, but there was no sense in arguing. "Fine. You were the calm one."

"I was. I ate my candy and waited for you to come save me. I knew you wouldn't fail me."

"I'm glad I didn't fail you." I paused long enough to lay my hand against his cheek. "In truth, the magic that was used against us wasn't that strong. I really could've saved us without the ghosts. They were just the most expedient way to go."

He cupped my hand and kept it in place, desperate to prolong the contact. "Okay. So, what are we dealing with?"

"I don't know. That's why I need help figuring it out."

Landon sighed. "Fine, but if we get haunted by freaky giggles again, I'm going to be really upset. I don't like the feeling that we're trapped in a horror movie."

WE DROVE TO THE INN BECAUSE NEITHER of us wanted to risk the walk, despite the fact that it was a sunny—and for this time of year warm—Michigan morning. The walk would've left us exposed.

Aunt Tillie was the only one in the dining room when we entered. The sharp cut of her jawline told me she wasn't in a good mood, despite being alone, which was often her preferred state.

"What's up with you?" Landon asked as he headed toward the coffee carafe.

"I've decided that maybe it's time to build myself a house on the property," Aunt Tillie announced. "Nothing too big or ostentatious. I don't want the *Yellowstone* ranch or anything. I do, however, want space away from your mother." Her eyes were dark when they landed on me.

"Let me guess," I drawled, smiling encouragingly at Landon as he brought me a cup of coffee. "Mom found out exactly how bad the Christmas decoration situation is and chewed you a new butt this morning."

"I'm not afraid of your mother," Aunt Tillie shot back quickly. "However, she is a complete and total itch in a hard-to-reach place, and I don't need her crap. I've got the Christmas decorations under control."

As if on cue, Mom swept through the swinging door with small black skillets clutched in both of her oven-mitt-covered hands. "Is that so?" she challenged.

"What's that?" Landon leaned forward to get a look at what Mom was holding.

"We're trying something new," Mom replied, inclining her head to Landon. "You guys are guinea pigs this morning."

Landon didn't look happy. "Um ... pass. I'll suffer through the usual. Where is the bacon?"

"In the skillet," Mom replied. Normally she doted on Landon, but a warning lined her face this morning. "Sit down," she ordered.

I was familiar enough with my mother's moods to immediately do as she demanded. I took my chair without complaint, made a mental note that there was a trivet in front of my chair, and waited until she'd slid one of the skillets in front of me.

Landon didn't move nearly as fast, and the derisive look he shot the skillet when Mom set it before him indicated he was about to make a massive mistake. Maybe it was because he was tired. Perhaps it was because he was a creature of habit. Either way, he was about to infuriate my mother ... and that was a problem none of us needed.

"Don't." I grabbed Landon's wrist and gave it a warning squeeze. "Just don't." I turned a set of imploring eyes on my mother before Landon could respond. "He didn't sleep. We had an *incident* last night."

"I heard." Mom turned her accusatory glare to Aunt Tillie. "Rudolph almost used his shiny nose to snort half the town."

"Not that." I let loose a haphazard wave. "That was more of a curiosity than anything else."

"That's not what Terry said."

"No offense to Chief Terry, but he's prone to histrionics where the decorations are concerned," I replied.

"Yes, because Chief Terry is receiving ten calls a night when he's supposed to be sleeping," he barked as he joined us in the dining room. There were shadows dogging his eyes, and the slope of his shoulders told me he was exhausted.

I shot him a guilty look. "Sorry."

"You should be sorry. You helped her do this."

"Nobody cares about the decorations," Landon replied. "Turn off your phone. The spell will run its course and the decorations will go back into hibernation in a week and a half. We need to talk about something serious."

"We were magically attacked at the guesthouse last night," I said when several sets of eyes turned to us.

Landon looked appalled. "Not that. I'm talking about this." He gestured to the skillet. "What happened to regular breakfast?"

If looks could kill, he would be dead. The slant of my mother's eyes indicated she was wishing for her butcher knife. "That is the same breakfast you normally eat," she growled. "It's just in a different configuration."

Landon's lower lip poked out as he surveyed the skillet. "All I see are scrambled eggs."

"Look under the eggs," Mom growled.

I watched as Landon used his fork to poke beneath the eggs.

"That's potatoes, cheese, and bacon for you," Mom snapped. "All of your favorites. I just put them in an individual meal because I thought it would be a nice change of pace. The only thing that's different is that you've got diced hash browns instead of shredded."

Landon shot me a curious look. "She could be trying to fool me."

"You won't know until you try it," I replied. I started poking at my breakfast. "It's different," I said.

"That's part of the charm," Mom explained. "It's like making individual omelets for people—they can put their orders in the night before—but we don't waste as much making it for everybody. You love tomatoes, onions, and mushrooms in your eggs. Those are mixed in your skillet. We left out the cheese because you don't tend to be a big cheese fan when it comes to your omelets."

I forked some of the mixture into my mouth. It was delicious. "Awesome," I encouraged her around a mouthful of food.

Mom relaxed, although only marginally. "I'll be right back with your skillet, Terry," she promised as Chief Terry took his normal spot next to me. "Marnie and Twila are finishing up the last of them right now."

"Thank you." Chief Terry beamed at her, love naked on his face. There were times he looked at my mother like Landon looked at his bacon. "I'm sorry I was such a grouch this morning."

Mom leaned over and kissed his cheek. "Don't worry about it. You're allowed to be angry about not getting any sleep." Her eyes were dark when they moved back to Aunt Tillie. "We're all angry about that."

She disappeared into the kitchen, leaving a sulky Aunt Tillie behind. That's when I remembered that nobody had reacted to my news that we'd been magically attacked at the guesthouse.

"Hey, does nobody care that we were attacked last night?" I complained.

Landon was elbow deep in his skillet—apparently, he was over his resistance to change—and he merely shrugged. "It was only a little attack," he said around a mouthful of food.

I glared at him before turning to Aunt Tillie. "We heard giggles again. I got thrown against the Explorer and magically held in place for about two minutes, until I called Viola to help free me. Landon was frozen in the snow during that time."

"Are you okay?" Chief Terry looked concerned as Mom reappeared with two more skillets. She let one drop with a thud in front of Aunt Tillie, the contents bouncing, and then delivered Chief Terry's with the sort of delicate love that made me uncomfortable.

Marnie exited the kitchen behind Mom with two skillets. She put one down in Mom's regular place and then sat with her own. Twila brought up the rear. She had a platter of toast and a final skillet for herself.

"What are we talking about?" Mom asked after a few seconds of staring soulfully into Chief Terry's eyes.

I repeated what I'd said when she'd been out of the room. By the time I finished, she was seated and digging into her breakfast.

"It doesn't sound like it was all that terrifying," Mom noted. "I mean ... you've been in far worse situations."

"I have," I agreed. "Far worse. That doesn't change the fact that someone made it onto the property twice. They threw magic at the pot field when Landon and I were there the other night. They're clearly testing us."

Landon got up long enough to pour two glasses of juice, but he dug back in as soon as he sat down again. He was inhaling the contents of his skillet as if he was about to die of hunger.

"They were giggling," Landon volunteered between bites. "They were watching and laughing."

"Except the giggles sounded ... manufactured," I replied. "It's possible the giggles were designed to be unnerving, and it could just be one person."

"Or it could be several people testing you," Aunt Tillie countered. She was methodically plowing through her skillet, and if Mom's disdain bothered her, she didn't show it.

"You said several girls at the school are witches," I said.

"Yup."

"How do you know that? I didn't feel anything magical about them."

"They've just got that look."

My eyebrows moved toward one another as I tried to contain my temper. "Aunt Tillie—"

"Oh, don't get your kvetch on so early in the day," she complained. "Pace yourself, Bay."

I moved to stand—I had no idea what I was going to do—but Chief Terry grabbed my arm.

"It's not worth it," he said in a low voice. "She's digging her heels in because she screwed up with the decorations. Pushing her will only make things worse."

He was always so good at reading us. *All* of us. When I was a kid, he would take Clove, Thistle, and me out for adventures. He tailored his reaction to each of us. Even though I hadn't realized it at the time, he also tailored his reactions to Mom and my aunts. Even Aunt Tillie wasn't capable of escaping his shrewd machinations.

I sat back down and forced myself to focus on my breakfast. "Whether they're an immediate threat or not, they could grow into one without realizing it," I said, choosing my words carefully. "The harder they try to take me down, the more dangerous they could get. I don't want to risk that ... for any of you or myself."

"Do you think they killed the headmistress?" Marnie asked.

"The headmistress was infatuated with the father of one of the students. It's possible that the kids realized this and were trying to pay her back or something."

"Like ... they think that Kevin Dunne only cheated with Enid and nobody else for some reason?" Landon asked. He'd practically inhaled his breakfast. "That's interesting."

"I don't know what they're thinking. I don't know if they're involved in what happened to Enid, but it seems that she had to be poisoned at the school," I said.

"And you think one of the students did it?" Chief Terry queried. He sipped his coffee. "The lab is trying to trace the poison. They don't have much to go on. All they'll say is whatever killed her, they don't know how fast it worked, or if it was administered over time."

"Maybe it's something the girls concocted," I suggested. "Is there a greenhouse on the property?"

"There is," Chief Terry replied.

I nodded. "Then we need to get a look at the greenhouse. Aunt Tillie will be able to ascertain if anything grown there is dangerous. I'll take her with me."

"Aunt Tillie is supposed to be dealing with the decorations," Mom said.

"I thought we were stuck because of the timeline she included when casting the spell."

"She can still try." Mom's frustration was palpable. "It's getting out of hand, Bay."

"We need to go back to the school. I'll take Clove and Thistle too. While we're there, we'll try to come up with a plan to deal with the decorations. If we all put our heads together, I'm sure we'll come up with something."

"And if you don't?" Mom demanded.

"Then it's going to be a very loud Christmas."

Mom threw up her hands. "Bay, if you want to take Aunt Tillie with you, then I'm going to make the decorations your problem too."

I thought of Childs's triumphant face the previous evening and sighed. "I swear I'll figure something out. Somehow."

20
TWENTY

Clove was more than happy to join us for the trip to the school—she was a busybody like the rest of us, after all—but there was one little problem.

"You can't take a baby to a magic fight," Aunt Tillie said when she caught sight of Calvin. Unlike the others in the family, she wasn't anywhere near as enamored with the baby as we expected ... especially since he was named after her late husband. She wasn't even simply indifferent. There were times I could've sworn she disliked her great-great-nephew.

"He's not old enough to stay home on his own," Clove replied. She had Calvin lodged on her hip. He was finally starting to show some personality and shot a gummy grin at me. "What do you suggest I do with him?"

"Get a babysitter." Aunt Tillie frowned at the baby, which only made him grin wider. "Why is he staring at me?"

"Because babies like other babies," Thistle replied. She plucked Calvin off Clove's hip and moved to the kitchen. "We're not taking him with us, so chill out." She smiled at the baby, who returned her smile, and carried him into the kitchen. I watched through the opening as she shoved Calvin toward his grandmother. "We're going on a mission to fight potential witches. He can't go with us."

"He is safe with us," a delighted Marnie promised as she took her grandson.

I caught Mom's steady stare through the open door. "You will be careful." She didn't look particularly worried, but there was an edge to her stance.

"You don't have to worry about us," I promised. "We're going to handle the junior witches. Then we're going to figure out what to do with the enchanted decorations." *Even if it involves magically sealing them in a cave until the spell is finished,* I silently added.

"Okay." Mom smiled. "Don't worry about Calvin."

"I'm not worried about Calvin," Clove said. "I'm worried about us. I haven't been in the thick of a magic fight in months. What if I'm rusty?"

Aunt Tillie shot Clove a look of disgust. "It's not as if you're ever important in a fight. You're always there just to be there. In fact, if we were the Donner Party, you would be the first one eaten."

Clove sniffed. "Are you trying to make my eyes leak?" she demanded. "If so, good job."

"Don't," I warned, extending a finger. "We're doing this as a group. Don't give her any grief."

"Do you know what I heard when you opened your mouth just now?" Aunt Tillie challenged.

"A good idea?"

"Blah. Blah. Blah." Aunt Tillie shot me a challenging look. "That's what I heard. You were channeling the teacher in a Charlie Brown cartoon."

I narrowed my eyes. "How far do you want to push me today?"

"I don't know, but I guess we're going to find out, aren't we?"

That was a challenge. Unfortunately for her, I was looking forward to it.

· · ·

THIS TIME WHEN WE INVADED STONECREST, WE didn't bother stopping at the administration building. Bianca might've been looking out the window for all we knew. If she came for us, we would deal with it in the moment.

"Do you know who works here?" I asked Clove as we started toward the dormitory. "Remember Bianca Golden?"

It took Clove a moment to put a face with the name. "Really?" Clove looked horrified. "That ... *pom-pom shaker* ... works here?" The absolute vitriol that dripped from Clove's mouth had me grinning.

"She remembers you fondly too," I teased.

"What did that whore say?" Clove demanded.

I darted a questioning look to Thistle.

"Tommy Brennan," Thistle explained. "Clove wanted him. She even went out on a date with him her senior year. You would've been in college at the time. Bianca swooped in and made out with him under the bleachers when her school was playing our team."

"They even did it under the home bleachers, which is a gross betrayal," Clove snapped. "Everybody knows you don't steal someone and then taunt the other party under their own bleachers."

"I wasn't actually aware of that rule," I admitted. "It's good to know."

"Right." Thistle smirked. "Where does Bianca work?"

I pointed at the administration building. "She's in there, but I think she has her hands full. That's the classroom building." I pointed again, this time to the other side of the lot. "We're heading to the dormitory, which is between the two."

"I thought we were going to the greenhouse," Aunt Tillie said.

I hesitated. I wasn't opposed to checking out the greenhouse. I stopped long enough to look around the grounds. Not everything on the campus was visible from our location.

Aunt Tillie wrinkled her nose. "We could wander around."

"It's cold," Clove complained.

"And here we go." Aunt Tillie pinned Clove with a death glare.

"You need to suck it up if you're going to be part of the team. Just because you had a baby doesn't mean you get special treatment. It's winter in Michigan. You should be tough enough to deal with it at this point."

"Don't take it out on me just because you're in trouble with Aunt Winnie," Clove fired back. "I get that you're still irritated that Calvin wasn't a girl, but you need to suck it up."

"You're not still mad about that, are you?" I demanded of Aunt Tillie, assuming Clove had to have gotten it wrong. "Why does it matter?"

"We have girls in this family," Aunt Tillie replied simply. "We've always had girls. Girls are magically stronger."

"Is that a real thing or are you just making it up?" Thistle asked.

Aunt Tillie turned on Thistle so quickly I was surprised she didn't give herself whiplash. "It's real!"

"How can you know that if we've only ever had girls?" I asked.

"Because ... because..." Aunt Tillie worked her jaw, and I could feel the fury washing off of her. "I'm done talking to you," she said finally, folding her arms across her chest. "Just ... done."

I was struck in the moment by what her refusal to engage truly meant. "Did I just win an argument?" I asked Thistle.

"It sure sounds like it," Thistle replied. "Do you feel stronger? More magically inclined? Wait." She held up her hand. "Do you feel the irresistible urge to put on a combat helmet and beat someone with a stick?"

Clove dissolved into giggles as I bit the inside of my cheek to keep from laughing.

"I see how it is." Aunt Tillie huffed. "Guess what, little mouths. I've been taking it easy on you for months because you've all been dealing with nonstop crap. Well, that's done. If you want the bull, you'd better be ready for the horns!" She shook her fist at us.

"So you don't want to wear a combat helmet?" Thistle drawled.

"Not last time I checked," I replied dryly. "Never say never, though." I decided to get the train back on the tracks. "We don't know where the greenhouse is so let's head straight in to talk to the kids. One of them will be able to tell us where to look, and if we're lucky, we'll lock in the kids right away and be done here."

"How often do we get that lucky?" Clove asked.

"Almost never," I conceded, "but there's a first time for everything."

WE GOT COMFORTABLE IN THE COMMON ROOM. It was quiet when we first arrived, which allowed Clove and Thistle to look around. It didn't take long for the students to make their way to us. Unlike the previous day, nobody was shy about our presence.

"Are you in love with us or something?" Violet asked as she moved to stand in front of us. She was obviously feeling sure about herself as she planted her hands on her hips and stared us down. "Are you predators? My dad warned me against predators."

Autumn let loose a mocking laugh as she crossed behind Violet. "Your dad only said that because he didn't realize you were the predator. If he knew the truth, he'd be telling these old ladies to run."

"Did she just call me old?" Aunt Tillie demanded.

"Screw you," Thistle shot back. "She just called me old. What in the actual Hecate? I mean ... come on. I'm in my prime."

Rather than rise to the bait the girls were dangling, I allowed my magic to ooze out and take a look around. I was looking for proof we were dealing with witches. When my inner danger alarm finally dinged, it was with as little zip as possible.

Slowly, I tracked my gaze to Aunt Tillie. She was right. They were witches ... but just barely.

"Told you." Aunt Tillie said.

"What did she tell you?" Autumn asked.

Rather than immediately answer, I shifted my attention to Katie. She was in the common room, hanging back by the door. Violet and Autumn might've been full of bravado, but Katie was a survivor.

"We should talk." I made sure the two uninvolved girls hanging around the common room had left before continuing. "I know you were outside my house last night. I have some questions."

"You think we were outside your house?" Autumn was the picture of innocence. "This is a closed campus. How would we have managed that?"

"I'm guessing it wasn't that hard," I replied. I leaned back on the couch. Despite the fact that they'd attacked, I wasn't all that worried. "Where did you get the magic?"

"You have to be more specific," Violet argued. "We're not fanciful kids who believe in magic. We're adults."

I cocked my head as I took in the safety pin attached to her shoe. There were beads on it and a little ribbon.

"What?" Violet sounded annoyed now. "Adults crave color too."

"It's not our fault these uniforms are boring," Autumn noted. "Sometimes you need a splash of color."

"I've been telling them that." Aunt Tillie held up her fist for Autumn to bump, earning a wrinkled nose for her efforts. "I'm just like the kids, Bay. You keep calling me old, but I'm young at heart."

"You're deranged is what you are," Thistle shot back.

Thankfully, Aunt Tillie didn't have the sort of fire magic that could just be thrown around willy-nilly, otherwise Thistle would be the human equivalent of a chestnut roasting on an open fire right about now.

"We're not here to talk about who is old and who is young," I started.

"I'm young," Aunt Tillie volunteered.

I ignored her. "We're here to talk about the fact that you have been at my house. Twice."

Violet and Autumn managed to keep straight faces. Katie was another story. She looked downright horrified at having been caught. Aunt Tillie had been right about them being witches. Just once I wanted Aunt Tillie to be wrong.

"Katie, come over here," I ordered when it looked as if she might bolt. "We want to talk to you especially."

Katie let loose a squeak. "Why me especially? I didn't go to your house. I didn't hang out around your field."

Given how nervous she was, I almost felt sorry for the girl. Then I remembered Landon's worry and forced myself to remain strong. They knew about the field. That was all the proof I needed. "Listen, we need to talk." I touched my tongue to my top lip as I debated, then barreled forward. "Where did you get your magic?"

"Where did you get yours?" Violet fired back. "Maybe that's the question we should be asking."

"I was born with it," I replied. There was no reason to lie at this point. "Magic is in our blood. Your magic ... was bestowed upon you."

"I don't know what that means," Autumn said with a snotty smile.

"It means someone gave you the magic," I said. "I want to know who." I was also curious about the how, but one thing at a time.

Autumn held her hands palms out and shrugged. "Sorry."

She wasn't sorry in the least. "Katie, were you aware your father was having a relationship with Headmistress Walters?" It was a brutal question to ask, especially in front of her schoolmates, but I was fairly certain they already knew.

"My father sleeps with anybody and everybody," Katie replied dully. "It would be more appropriate to ask who he hasn't slept with. He likes getting around."

I nodded. "Did he send you here because you knew that?"

Katie hesitated, then shook her head. "It's not that simple. I knew he was having affairs and I started ... mouthing off. I guess that's the best way to put it. My father said I was difficult. My mother was too hurt by what my father was doing to stand up for me. That's how I ended up here."

I leaned back and crossed my legs. "Did you know about Headmistress Walters?"

"I knew that she had feelings for my father," Katie replied. "She would make excuses to get him to visit the school. Not me, but the school. She wanted private meetings with my father, and she would say she was doing it to make sure I got a proper education, but I was the only student she was treating this way."

"It was way gross," Violet said. "We felt bad for Katie. That's why we joined her when ... well, when she thought we should become a group."

"Where did you get the magic?"

The girls exchanged looks, something unsaid passing between them. Ultimately, Autumn responded, although the previous bravado she'd boasted had fled.

"We don't know," she replied. "One day we woke up and we could just do things."

I didn't know what to make of that. "And you weren't concerned?"

"Concerned? No." Autumn's sly smile was back. "It's more like we were excited. I mean ... we woke up with special powers. Who wouldn't be excited about that?"

"Anyone with a brain," Thistle replied, earning a trio of glares. "You have no idea what you've gotten yourselves into."

"Did you tell anyone what was happening?" I asked.

Katie shook her head. "We were afraid to. Especially after the shadow started showing up."

"The shadow?" Now she had my full attention.

Katie shrugged. "It was dark. We'd see it on the lawn from our room window."

"You all share a room?"

"Yeah," Autumn confirmed. "The shadow would sit under our window and watch us. It would tell us to do things."

"Did it tell you to come to my house?"

"It said you were witches, and we should make sure you didn't do anything evil," Violet replied. "It said we were good witches, and you were bad witches." She gnawed her bottom lip.

"Crap." Briefly, I shut my eyes and pinched the bridge of my nose. "This is not good."

"Nope." Even Aunt Tillie was agitated. "Girls," she scolded, "in what world did you think it was okay to take orders from a shadow you've never seen? Did it ever occur to you that the shadow was the malevolent force, and you were on the wrong side?"

"Not so much." Katie pressed her hand to her stomach. "Is that true?"

"Yes," Aunt Tillie answered.

"No," I countered, shooting my great-aunt a quelling look. "We're saying that you should have considered the ramifications of what was happening a little sooner than you did. Most people have questions when they suddenly wake up with powers. They don't attack people for the fun of it."

"What should we do?" Katie asked.

That was a very good question. I only had one answer. "Well, for starters, we need to see your greenhouse." I was stern as I regarded them. "You didn't poison Headmistress Walters?"

"We would never," Violet replied solemnly. "We didn't particularly like her, but we didn't want to hurt her."

"She didn't pay attention to us," Autumn explained. "She was too busy paying attention to Mr. Dunne. Why would we want to risk somebody else coming in?"

"Because this was her school," I replied. "It might go away now that she's gone."

"We don't hate the school," Katie countered. "We hate why we were sent here. The school actually isn't so bad."

"The food is good," Violet volunteered.

"And being away from our parents is awesome," Autumn added.

"We don't want to lose the school," Katie insisted.

That made an odd sort of sense. "Okay, well, you girls are working with us now. We need to see your greenhouse, and then we'll go from there."

"We can take you to the greenhouse," Autumn supplied. "You're not going to kill us or anything, right?"

"That's not the plan," I replied, "but try not to give us too much attitude."

"We can't promise that," Violet replied.

21
TWENTY-ONE

The greenhouse was at the back of the grounds, next to a former chapel.

"There's no church here now," Autumn explained. "It's not a religious school."

"What's in there?" I asked.

"Just storage," Violet replied. "We're not allowed in there because they're afraid we'll steal."

I slid my eyes to Thistle. "Or that's where Enid was keeping more stuff," I suggested.

"That's possible," Thistle agreed.

"Let's do the greenhouse first," Aunt Tillie interjected. "We'll check the church after."

"It's locked," Katie argued. "We've tried to get in there to … hang out."

It only took a second for me to figure out what she meant by "hang out", and I had to hold back a laugh at how prim and proper she turned. "Aunt Tillie likes 'hanging out' a lot too," I said. "She has a whole field for hanging out."

"We heard," Autumn replied. "Why do you think we were at your house that first night?"

"I thought it was because the shadow told you to go," I pressed.

"It did," Autumn conceded. "It told us to go to your house. The field is famous. We wanted to check that out while we were waiting for you to be alone. We kind of knew where the field was, but we couldn't figure out how to get to it. Then you guys disappeared."

"Of course." I shook my head and made a tsking sound with my tongue. "You guys really need to start questioning people's motivations."

"Yeah." Aunt Tillie gave Autumn a dirty look. "How did you end up at the bad girls' school when you can't even tell the difference between good and bad people?"

"The shadow said you were bad people," Autumn insisted. "How were we supposed to know it was lying?"

"It's a freaking shadow," Aunt Tillie replied. "It's not like *Peter Pan*. There are no good shadows."

"Is that true?" Autumn turned her questioning eyes to me. Apparently, I was the voice of reason today.

I shrugged. "There are no absolutes in this business," I explained. "In general, shadows are bad. It's kind of stereotypical, but certain stereotypes persevere for a reason."

"Like Italians loving bread," Aunt Tillie interjected. "That's totally true."

"You love bread," Thistle snapped.

"I'm one-seventy-eighth Italian." Aunt Tillie shot Thistle a haughty look. "Can we look inside the greenhouse?"

"That's a fabulous idea," I said. This conversation was due to take an unfortunate turn if we allowed Aunt Tillie to keep unleashing stereotypes. The one about Greek people and beets was particularly odd. "Let's hit the greenhouse first. Then we'll check the chapel."

. . .

THE GREENHOUSE WASN'T OUT OF THE ordinary. Even though it was winter, the glass plates allowed for some growth. This was Aunt Tillie's forte, so I turned to her and arched an eyebrow.

"Why is it so much hotter than your greenhouse?" Clove asked as she fanned her face.

"It's heated," Aunt Tillie replied. "You have to be careful what sort of crops you put in one of these things over the winter. Certain plants won't grow no matter what. Why do you think I worked so hard on perfecting a field that can grow everything in the dead of winter?"

"I thought you were just flexing," Clove responded honestly.

Aunt Tillie rolled her eyes. "You are a complete and total pain sometimes. Has anybody ever told you that?"

"Just you." Clove's smile was triumphant. "Everyone else loves me."

"You keep telling yourself that." Aunt Tillie rolled her eyes. "It's mostly root vegetables, as you can see. Carrots. Turnips. Parsnips. Radishes." She leaned over a few leafy offerings. "Spinach. Kale. Cabbage. That Chinese thing they put in my stir fry dishes that I hate."

I looked over her shoulder. "Bok choy."

"Whatever. It tastes like water that's been formed in a Jell-O mold."

"Anything else of interest?" I asked.

"Some herbs." Aunt Tillie gestured to a different section of the greenhouse. "Standard stuff." She tracked her eyes to the girls. "Is there a part of the greenhouse you're not allowed into?"

Autumn pointed to the back of the building.

"Here we go," Aunt Tillie noted. "Belladonna." She pointed. "Also known as nightshade," she explained to the younger witches. "It's helpful in modern medicine, but if you use too much it could kill you."

I thought of Enid. "I'll tell Landon to ask the lab to run a panel. Anything else?"

"Lily of the valley." Aunt Tillie pointed again. "That mostly causes severe gastrointestinal issues, but it can kill if it's not regurgitated in time."

"So there's more than one thing here that can kill," I said.

Aunt Tillie nodded. "Yup."

"Okay. Let's hit the chapel. Then I need to make a trip to Traverse City."

"Why are you going to Traverse City?" Thistle asked. "You know we can't go with you. We have to open Hypnotic one more time before Christmas. It's the last shopping rush this afternoon, and we're opening with the other businesses."

I knew this day was important to them. They would move a lot of merchandise to last-minute panic shoppers. I would never put them in a bind and ask that they come with me. "It's fine," I promised. "The trip I plan to make doesn't require backup." I cast a pointed look to Katie. "I need to talk to Kevin and see who might have reason to be jealous ... and who might have the ability to call on a shadow to help. It's going to be a quick conversation. Then I plan to come home and get comfortable before the blizzard hits."

"I was kind of hoping we would get by without the blizzard," Thistle admitted. "When I'm finished at the store, I have to help Marcus get the animals secured. Are you sure you don't need help?"

"I can help," Aunt Tillie offered.

Thistle, Clove, and I grimaced.

"You need to handle the decorations," I argued. "We have to figure out a way to at least hide them for the next week and a half. I can handle Kevin. I very much doubt he's a threat."

"The only thing threatening about him is the way he wields his penis," Katie said darkly.

I patted her shoulder. "Don't worry," I said. "I'm not afraid of your dad. I don't even think he's responsible for this. I do think he knows who is responsible, even if he doesn't realize it yet."

Katie nodded. "I don't care what you do to him." She said it with enough bravado that others might have believed her. I didn't.

"It's going to be okay," I promised. "I'm going to get to the bottom of this. You have my word."

WE USED OUR MAGIC TO BYPASS THE LOCKS on the chapel. Someone had obviously been using it as an office of sorts, but there was nothing of interest inside.

My problem was that it made the most sense for someone at the school to poison Enid. I didn't believe it was one of the girls. It could very well have been the shadow that had been sent to communicate with them, though. The shadow was either sent to the school to throw people off, or the person who was really behind all of this wanted to deflect attention away from him or herself. I was leaning toward a woman, because the one thing that made sense as a motive was jealousy over Kevin. But I couldn't rule anything out.

At least not yet.

I dropped Thistle, Clove, and Aunt Tillie back in town. The latter was seemingly annoyed about being cut out of the action. Or, that's what she pretended. I knew beyond a shadow of a doubt that her real problem was that she didn't want to clean up the decorations she'd unleashed. She had no choice. The last thing we needed during a blizzard was out-of-control Santas and reindeer tromping through town.

Once I was on my own, I headed to Traverse City. I texted Landon to tell him my intentions—and promise that I would be home well before the storm—but I didn't wait for a response. I knew he would try to talk me out of my plan of attack. It was too late for that. I wasn't going to play games with Kevin. Not a second time.

His office was sparsely populated when I walked through the front door. The woman sitting at the front desk looked surprised that someone would bother to shop for real estate with a blizzard barreling down.

"I need to see Kevin," I announced with purpose. I didn't want her questioning me. There was a reason Thistle and Aunt Tillie always got their way, even when it ran counter to what the person they were addressing wanted. They didn't allow anyone a choice when it came to what needed to be done.

"We're closing the office," the woman said. "Can this wait?"

Apparently, channeling Aunt Tillie and Thistle wasn't working. I needed to be more forceful. "No, it cannot wait. I need to talk to him now."

"Well—"

I didn't wait for her to spit out whatever she was going to say. I took off to the left and stormed into Kevin's office.

"Hey," I said when his eyebrows practically flew off his forehead. "We need to talk."

"Did you decide on one of the properties for your aunt?" he asked hopefully.

"Honestly, if we could move her to a different house so she can train raccoons without getting in the way, I would do it. But that was a cover."

"A cover?" Kevin steepled his fingers on his desk. "Were you checking me out because you want to move some of your family property?"

The look of glee on his face made me want to punch him. "That's never going to happen."

"I'm confused." Kevin was no longer feigning patience. "If you're not here to buy or sell, why are you here?"

"Because you were having an affair with Enid Walters, and she's dead." I decided that dragging things out wouldn't help anyone. I needed to get home before the storm hit. "I believe one of your current mistresses killed Enid, and I need to know which one is more likely to have carried out the deed."

"I don't know what you're talking about," he replied. His body was straight, his expression stiff. He barely reacted to the charge.

"Listen, you little jerk." My magic escaped before I realized what I was going to do, and I sent his chair careening backward. It hit the wall with a tremendous clang. Then, rather than allow the secretary to rush in and make a scene, I shoved enough magic at the door to slam it hard enough to shake the small office.

"I'm done screwing around," I announced.

Kevin, for the first time since I'd met him, looked afraid.

"There it is," I drawled, letting loose a feral smile. "I can't tell you how happy I am that you're finally grasping that something bad is happening." I took a threatening step toward him. "Which of your current crop of mistresses would kill someone to secure your affections?"

"I don't know—"

I cut him off by throwing his chair against the wall yet again. "Do. Not. Push. Me." I gritted out the words. "If you keep denying who you are, what you are, you're going to make me mad. And much like the Hulk, you won't like me when I'm mad."

Kevin stared into my eyes for a long time, as if trying to ascertain whether I was telling the truth. Ultimately, he shrugged. "None of my girlfriends would do what you're suggesting."

It was a step forward, even if it was yet another denial. "How can you be sure of that?"

"I don't date psychopaths."

"Date?" His word choice rankled me. "That is ... just weak. You don't date them. You use them for sex and then you walk away."

"They're very aware of my stance before we even take the first step," he insisted. "I only entertain a certain type of woman."

"What type of woman is that?" There was no doubt I would hate his answer, but I wanted to hear him say it.

"The sort who understands that I'm only in this for one thing," Kevin replied. "I don't know what you think of me—I'm guessing it's not good from that little display you just put on—but I'm open and upfront with these women. I'll never leave my wife."

"Of course not. Your type never does. You gaslight the women you're dating despite your proclamations to the contrary. You might tell them you're never leaving your wife, but you do enough to keep them on the hook.

"You look for emotionally vulnerable women," I continued. "You want women who will have sex with you and keep up the charade they don't want more. All the while, you text them and tell them things like you wish you could give them what they truly want but your shrew of a wife won't allow you to live the life you deserve."

Annoyance ran roughshod over Kevin's face. "Who told you that? I told them to keep it a secret. There will be repercussions for letting that slip."

"Nobody told me." I thought of Georgie. "You've had more than one mistress take things a step too far over the years. Don't bother denying it. Someone got fed up with Enid and decided to take her out.

"I have theories on your culpability in this," I continued. "Part of me wonders if you fired one of them up to go after her because you found out she was stalking you." There was a glint in his eyes, but he didn't respond. "Don't pretend you didn't know she was infatuated with you."

"I have no idea what you're talking about," Kevin insisted. He was a good liar. As a reporter, I'd seen my fair share of good liars over the years, most of them attorneys and politicians. Kevin wasn't special. "While I admit that I had a very brief dalliance with Headmistress Walters, the rest of it is pure nonsense. I told her what I could and could not give her. She wanted more and became quite insistent. I broke things off right away when I realized that she would end up being hurt in the situation."

"How magnanimous," I drawled. "You're a real prince."

"I'm a man who has very limited offerings," Kevin replied. "There are still women out there who want to partake in those offerings. Who am I to deny them something so joyous?"

"Joyous?" I wanted to wring his neck. "Have you ever wondered what sort of horror you've left in your wake? I hate to be the bearer of bad news, but you're probably the source of more than one therapy bill."

"That's not my fault." Kevin was belligerent. "I tell them exactly what to expect at the start. If they're surprised when the end comes, it's on them."

I narrowed my eyes. "Listen, you're a piece of crap, and I'm betting you have a penis the size of a light switch. I honestly don't care about that. You've deranged some poor woman to the point of no return, and that woman has magic at her disposal. I need to know who she is."

"Magic?" Kevin's laugh was haughty and grating. "Perhaps you're the one who needs to talk to someone."

The fact that he could say that with a straight face given what I'd done in throwing him against the wall and slamming his office door proved how delusional he was.

"This isn't over," I said as I started for the door. I couldn't risk the secretary calling the police. If I was stuck in a Traverse City jail for the storm, Landon would melt down. "Just understand that I know you're part of this." I paused with my hand on the door handle. "We saw Enid's boards, how she was stalking you. There's no way one of your other mistresses didn't figure it out. Perhaps Georgie."

It was the only name I knew, so I threw it out there. When I looked over my shoulder, I found Kevin swallowing hard.

"We're pretty far from done here, Kevin. Take the blizzard to think about things, because I will be back."

With that, I headed out, saluting the receptionist before disappearing. "Have a nice Christmas."

22
TWENTY-TWO

I was angry when leaving Kevin's office, distracted when my phone rang back in my car. I put it on speakerphone without thinking when I saw Landon's name.

"Men are stupid," I offered by way of greeting.

"And hello to you, too," Landon drawled. "The love is clearly flowing today."

"You're not stupid," I assured him. "Just other men."

"Chief Terry?"

Okay, now I was irritated with him too. "What do you want?"

"What do I want?" Landon sounded as frustrated as I felt. "I want you home."

"It's fine," I assured him. "It's barely snowing."

"Bay, I just saw the weather update. The blizzard is early, and it's directly on top of you. It's sweeping west to east. It's going to chase you the whole way home. Unless ... are you already home?"

His tone told me that he already knew the answer. "I am almost there," I replied as I snapped my seatbelt into place, a noise that he would definitely hear on the other end of the call. "I'll be there in thirty minutes."

"Are you still in Traverse City?"

I couldn't lie to him. Especially if I ran into trouble and had to call for help. I kept my voice light and calm as I pulled away from Kevin's office. "It's barely snowing here, Landon. I'm on my way."

"In a tiny car with a blizzard raging."

"What did I say? It's not blizzarding."

As if on cue, the snow quadrupled in intensity. "Crap!" I hadn't meant to say it out loud, but once the word was out, there was no bringing it back.

"It's snowing, isn't it?" Landon didn't sound happy.

"It's fine," I assured him. "I've been driving in snow my entire life."

"I'm staying on the phone with you." There was no give to his tone.

"Landon, I'm going to be furious by the time I get home if you don't stop. I need to concentrate on the road. If you want to stay on the phone, that's fine, but don't yell."

His tone softened. "I'm not trying to be difficult. I just ... want you home."

"Where are you?" I asked. I was trying to relax after my interaction with Kevin. The best way to do that was to imagine him eating a doughnut in his Explorer as he waited for me.

"I'm at the police station. We went to the festival to make sure they were shutting down. We're clearing the downtown streets next so the plows can get through. Then I'm just waiting for you."

"Aw, so sweet." I smiled despite my bad mood. "Do you want to stay at the guesthouse or the inn? We don't have much food at the guesthouse."

"That shows what you know. Your mother has put together a huge picnic basket. We have more than enough to get through the next three days. We're talking chicken, leftover pot roast, soup, and pie."

"What kind of pie?"

"Blackberry. Where are you?"

I scowled. "I'm still in downtown Traverse City. I'm almost at the turn-off to M-72. Then it's a straight shot home."

"What's the traffic like?"

"Since when are you a traffic watcher?" I tried to keep my tone light even as I gripped the steering wheel tighter. The snow was falling heavier now.

"I want you home, Bay. The forecast says this is going to be a particularly bad storm. We can spend all of tomorrow in bed."

"Doesn't law enforcement have to go out no matter the weather?"

"I'm the FBI, ma'am," he replied in his sternest voice, making me grin. "I go out when I want ... and tomorrow I want to be with you."

He was so earnest it tugged at my heartstrings even though I wanted to be angry with him. "We'll have a quiet day in front of the fireplace."

"Screw that. We'll have a quiet day in bed. I got more reindeer candy at the festival."

Of course he did. "Well, that's something to look forward to."

"Where are you now?"

It was only then that I realized he was tracking me. Rather than give him grief over it, I decided to play along. "I can see the Grand Traverse Resort. I'm about to turn on to 72. It won't be long. Try not to panic."

"I can't help it, Bay. I'm kind of fond of you."

I gripped the steering wheel tighter as the wind picked up enough to rock my car a bit. Maybe Landon's suggestion that I get something new, something sturdier, wasn't the worst thing I'd ever heard.

"Talk to me, Bay," Landon instructed when I'd been quiet for a few minutes. "Tell me what happened with Kevin Dunne."

I told him, and not just because he asked. I was frustrated and needed to vent. When I finished, he sounded annoyed.

"Why would you use your magic on him, Bay? What if he tells someone?"

It took everything I had not to laugh. "Who is he going to tell? Is he going to walk into the police station, tell them I came in threatening him about his mistresses, and then describe how I used magic to slam his office door? Who would believe him?"

"It's unlikely, but it's not impossible. If enough people tell the same story, Bay—I'm talking Dunne and Childs—then people might start giving you side-eye."

"Everybody believes that Hemlock Cove is full of magic," I argued. "I'm just playing the game. And will you look at that?" I pulled my foot off the accelerator and tapped my brakes.

"Don't say things like that when I can't see what's going on," Landon ordered. "What is it?"

That was a very good question. The snow was swirling badly, and even though the road was still mostly clear, visibility was declining rapidly. Still, I saw the shadowy figure that had appeared in the middle of the road.

I looked forward and back on the road. Apparently, I was the only one on the highway. Everybody else had actually thought better of it and had seemingly gotten home at a reasonable hour.

"Landon..." I trailed off, uncertain what to say.

"You're going to say something that will drive me insane," Landon sounded as if he was about to lose what little cool he had left. "Bay, I don't want bad news. I bought all of the reindeer candy. A*ll* of it."

"I'm in trouble," I announced. "There's a magical shadow in the middle of the road, and it's staring right at me.

"Where are you?"

"You can't come and get me. I don't have that sort of time." What I didn't add was that there was nothing he could do for me even if he should manage to get here in time.

"Turn around," Landon ordered. He sounded as if he was running. "I'll come to Traverse City and get you. We'll stay in a hotel if we have to. I'm on my way."

It was too late for that. "Don't get on the road, Landon."

"Don't you tell me what to do." He was outside now.

"I need you to listen to me." The shadow was heading in my direction with a Jason Voorhees- steady stride. "I'm really close to Baggs Road now. I want to say I'll be heading in your direction shortly, but I don't think I'm that lucky.

"You cannot come looking for me yourself," I insisted. "You need someone with magic. Have Aunt Tillie send Evan if she can. The cold won't affect him."

"Bay." Landon sounded anguished. "Baby, don't do whatever it is you're about to do."

"I love you, Landon."

"Don't you say your goodbyes."

"This isn't goodbye," I assured him as I pumped my magic into the car. It had been a good car and it was about to sacrifice itself. "Make sure you send someone magical, Landon. Promise me."

"No. I'm coming for you right now."

"Promise me," I ordered.

"I promise." He sounded wretched. "Why didn't you stay here?" He caught himself immediately. "I don't mean that. I love you. Don't get hurt."

"Send Evan," I ordered. He was the only one I knew who would be safe in this snow. "I'll see you soon."

"Bay!" That was the last thing I heard before I ended the call and unplugged my phone. I put it in my bra for safe keeping. Then I increased the magic flowing into my car.

The shadow was almost halfway to me. It probably thought I was going to flee. Someone else might've done just that. I was a Winchester, though. Instead, I stomped on the accelerator, got my tires spinning, and then careened toward the shadow.

There was one brief moment when the shadow appeared to realize what was about to happen, but it was too late for either of us to escape the crash.

When my magic collided with the shadow, it was followed by a magical explosion. My car went airborne and then started to roll.

My heart threatened to beat out of my chest.

My breath came in short gasps.

The snow continued to fall as the engine died.

Then the world went black.

I WOKE TO THE SOUND OF METAL RIPPING apart. When I forced my eyes open, I was face to face with Evan.

"You came," I said dumbly. Every muscle in my body ached.

"Of course I came." He was tentative as he reached in and slid his arm under my legs. "We're in the thick of it now, Bay. It's not even the big part of the storm yet. It's cold, and you've been in an accident. What hurts?"

"Everything."

"What's broken?"

"I don't think anything is broken." That was the truth. "I'm going to ache for days, but I'm not going to die or anything." Perhaps I just hoped that was true. "Where is Landon? Is he okay?"

"Tillie wrestled him to the ground and sat on him," Evan replied as he hefted me out of the car. He was effortlessly strong thanks to the vampire thing. "Listen to me very carefully." He stared into my eyes. "I'm going to run the whole way to Hemlock Cove. It's going to be weird for you."

I was already out of it, so I just nodded. "I need to get you to Landon. He's going to melt down if I don't get you to him quickly."

I was open for anything at this point. Then, I remembered the shadow. "Did you find a dead monster?" I asked.

Evan looked taken aback. "No. Was I supposed to find a dead monster?"

I shook my head. "I thought maybe..."

Evan jerked his eyes left and right. There was nothing but snow. "I don't see anything. I can come back later."

"Don't bother. It will find me. Whoever is doing this has marked me as an enemy. The shadow will come again."

"Great. Shove your hands inside your shirt to keep them warm."

I did as I was told. "How long?"

"Well, I can't quite run like a *Twilight* vampire, but I could win a couple of gold medals." He showed me his teeth when he smiled. "Just hold on."

I ZONED OUT FOR MOST OF THE TRIP back to Hemlock Cove. There was nothing to focus on, no color or sound, other than Evan's feet tirelessly thumping. I lost track of time and couldn't even fathom where we were at certain points.

Eventually, I heard voices in the background. Evan handed me over to someone warmer. We were in a vehicle. Then I was plunged into a hot tub. When I finally became fully aware of my surroundings, I was in the guesthouse ... and I was pretty far from alone.

"Why is everybody in the bathroom?" I snapped, crossing my arms over my chest in a belated move for modesty.

"We want to make sure you're okay," Mom replied as she stared down at me. "Oh, what are you doing?" She made a face when she realized I was squirming. "I brought you into this world, Bay Winchester. I've seen you naked."

"Not recently you haven't. Get out."

Mom rolled her eyes and smiled. "I'll send Landon in to help you get dressed."

"I can dress myself."

She ignored me. "Then we'll talk really quick before you go to bed."

I glared in her wake. The last thing I needed was this much active parenting. I didn't have the energy to fight her, though. She was right about that.

Landon managed a smile when he walked into the bathroom and shut the door behind him. "Come on, baby. Let's get you dried off."

I let him pull me to a standing position. I felt oddly drunk as he helped lift me out of the tub and then let me lean on him once my feet were on the floor.

"Here we go." He took extra care drying me. Then he did all the work pulling on a pair of jogging pants and an oversized shirt. He showed tremendous patience running a comb through my wet hair, and then he led me from the bathroom.

I couldn't believe all the people in the living room. It was the whole family, sans Clove and Thistle, along with Evan. "Why aren't you all home?"

"We wanted to make sure you were okay," Mom replied. She was calm despite what had happened.

What had happened? It was all a little fuzzy.

"Are you okay?" Marnie asked.

I nodded, even though I wasn't certain that was true. "I'm fine. You don't have to worry about me."

"What happened in the storm?" Aunt Tillie asked. "Landon said you knew trouble was coming. Evan said it looked as if you'd tried to run over a giant. Your car is a dead loss, by the way."

That was hardly surprising. "I guess Landon gets his wish about a new vehicle," I murmured as I sank down onto the couch. "As for what happened, I was fine. The roads weren't great, but they weren't terrible. I would've made it home without any problems."

"Then what?" Mom prodded.

I told them what happened. Or, what I remembered. When I was done, Aunt Tillie was annoyed.

"What sort of shadow stands in the middle of the road like that during a blizzard?" she complained. "That's just wrong."

"It's over and done with. Although ... won't emergency responders launch a search for me when they find my vehicle?"

"We already called them," Landon replied. He'd been oddly standoffish since I emerged from my reverie. "They know you wrecked, and we picked you up. Or, they think we did. We told them not to risk anything to save the vehicle and we would deal with it after the storm."

I was sad about the wrecked car. "Then we're good for the blizzard? I can get some sleep and there's nothing to worry about."

The look Mom shot Landon suggested there was something to worry about. She nodded all the same. "Everything is fine. Get some rest."

I flicked my eyes to Evan. "Thank you for coming for me."

His smile was soft and easy. "I like being the hero, so it worked out for me. At least now I know I'll be able to retain my spot as Tillie's number one sidekick."

"And for a good long while," Aunt Tillie confirmed. "Easton couldn't have done what you did today."

I was exhausted and closed my eyes. "Thank you, everybody. I'm fine."

"She needs rest," Landon interjected. "I'll take it from here."

23
TWENTY-THREE

All I wanted was to sleep. Landon's quiet nature had me fighting the urge to pass out, however.

"How long are you going to be mad at me?" I asked as he tucked me in.

"I'm not mad." His smile was tight. "Why do you assume I'm mad?"

"Because I've met you."

"I'm not mad." He tucked me in tight and moved to walk away from the bed. "Get some sleep."

Well, that just tore it. "Oh, no way!" I threw a pillow at his back.

When he turned, there was irritation—and something else—lining his features. "Did you really just throw a pillow at me?"

"I did," I confirmed. I had no intention of going to sleep until things were settled between us. "Do you want to know why?"

"I'm guessing you want to pick a fight."

That wasn't entirely the wrong answer. "Kind of," I confirmed. "What I really want is for you to lose your temper, lambast me for being stupid, and then call it a day."

"I'm not going to lose my temper. There's nothing to be angry about." His affect was flat, and it bothered me so much more than a lecture would have.

"Landon, you're mad. You're mad that I went to Traverse City with a blizzard bearing down on us. You're mad that I got attacked. You can't say you're mad, though, because I was in an accident and in your head, you think admitting you're mad is the same as somehow smacking me around or something."

"I have no problem admitting when I'm mad." The way he crossed his arms over his chest was defensive. "We fight all the time."

"We don't following a serious incident."

"Perhaps not but ... I'm fine." He smiled but there was no life to his eyes.

I decided to take a different tactic. "I need you to love me."

Well, that had him shifting. His eyes went from carefully neutral to fed up. "Is that what you think our problem is? You don't think I love you?"

"No," I replied without hesitation. "Not even a little. Right now, though, I need to be coddled. You're not in a good place mentally to do it. So, to get you to that place, I need you to yell at me and then get over it."

"Really?" Landon narrowed his eyes, and it was the first sign of true anger he'd allowed himself to show. "See, from where I'm standing, I can't decide if I have the right to be angry."

His response threw me. "I ... don't understand. Why wouldn't you have the right to be angry?"

"Because you did what you do. You did what you needed to do. You needed to talk to Kevin Dunne. I can't tell you not to do that when it's what had to happen. It's not fair."

"I guess." I considered where he was coming from for several seconds, then sighed. "You know what? You're right. It's not fair to be mad over that. You can be mad over the timing, though."

"You know what? Screw that. I'm mad you went over there without backup." Landon lost all pretense of trying to pretend he was above it all. "If you'd had backup, this wouldn't have happened."

"How do you know that?" I was honestly curious.

"Because it just wouldn't have happened. I know."

"What if I'd taken Clove?" I had no idea why I was pushing things the way I was. I couldn't seem to stop myself though. "Like ... what would she have done to stop it? I agree that if I'd taken Scout or Evan, I would've likely been fine. Thistle wouldn't have been able to do much to help, though, and Aunt Tillie likely would've made things worse."

"I don't care. You should've had backup. Once you knew there was a murderous shadow thing wandering around, backup should've been your first thought."

"I didn't know the murderous shadow thing was going to follow me to Kevin Dunne's office ... although, in hindsight, I have to wonder if I should've known that." I was thoughtful for a beat. "You don't think he's conjuring the shadow, do you?" It was something I hadn't considered until this very moment. "Like ... maybe he's the magical one." The moment it escaped my mouth, I knew it was the wrong assumption. "If he was the magical one, he would just magically kill his wife. As it is now, he has to worry about losing half of everything. If he was magical, that wouldn't be an issue. Forget I said that."

"At this moment, I don't care who is conjuring the shadow," Landon shot back. "What I care about is that you could've died."

I opted to be reasonable. "Why do you think I told you where I was? I was making sure I wouldn't die. As long as you knew where I was and could send Evan, I felt I was safe."

"Yes, Evan." Landon made a face. "Do you have any idea how frustrating it was to have to call him to rescue my wife?"

"Wait ... are you angry about me not having backup, or the fact that Evan was the one who had to come save me?"

His expression reflected incredulity. "Yes."

I pressed my lips together to keep from laughing. He was too worked up for that. Instead, I leaned back and opened my arms. "I want to hug you."

"I'm not in the mood."

"Fine. I need you to hug me." I knew he couldn't turn me down, and I was gratified when he rolled into bed next to me. His arm was gentle when it slipped under my waist, and he committed fully to the embrace when he pressed me against his side.

"I really didn't expect that to happen," I said after a full minute of silence.

"I know." His hand moved to my back, and he began to trail his fingers up and down my spine. "I just ... hate feeling helpless, Bay. You have no idea the terror I felt hearing you say your potential goodbyes and knowing there wasn't a thing I could do to stop whatever it was that you were facing."

"I wasn't saying my goodbyes," I assured him. "I was doing my best to make sure I would get back to you. There was no turning back, Landon. Had I turned my back on that thing and not taken it on, then I would've died because it would've attacked from behind. As it was, I took it out at the same time I essentially hobbled myself. It was the only option I had."

He was quiet long enough to consider it. "You're safe, and that's the most important thing," he said finally. "I just hate that it happened, and I really hate that I couldn't go to you. Evan had to be the one to do it."

"Evan could get there quickest ... and if the shadow had still been around, he could've handled it."

"Yeah."

"I'm sorry you were afraid."

"I'm sorry you were hurt." He snuggled me in tight at his side. "We still need to talk about what that shadow thing is."

I didn't disagree. "Yeah. Can we get some sleep first? I'm exhausted, and I swear I'm going to be in pain tomorrow when I wake up."

"See, that doesn't make me feel better."

"I'm sorry." I was already floating toward sleep. When he shifted to move away from me, I gripped him tighter. "Where are you going?"

"I'll be right back, Bay. I have to turn off the lights and kill the fire."

"I don't want you to go away."

"Baby, I'm never going away." His fingers moved over my cheeks. "You're exhausted. Go to sleep. I'll be right behind you."

I believed that, but I was still wary. "You're not mad?"

"We'll talk about it in the morning."

"Landon—"

"Shh." He pressed his finger to my lips. "Go to sleep, Bay."

I WOKE SLOWLY THE NEXT MORNING, IN increments. When I finally woke up, I found Landon watching me. He had a box of candy on his chest—the same one I'd bought him several nights before—and he seemed interested in watching me greet the day.

"What?" I was grouchy, which didn't seem warranted, but that didn't stop me from frowning as I wiped the corners of my mouth. "What did I do?"

"Oh, so many things." He popped a reindeer in his mouth as he regarded me. "How are you feeling?"

That was a loaded question. I wasn't an idiot. He was feeling me out. "Go ahead." I rolled to my back. "Get it out of your system."

"Get what out of my system?"

"You want to yell. I'm perfectly fine with you yelling."

"What would I want to yell about?"

I narrowed my eyes as I slid my gaze to him. "Are you purposely trying to mess with me?"

"No. I'm debating if I should get up now and heat up the breakfast burritos your mother left or stay here a few minutes longer because you're warm and snuggly."

I rolled back to cuddle with him. "I thought we were spending the day in bed."

"You certainly are." He kissed the top of my head. "I'll be around here and there to take care of you." His gaze moved to the window. Apparently, he'd closed the blinds when I'd been sleeping. "I wonder how much snow we got. It should be almost done by now. Then we just have to wait it out until all the streets are cleared."

I waved my hand, letting just a little bit of my magic loose, and the blinds opened to reveal a winter wonderland. "Holy..." I lifted my chin so I could get a better view. There was nothing but white as far as the eye could see. "We're really snowed in."

"Is that a problem?" Landon was giving me some serious side-eye as he regarded me.

"Nope." I shook my head. "Not a problem in the least." I snuggled closer to him, which shouldn't have been possible because I was practically on top of him. "Do you want to play under-the-covers games with me all day?" I already had a few ideas on that front.

"Um ... you're recuperating."

My excitement disappeared. "I'm fine."

"Oh, no." Landon wagged a finger directly in front of my face. "You almost died yesterday ... and you made the choice how you handled things. That means you're going to be in bed recuperating all day because of that choice."

Of course. I should've seen it coming. This was how he was going to punish me. "Landon—"

He was firm when pulling away from me. "I thought I'd start with heating up the breakfast burritos. Your mom put everything in them. Then I thought we'd get you in a warm bath. Then we'll tuck you back in tight, and you can sleep all afternoon."

I glared at him. "That's not happening."

"Oh, but it is." The set of Landon's jaw told me he wasn't going to change his mind. "You, my darling wife, had a very close call yesterday. I'm home with you today, so it seems only fitting that I should take care of you in the manner I believe will be most conducive to your recovery."

Yup. He was punishing me. "Well played." I propped myself on my pillow and stared him down. If he wanted to play the game this way, so be it. I could be just as hurtful. "I didn't expect you to take this tack. I mean ... I thought you loved me."

His mischievous smile disappeared. "Don't push it. I'm the one who gets to be obnoxious today."

"It's fine." I allowed my lower lip to start trembling. "You do what you need to do." I sniffled. "I thought we were going to spend the day cuddling, eating candy, and having sex, but if you have a better idea..."

I wasn't expecting anybody else to hear what I had to say, but Aunt Tillie picked that moment to let herself into our bedroom. "Oh, gag me," she exclaimed from under her knit cap. "What is the matter with the two of you? How could you say something like that, and in public no less?"

I turned my glare to her. "We're not in public."

"We're in our bed, in our house, minding our own business." Landon folded his arms over his bare chest and angled his chin in such a way he was practically daring Aunt Tillie to pick a fight. "Why are you out so early?"

"I'm always up early. I have the bladder of a small child." Aunt Tillie delivered the news blandly.

I opted to ignore her and turned back to Landon. "I want my cuddle time and the other things I mentioned."

"Sex," Aunt Tillie barked. "She said she wants sex. She's a regular little heathen these days. I blame you."

"Thank you," Landon replied. "I enjoy being blamed for turning my wife into a heathen." He shot her a thumbs-up. "You still haven't told us what you're doing here."

"Who says I have to tell you anything?" Aunt Tillie challenged. "This is my property."

"Which we happen to be living on," Landon argued. "I pay rent."

Aunt Tillie snorted. "You pay like fifty bucks a month. Give me a break."

"I pay way more than that!"

"Winnie gave you a break, so you'd have extra money for the new house," Aunt Tillie challenged. "I didn't come here to argue about that."

"Great." Landon bobbed his head in such a way I knew he was growing more and more agitated. "Then you have no reason to be here."

"I'm here for your wife."

Landon immediately started shaking his head. "No. Whatever you have planned..."

"And why not?" Aunt Tillie crossed her arms and cocked her hip. The stance only lasted a few seconds. "Ow! I swear your mother is shrinking all of my clothes. Now my snow pants don't fit correctly, and it's affecting my hip."

"Or your hip hurts because of your age and your pants don't fit because ever since you cast the spell on your field, you've been smoking way more pot, which means you've had the munchies twice as often," I countered.

"You are so on my list."

For some reason, that struck me as funny. "What do you want? Landon and I are going to enjoy the blizzard and spend the day in bed."

"Yes, having sex. I heard you. I don't need to hear it again."

"You should be going," I prodded.

"We're not having sex anyway," Landon argued.

"Yes, we are," I countered.

"No, we're not." He was firm. "You're recuperating. You need to rest. That's all there is to it."

"Oh, really?" I didn't like his tone. "Is that your final stance on the subject?"

"It is," he replied stubbornly.

"Awesome." I turned back to Aunt Tillie. "What do you have behind door number two for me?"

"The decorations have apparently taken over downtown," Aunt Tillie replied. "The blizzard wasn't enough to hold them back. They've cut off access to the plows and refuse to let the workers get to the festival grounds so they can be cleared for tomorrow. Terry has gotten three calls since four o'clock this morning. He's threatening to kill me."

"Perhaps you have it coming," Landon suggested.

"Perhaps *you* have it coming." Aunt Tillie mimicked him in a whiny voice. "Nobody is talking to you, whiner. I'm talking to Bay." She was serious as she locked gazes with me. "We have to do something."

"Who is this 'we' you're talking about?" I countered. "Why do 'we' have to fix 'your' spell?"

"Because you were there when I cast it, and it's on you, too," Aunt Tillie shot back. "Also, the gnomes from the previous spell are not dormant as they're supposed to be. They've joined with the Christmas decorations. Apparently, this morning they were singing 'Who Let the Drendel Out.' People are going to accuse me of being antisemitic when that wasn't my intention."

"And what do you plan to do to stop this?" I asked.

"I was thinking I'd lure all the decorations to the barn on the south side of town and lock them inside until the spell expires," she replied. "Then, even if the gnomes stick around, we'll be able to handle them easily enough."

It was an interesting proposition. "You said the plows haven't been out," I reminded her. "How are we supposed to get downtown."

"I happen to have two new, shiny snowmobiles."

I jerked up my chin. "Mom said no more snowmobiles after that last incident."

"Do I even want to know what the last incident involved?" Landon asked.

"Probably not," I replied.

"It was one little accident," Aunt Tillie replied. "The snow shadow—the one that only comes out a few weeks every year—was stalking me. I decided to take it for a ride to the bluff. I couldn't stop in time." She held out her hands and lifted her shoulders. "It wasn't a big deal."

"Does Winnie think it was a big deal?" Landon asked.

"Winnie thinks everything is a big deal," Aunt Tillie answered. "It doesn't matter. She's not the boss, and the snowmobiles are shiny and new. You guys can cuddle on one and everything."

Landon shifted his eyes to me. I could tell he was torn. On one hand, he wanted me to rest. Torturing me was part of the deal. On the other, like a typical man, he liked playing with new contraptions.

"I guess it can't possibly hurt to check out the situation downtown," he hedged.

"And then we'll come home and spend the afternoon in bed?" I challenged.

"Maybe." Landon's smirk told me he'd already been won over. "You really are turning into a heathen, baby. It's a little distressing."

"Unbelievable," I muttered. "I can't believe you of all people are giving me grief about wanting to spend the day in bed."

"That's what happens when you almost die on me. Don't let it happen again, and I won't have to torture you."

"I'll keep it in mind."

24
TWENTY-FOUR

"I'm driving."

Landon was surprisingly gung-ho for the trip into town. He almost did a little dance when he saw the snowmobiles. When I climbed into the driver's seat, he balked.

"Why do you want to drive?" I demanded as I adjusted my knit cap. I had no intention of driving fast enough to get windburn, so a mask wasn't necessary. "Is this an 'I have a penis' thing?"

"It most certainly is not." Landon yelped. "It's a 'my wife was injured in a car accident yesterday, and I don't want her driving with a potential brain injury' thing."

I narrowed my eyes. "That was quite the mouthful."

He grinned. "It's the truth. I want to drive."

I remained unconvinced. "How about I drive half the way and you drive the other half?"

"No. I want to drive."

"Because you think I have a brain injury?"

"Because driving is fun and the only thing that could possibly propel me out of my warm bed with you following a blizzard and your accident is the opportunity to drive. I'm driving."

I considered pushing him further, but I slid back on the seat. "Fine. Not too fast, though. I don't want windburn, and I prefer not getting in a second accident. No vampire is going to come to our rescue today."

"Speak for yourself," Aunt Tillie said as she got comfortable in the driver's seat on the second snowmobile. To my surprise, Evan hopped on behind her.

"Someone has to keep Tillie out of trouble," he said. "Plus, I'm bored."

"I should thank you for coming for me yesterday. You were gone when I regained my faculties. I owe you."

"You don't owe me anything, and you did thank me yesterday even if you don't remember." Evan looked decidedly uncomfortable as he waved off the offer. "I was happy to help. It gave me a good reason to take a break from your great-aunt."

"I heard that." Aunt Tillie glanced over her shoulder. She'd found protective ski goggles somewhere and looked as if she was about to go diving rather than on a leisurely ride through the snow. "Don't think I won't put you on my list just because you're my sidekick."

"If you say so." Evan didn't look bothered in the least and flashed me a smile. "I guess we'll see you downtown." The words were barely out of his mouth before Aunt Tillie sped off like a bullet.

"Don't go that fast," I ordered Landon as I wrapped my arms around his waist.

He chuckled. "I've got it, Bay."

Because I knew that was true, I could relax for the ride. "Let's do this."

IT TOOK US TWENTY MINUTES TO GET downtown. We could've gone a little faster, but Landon relaxed into the ride after a few minutes, and we enjoyed ourselves and the scenery. Almost two feet of snow had blanketed the region.

The stillness of the landscape changed when we reached the

downtown area and found it had been overrun by Christmas decorations ... all singing different carols in an attempt to drown out the others.

"No way." Landon killed the engine on the snowmobile and stood.

In front of Mrs. Little's store, the three polar bears that Chief Terry had been worried about escaping from the Bunton family's yard stood on their hind legs and stared through the window of her store while singing *Jingle Bells*.

In the lot next to the town square, the huge Rudolph inflatable sang his own theme song as someone's Frosty inflatable followed suit with his theme song on the other side of the lot.

The creepy Cabbage Patch Kid that had been used as Jesus in someone's manger—the one missing a leg—swayed back and forth while crooning *Away in a Manger* in a voice only a mother could love.

Oversized Christmas bulbs rolled around Main Street belting out *The First Noel*.

White wicker reindeer galloped all over the place screeching *Joy to the World*.

Three Santas sang *Up on the Housetop* in front of Hypnotic, all of them singing different parts over each other.

The Grinch inflatable I was almost positive I'd seen on a front yard during our first drive to Stonecrest sang his own theme song while giving two posable elves some serious side-eye.

Then there were the angels I'd been worried about taking flight. They buzzed above us while singing *Hark! The Herald Angels Sing*. They, not surprisingly, had the best voices.

"This is what I picture the inside of your brain looking like," Evan said to Aunt Tillie as he circled to take everything in. "Chaotic, loud, and I think I might throw up if I spend too much time thinking about what that Santa is doing with that stick."

I jerked my eyes in the direction he was looking, and sure enough, the Santa from the roof of The Overlook had joined the fray.

"Aunt Tillie." My tone was full of warning. "You have to do something."

Ever blasé in the face of a crisis of her making, Aunt Tillie avoided eye contact and pretended to be fixated on cleaning her goggles. "I don't know why you're so worked up. It's just a few Christmas decorations having a good time."

"A few?" Landon screeched. "There must be more than a hundred decorations here."

"And that's not counting the gnomes," Evan added. "You can see the snow shifting here and there but no sign of what's moving beneath it. That's the gnomes. They're so short they're running around beneath the snow like weird little sharks."

I cringed at the picture. "Can we not talk about that?" I demanded. "I don't want to deal with snow sharks. The time she trapped us in the soap opera, we had to deal with snow sharks, and I'm not playing that game again."

Landon shuddered next to me, and not because of the weather. "No snow sharks. No soap opera either. I don't want to spend Christmas trapped in anything resembling a fairy tale, a soap opera, or the past." He ticked them off on his gloved fingers. "I'm going to be really mad."

"Oh, well, if you're going to be mad," Aunt Tillie drawled. "I guess I know what I'm getting you for Christmas." There was a threat beneath the words.

I jabbed a finger in her direction before she could get ahead of herself. "Don't even," I warned. "We're not doing this. We have too much going on. In fact..." Before I could suggest we start knifing inflatables, my phone sounded from inside my coat. I grumbled as I dug for it, finding it on the third ring. I didn't recognize the number. "Hello?"

"Bay?" The voice was young. It was one of the girls from the school—I wasn't certain which one—and the dread inside of me doubled when I thought about what might be going on at Stonecrest. "It's me," I assured the girl. "Who is this?"

"It's Katie," she replied. I'd given them my number in case of emergencies before leaving the previous day. I'd promised that I would get back to them when I had a plan. "Um ... can you come to the school?"

"To the school?" I darted a look to Landon. "Do we have enough gas to get out to the school?" I asked.

"Sure," he replied. "It's not that far. I don't know if we have enough gas to get back home from there. The gas station at the end of town is closed because only in Hemlock Cove is it okay to shut down the only gas station in town because of snow."

"What about the pump behind the police station? Can we get gas there?"

Landon nodded. "I just need the code from Terry."

"Oh, don't worry about that." Aunt Tillie waved her hand. "I've got the code."

"Do I even want to know why?" Landon whined.

"Probably not, but I don't care either way." Aunt Tillie was blasé. "What's going on out at the school?"

That was a good question. I repeated it to Katie and waited for her response. After listening to her story, I said, "Give us about thirty minutes. Don't leave the dorm."

WE PULLED TO A STOP in front of the dormitory within thirty minutes. Landon and Aunt Tillie had spent ten of those minutes arguing about why she knew the code to unlock the gas pump behind the police station, but once I screamed at both of them to shut up, they let the argument go.

At least for now.

Katie met us at the door. "It's locked," she explained as she let us into the dormitory. The common room was full of worried girls in their pajamas. "The timer hasn't switched off."

I removed my gloves and rubbed my hands together.

"All the buildings are on a timer," Violet volunteered. "The doors to the classroom building automatically lock at five o'clock. Same with the administration building. They automatically unlock at nine o'clock the next morning ... unless it's a weekend or holiday."

"The dorm locks at eight o'clock every night and opens again at eight every morning," Katie explained. "It locked like normal last night. It hasn't unlocked yet this morning."

I still wasn't certain what we were dealing with. "Okay, well ... why is that important?" I shot Autumn a rueful smile when the girl rolled her eyes.

"We were supposed to have classes today," Autumn replied. "It's the last day of classes before the holiday."

I ran the calendar through my head. "You guys are done after today until the new year, correct?"

"Yeah, but the classrooms aren't open."

"How can you know that?" Landon asked.

"The lights didn't come on," Katie explained. She moved to the window and pointed. "Do you see the front of the classroom building?"

I nodded as I looked through the window with her.

"There's a green light on the front porch that illuminates when the building is open," Katie said. "It's so we know if the building is actually open when there's a rare night astronomy lab or something. It's not on. It's always on when the building is open."

"So the building isn't open but should be," I said. "What does your dorm monitor say?"

Katie and Violet exchanged looks heavy enough that my stomach constricted.

"Just tell me," I ordered.

"Ms. Duncan isn't here," Violet replied. "She left last night to go home and spend Christmas with her family."

"Was that already scheduled?" Landon asked.

"No, but ... we told her it was fine," Violet said. "Bianca was going to make her stay, but Ms. Duncan hasn't seen her family in months. It was arranged before Ms. Walters died that Ms. Duncan would be able to go and Bianca would stay with us. But after Ms. Walters died, Bianca ordered Ms. Duncan to stay ... and that wasn't fair."

"We told her to go," Katie interjected. "We told her it would be fine. We wanted her to get time with her family. She earned it."

"It's okay," I promised them. "We're not here to get Ms. Duncan in trouble. I'm just confused. When are you supposed to go home?"

"We're not," Autumn replied. "We're stuck here over the holidays because our families don't want us back."

If I thought I felt bad for them before, now I felt sick to my stomach.

"Some of us go home," Violet said. "About half the students." She gestured around the room. "They've already left. Bianca arranged for them to be picked up yesterday before the storm hit."

That made sense, but there were still fourteen girls in the room. "So ... this is everybody still here?" I asked.

"Yes," Katie replied.

"Your parents are only one town over." I didn't mean to sound so accusatory. "How could they leave you here for Christmas?"

"I asked to stay," Katie replied. "I don't mind seeing my mom, but I don't want to see my dad."

"And they said that was okay?"

"It's not a big deal."

It *was* a big deal, but we couldn't hash it out now. "What about your cook?"

"Gone for the holidays," Violet replied. "They left leftovers that we can heat up."

"And the security guards?"

"We rarely see them anyway," Katie answered.

"And Bianca?" Landon demanded.

"That's just it," Autumn said. "She was supposed to be here this morning. We thought the snow slowed her and we'd be on our own for a few hours, but she's not answering. There's nobody in the administration building."

"It's just us," Katie whispered. She looked terrified.

Even though she'd caused innumerable problems—seriously, who listened to a dark shadow without knowing who it was?—I felt bad for her. These kids had been discarded, first by their families and then by the school officials who were supposed to take care of them.

"Okay, everybody needs to remain calm." I pulled my phone out of my pocket and blew out a sigh to center myself. "See if you can track down Bianca," I instructed Landon.

He already had his phone out. "What if she can't get here?"

"I don't really care if she can," I admitted. "I want to know where she is."

"Why?"

"Because someone attached to this school conjured a shadow and likely dosed these girls with secondary magic," I replied in a low voice. "Bianca is as good a possibility as anybody else."

Realization dawned on Landon. "Oh."

"Oh," I echoed. "Where the hell is she? I can't imagine leaving these girls to fend for themselves last night. What sort of monster does that?"

"Maybe she's not a monster," Landon argued. "Maybe she's just in over her head."

"Maybe," I acknowledged, although I felt otherwise to my very bones. "If she needed help, she should've asked for it. This is unacceptable."

"What are you going to do?" Landon inclined his head toward the phone I had clutched in my hand.

"I'm calling in reinforcements." I did the one thing I never thought I would do and called my mommy.

"What's wrong?" Mom asked.

I filled her in on the new development. As expected, she was furious.

"So, let me get this straight," Mom said darkly. "The people who were supposed to take care of those girls—girls abandoned by their own families—have abandoned them again?"

I knew that would get to her. "That seems to be the case," I confirmed.

"Well, that can't happen." Mom sounded brisk now. "We need to pack some food. How many kids are we talking about?"

"Fourteen," I replied.

"Well, we'll get our supplies together. We'll take enough to provide them food for all three meals today. Will you have this handled by tomorrow?"

That was a good question. "I think we need to bring this to an end regardless," I replied. "If this is the end of the school, the girls need to go home and make plans for the next semester."

"Okay, give us an hour. We'll take Aunt Tillie's plow truck."

I tried to picture Aunt Tillie's face when I gave her the news, and it took everything I had to bite back a laugh. "That sounds like a great idea. I'll tell the girls to expect you."

"What are you going to do?" she asked.

"I'm going to find Bianca."

"And kill her?"

The question threw me. "That wasn't on the agenda. She has a few things to answer for, though."

"If you don't like her answers, you have my permission to kill her."

"That sounds a little harsh."

"You don't abandon children at Christmas. Do you want me to bring Terry with me?"

That was an interesting offer. "Actually, we're going to need a real vehicle." A plan was starting to take shape. "We're going to need Aunt Tillie's plow after you use it to get here, so you'll need a separate vehicle."

"How did you get there?" Mom asked.

I answered without thinking. "Aunt Tillie's snowmobiles."

"Really?" Mom's voice was icy cold. "I didn't realize she had snowmobiles."

When I glanced at Aunt Tillie, she glared at me. "This isn't my fault," I insisted. "I forgot."

"You're so on my list," Aunt Tillie growled.

I could see that, but it was a problem for another day. "We're going to search the campus just to be on the safe side," I told Mom. "We'll see you in an hour."

25
TWENTY-FIVE

I went with Evan to search the campus. Landon seemed annoyed that I wanted to search without him, but he needed to make some calls and had more questions for the girls.

"My wife," he said pointedly to Evan as we headed out.

"Oh, how cute are you?" Evan crooned in derogatory fashion. "As if I would try to steal your wife. Get a grip."

"No funny stuff," Landon insisted before leaning in to kiss me, eliciting sighs and giggles from the girls. "Be careful," he warned. "If there's trouble out there, come back, and we'll come up with a plan before you take on whatever it is."

"I'll be fine," I assured him. "I don't think we're going to run into anything."

"Why is that?"

"I think whoever we're dealing with has abandoned the campus."

"Bianca?"

I held out my hands and shrugged. "Or Ms. Duncan."

Shock registered on Landon's face. "We haven't even met her."

"That's why I'm leaning more toward Bianca," I admitted. "She's a known entity ... and as far as I can tell, she would have more motive for wanting Enid dead."

"Because she wanted to take over the school?"

"Maybe, or maybe because she got distracted by Kevin Dunne's shiny penis, just like everybody else."

Landon's eyebrows moved toward one another. "You think she was having an affair with him too?"

"Why not? Kevin apparently likes humping anything that moves. Why stop with Enid?"

"Especially when he might need eyes in this school because Katie was here," Landon surmised. "It sort of makes sense."

"Can you hold down the fort here while we take a look at the campus?"

"Sure, but my warning stands. If you see that shadow thing, come back. Don't take it on yourself."

I understood his worry, but I didn't share it. "It's okay," I promised him. "I've got this. Don't worry about me."

"Come back to me, Bay." Landon was deadly serious. "I'll give your Christmas gifts to somebody else if you don't."

"I'll always come back to you. We've got this. I'm willing to bet all the chocolate reindeer that there's nothing supernatural left on this campus."

He gave me a kiss. "Check in as you move from building to building. Just in case."

"I can manage that."

"You'd better. I'll melt down if you don't."

That wasn't an empty threat, so I nodded. "Try not to miss me too much," I teased as I turned.

I LET EVAN DRIVE SO I COULD SCAN THE CAMPUS with my magic as we progressed from one end to the other. As expected, there was nothing to report.

"No footprints, no magic trails, no signs of Christmas decorations run amok," Evan noted as we stood in front of the greenhouse. "I don't understand any of this."

"What confuses you the most?" I asked, breathless after wading through an almost three-foot-tall snowdrift. "I remember this being fun when I was a kid. What happened?"

"You got old." Evan grabbed me around the waist and lifted me. "Hold on." He was a machine as he powered through the snow, and I couldn't help but laugh when we reached the greenhouse door and he pushed us inside. "Don't tell Landon I carried you," he admonished as he lowered me to the ground. "He'll be jealous, even though it's ridiculous to think for even a moment that you'd be interested in anyone but him."

"It *is* ridiculous to think that," I agreed. "It's ridiculous to think you'd be interested in me. He would see that if he gave it some thought."

Evan smiled. "I wondered if you guys had figured it out."

"That you're gay?"

"I like to think of myself as the sort of person who falls for an individual, not a gender, but that notion has faded some over the years. When the people you fall for are all men, a pattern starts to emerge."

"Have you ever dated a woman?"

"A few. It never got serious."

"And Scout?" I asked, referring to his best friend. She'd healed him, brought him back from the brink, and they were as tight as ever, though I never detected as much as a stray vibe.

"It was never like that with us," Evan replied as he glanced around the greenhouse. "This is a nice setup."

"It's well put together," I agreed. "The witch herbs are over here." I pointed to the corner the girls had indicated the last time we were in the building. "They have some potent stuff here. I..." I trailed off. The witch section of the greenhouse had been disturbed. "Crap."

"What was here?" Evan asked.

"Belladonna, mandrake, bay leaves, cinnamon, yarrow, and rosemary. I didn't see all of it."

"Most of it is gone now," Evan noted. "I don't take that as a good sign."

"Somebody is putting together a spell or curse," I said. "I wonder who it's aimed at."

"Haven't you been the target more than once?"

"I was the target of the girls. The girls aren't responsible for Enid's death."

"The girls were directed to you by a malevolent shadow," Evan argued. "Whoever created that shadow knows who you are ... and that you're a threat."

He was right. "Well, they're not here now. That would seem to fortify my idea that Bianca is to blame."

"I don't know her, but I'll take your word for it."

I studied his handsome face for a moment. "You didn't get to finish your thought about Scout. You never even considered the idea of falling in love with her?"

"Some loves transcend others," he replied. "The love between soul mates, for example. The love between a parent and a child. My love for Scout transcends the romantic. Besides, Gunner is her soul mate. I know that."

"And you're not bitter about it?"

He shook his head. "Not even a little. She's one of my soul mates. Just in a different way. Eventually, I will find my other soul mate. I'm not in the best headspace for that right now."

"Because less than a year ago you were a soulless, blood-sucking vampire bent on murder?"

"Pretty much." He grinned. "Why do you care so much? I would've thought you would be Team Gunner."

"I am." I would never say that Scout and Gunner didn't belong together. I'd seen them and knew they were connected for life, much like Landon and me. "It's the other part that's getting to me. The part where I have to think outside the box about relationships."

He didn't hurry me to continue. He just waited.

"These girls were sent here by their parents, and even though Landon said I had an attitude about that from the beginning, I don't think I had enough of an attitude. These girls might be mouthy, and they might not get the best grades, and they might need counseling ... but none of them are so far gone that I can understand why their families sent them away."

Evan nodded in understanding.

"We were mouthy as kids too. Nobody ever sent us away."

"I bet Tillie threatened to send you away."

"Of course, but we knew it was an empty threat. As far as I can tell, Katie was sent one town over to keep her father's affairs a secret ... but his wife knows about the affairs."

"You hate the father," Evan surmised.

"So very much," I agreed.

"What are you going to do about it?"

That was a good question. "We have to go to Bianca's house," I replied. "We need to find her. She makes the most sense as an enemy. I bet she was sleeping with Kevin too. I bet he set the whole thing up when he realized Enid was careening off the rails."

"If you find her, will you kill her?" There was nothing judgmental about Evan's tone.

"I'm not sure yet."

"Then let's get back to the dorm. This day is only just starting. I think we should work together to finish it."

"Yeah. Let's see if we can deliver a merry Christmas to those girls."

CHIEF TERRY DIDN'T APPRECIATE WHEN the girls catcalled him as he raced to their rescue with Mom and my aunts. I found it entertaining. My mother's smile told me she did, too. Evan and Landon wisely ducked their heads and hid their reactions.

We left Evan and Aunt Tillie with Mom and the others. We needed guards there for the girls, and they fit the bill.

That left Landon, Chief Terry, and me to go to Bianca's house.

"Why is she isolated so far into the woods?" I asked as we looked around at the nondescript ranch.

"Some people might ask the same question about our new house," Landon noted.

"We're on a lake. The lake is the draw. Besides, we're outdoor people."

Chief Terry snorted, then quickly averted his gaze when I shifted to stare at him.

"We are," I insisted.

"If you say so. You're outdoor people who believe spending time outdoors includes hanging out in a magically controlled climate dome."

"Hey, outdoors is outdoors," Landon countered.

Chief Terry's eye roll was pronounced. "I maintain what I said. Some people like the great outdoors. Maybe Bianca does."

I thought back to what I knew about her from when she competed against Clove and made a face. "She's not."

We'd cleared a path driving up Bianca's driveway. Her Jeep Compass was in the driveway, buried in snow. There were tire tracks on the left side of the driveway, mostly buried to the point of being slight indentations.

"Maybe she had a visitor last night," Chief Terry suggested as he watched me take in the tracks.

"Maybe it was Kevin," I mused.

"We have no proof that they're romantically involved," Chief Terry argued.

"They are." I felt it to my bones, and that propelled me toward the front door. "Trust me."

We knocked, but nobody answered. There wasn't even a hint of movement inside. I used my magic to get us past the front door—

something that earned a dark look from Chief Terry. The house was silent when we entered.

"Look at this," Landon said as we walked into Bianca's office. There were only two bedrooms in the house, the master containing a bed that obviously hadn't been slept in the previous evening, and the other, a home office. Much like at Enid's house, Bianca's office was reserved for stalking.

"Oh, no way," I said when I realized that Bianca had set up a situation similar to that of Enid to follow Kevin's movements. "This is unbelievable." I threw my hands in the air at the sight of a candid photo of Kevin. He was in downtown Hemlock Cove—probably during the Fall Color Festival. He wasn't alone.

"That's Kelly Sloane," Chief Terry said, his forehead creased. "How old is she again?"

"She's an adult," I replied.

"Barely." Chief Terry's expression grew more sour by the moment. "She's not even old enough to legally drink."

"I think she's twenty," I replied. A memory niggled at the back of my brain. "Mom and the aunts were competing for ribbons at the Fall Color Festival."

"It's called the Orange Leaf Festival, but sure," Chief Terry replied.

"I don't think that's a good name, so I refuse to use it," I argued. "Anyway, I remember Mom and Aunt Marnie arguing over which could bring a blackberry pie. They both brought one—which was apparently against whatever rules they'd agreed upon—and they were fighting with one another. In the background, I watched Kelly argue with Mrs. Little about serving hard cider at the booth. Mrs. Little said she wasn't old enough and Kelly said she needed the money. Kelly said she would be old enough in a few months."

"That puts Kelly at twenty," Chief Terry noted. "Far too young for Kevin Dunne."

"And yet they were together at the festival." I tapped the photo for emphasis. "How much do you want to bet he has a lover in every town?"

Landon studied the photos. "She has photos of him with Joanie and Georgie both in Shadow Hills." He gestured to the two sections of the board. "She has photos of Kelly in Hemlock Cove. I'm not sure who that is, but the photo was clearly shot in Hawthorne Hollow." He pointed again. "Those two women were shot in Traverse City."

"And these are just the women we know about," I noted. "I'm sure he managed to keep one or two on the sly. Maybe he had a few one-night stands here and there." My anger grew with each photo. "He's a disgusting piece of filth."

"He is," Landon agreed. "But that doesn't mean it's okay to murder the competition."

"I'm not saying all these women are innocent," I replied, "but he's a pig."

"I'm all for unleashing one of Aunt Tillie's more inventive curses on him when this is finished."

I perked up considerably.

"For now, we need to find Bianca," Landon continued. "I have to think she's our murderer. Although ... you didn't catch a whiff of magic when you were talking to her."

"I didn't," I confirmed as I watched Chief Terry cut through the house. He looked to be heading toward the garage. "That doesn't necessarily mean anything. If people know I'm magical, they can shield themselves ... and I'm willing to bet Bianca at least had an idea that my family was magical, given the way Clove tried to curse her when they were kids."

"Okay..." Landon trailed off when Chief Terry appeared in the doorway, white as a sheet. "What is it? Oh, don't tell me she has some weird fetish collection in the garage. If she collects Dunne's toe gunk in jars, I don't want to know about it."

Chief Terry was pale enough I knew something was really wrong. He stepped back when I reached him and looked pained about me going into the garage.

I only took two steps before I pulled up short. Bianca wasn't gone after all. She was in the garage. She was dead, strung up from the rafters and put on display so it was impossible to miss her.

The dead woman's eyes were wide and sightless. The rope around her neck was tight.

"Well, she's not our killer," I said. I thought back to the tracks in the driveway. "Whoever was here didn't stop by for a random visit. Bianca was targeted."

26
TWENTY-SIX

We searched Bianca's house. Chief Terry called for the county to plow the road to her house, including the rest of the driveway, allowing the medical examiner to join us. He was wide eyed as he regarded the body.

"She was alive when she was hauled up there," he said.

"How can you tell?" I asked.

"Look here." The body had been lowered after a series of photographs. I could see into Bianca's eyes more closely now. He pointed to her neck, bruised and bloody. "She clawed at the rope."

"Which suggests she knew what was happening to her," Landon noted, his hand moving over my back.

The medical examiner nodded. "She would've been aware. I think you're looking for a man."

The declaration threw me. "What makes you say that?"

"It would take someone strong to haul up a body that way. No offense to the gentler sex, but I don't know many women with that kind of strength." He winked at me for good measure. He likely thought it would come across as charming. It made me want to smack him across the face.

"Good point." I returned the smile even though I wasn't feeling it, and then dragged Landon to a corner where nobody could hear us. "It's not a man. It was the shadow."

"I've got that," he assured me. "There's no way that guy ever considered a magical shadow. There's no point in mentioning it."

I rolled my neck. "I don't know what to do here, Landon. I feel as if the answer is right in front of me, but I can't see it."

"Maybe you should talk to Katie," he suggested. "She was familiar enough with her father's antics to get sent away. She might know who else he was seeing. She also might be able to give you some insight into her mother."

I balked. "Why are you assuming Joanie is to blame?"

"I'm not," Landon replied. "I just think it's wrong—lazy even—to disregard the wife because you feel sorry for her."

He was starting to bug me. "I just don't think it's her."

Landon folded his arms across his chest and regarded me with a piercing look. "Why?"

"Because she doesn't have it in her to kill someone." Even as I said it, I wasn't certain.

"She went after you, Bay. She didn't have proof that you were sleeping with her husband. All she knew is that you were looking at her, and maybe had asked some questions regarding her children."

"She didn't go after me all that hard," I argued. It sounded lame even to me. "She was surprised."

"Bay." Landon was clearly exasperated. "She didn't have cause to go after you. If she was suspicious, she could've asked if you were seeing her husband. But she attacked. What makes you think you're the first one she's done this with?"

I sensed Chief Terry move in behind me. His presence was warm and steadying. "Do you think I have a blind spot for the wife?" I asked him without looking over my shoulder.

"I think you feel bad because you can't help picturing yourself in her situation," Chief Terry replied.

Landon made a strangled sound.

"Knock it off," Chief Terry chided. "I'm not saying you would ever do that to her. In fact, if I thought that was a possibility, I would've encouraged Tillie to kill you and bury you in her pot field."

He was all smiles when I finally turned to him.

"You're loyal to a fault, Landon," he continued. "I've never doubted that. Bay can't help but feel sympathy for Joanie. That's who she is."

"But is it misguided sympathy?" I pressed. "Am I refusing to see her for what she really is?"

"I don't know, Bay." Chief Terry held his hands palms out. "I have questions regarding who she is as a person. It's one thing to accept that your husband is a dog running around on you—that's her choice—but it's another to have your teenage daughter sent away by your husband and not do a thing to stop it."

I stilled. I'd been casting all the blame on Kevin. "I hadn't considered that."

"We need to talk to Katie," Landon said. "At this point, she seems like our best shot. If she can't help, maybe the best route is to go through the shadow."

"You said we're dealing with magic," Landon continued. "You also said it wasn't very strong. Maybe you can take over her shadow and end this even if we don't know who we're dealing with."

I nodded and forced a smile. "That's a good idea, but we should check on the girls."

"We left Tillie in charge of them," Chief Terry said. "For all we know, she's already turned them feral, and we'll have a scene from *Yellowjackets* waiting for us."

I couldn't stop myself from grinning despite the presence of a body. "She never turned us feral. I'm sure they're okay."

"Let's make sure."

THE GIRLS SEEMED HAPPY WHEN WE got back to Stonecrest. Mom and my aunts had fed them breakfast, and now they were cleaning the dormitory from top to bottom, with a little help from the bossy threesome.

"Anything?" Mom asked when she detached from the group cleaning the baseboards.

I caught her up.

"Well, that's disturbing," Mom said. "I don't understand. Who killed her?"

"That's what we need to find out," I replied. "Where's Katie? I have some questions for her."

"She's upstairs in her room with Evan and Aunt Tillie. They're supposed to be cleaning, but you know Aunt Tillie."

I wasn't surprised that Aunt Tillie had decided to take over the room of witch acolytes. "Keep the rest of the kids busy," I said. "I need some privacy to talk to Katie."

"I can keep them busy," Mom volunteered. "This place is filthy. I can keep them busy all week if need be."

"It won't come to that," I promised. "Chief Terry is getting the parents on the phone. They're going to have to come pick up their kids tomorrow."

Mom balked. "Why?"

"Both women who ran the school are dead. There's nobody to take over on short notice. Someone else will have to take over, but that will take months."

Mom looked decidedly sad. "I didn't think about that. What about tonight?"

"I was thinking we'd stay here with them tonight," I replied. "We need to protect them in case the shadow returns."

"Right." Mom nodded. "I also didn't think about that."

"Neither did I." It was hard to admit. "I assumed Bianca was guilty and she'd taken the ingredients from the greenhouse. She didn't, and that means we have a bad witch out there and a nasty shadow to contend with. I don't think these kids are safe."

"We'll protect them." Mom was firm. "We can do that, can't we?"

"It's only one night. I'm hopeful Katie will be able to help me figure out who's behind this, even if..." I couldn't finish.

"Even if it's her mother," Mom surmised.

I wanted to deny it, but that would've been a waste of time. "Even if it's her mother," I confirmed. "I don't want to believe it's her—mostly because I feel tremendous pity where she's concerned—but I can't rule her out. It's possible Kevin's constant philandering drove his wife over the edge."

"Which is another form of tragedy."

"It's emotional abuse," I agreed. "I have no choice but to talk to Katie. After that, hopefully, I'll know better where to look. Either way, these kids are our responsibility for the next twenty-four hours."

"We'll take care of them," Mom promised. "You know me. I'm happy as long as I have someone to dote on."

I grinned. "That's why you and Chief Terry are such a good match. You both like to dote on each other."

"We do have that going for us," Mom agreed. "Now if I could just get the man to propose, we could dote on each other forever."

I was not expecting her to say that. In fact, it was something that had only vaguely crossed my mind. Now that she mentioned it, though, I had questions. "Well, maybe you'll get your Christmas wish," I suggested, an idea taking shape.

Mom's smile was wide and easy. "One thing at a time, Bay. Right now, these girls need us. After that, we'll take care of the personal stuff."

I HEARD AUNT TILLIE CHATTING with Violet, Autumn, and Katie as I headed down the dormitory hallway. She seemed more than happy to talk about magic with them, even though the girls were full of nonstop questions.

I stood in the doorway and watched them for several seconds as they peppered Aunt Tillie with questions. She noticed me first.

"Anything?" she asked.

The grim set of my jaw must've told her all she needed to know. "Unfortunately, yes." I entered the room. "Katie, we need to talk."

The look Katie shot me was full of fear. "Did something happen to my mom?"

"No." I sat on the nearest bed. I figured trying to cut her roommates out of the conversation was a mistake. "As far as I know, your mother is fine. I do have some questions about her."

"What sort of questions?" Katie sat on the bed across from me, Violet and Autumn immediately placing themselves on either side of her.

"Your mother knows about your father's affairs. I know that because I had a slight altercation with your mother at the festival the other day."

"What does 'slight altercation' mean?"

"She saw me watching her and assumed I was one of your father's ... um ... friends. She pulled my hair and made sure I was aware that he would never leave her."

Katie didn't look all that surprised. "Yeah, I can see her doing that. My mom has known about my dad's cheating for as long as I can remember."

"When did you find out about your dad's activities?"

"I guess I was about eleven or so. I knew my mom was upset with my dad all the time, but I didn't know why. I overheard them fighting one day. I understood what they were saying, but I couldn't quite wrap my head around it, you know?"

I did indeed understand.

"I started paying closer attention," she continued. "My dad slept on the couch most nights. My mother hated him. I never understood why they stayed married. All of my friends in Shadow Hills had parents who were divorced, and everybody seemed somehow happier. My parents stayed together and hated each other."

"At some point you obviously brought it up," I prodded.

"I knew about it for a long time," Katie confirmed. "I never said anything. I just sort of watched. Then, one day, my high school principal started being mean to me for no reason. I brought it up to my mom, and she said it was because my dad had been screwing her and then dumped her."

"Your mother just blurted it out like that?" Aunt Tillie demanded.

Katie nodded. "I think she was tired ... of all of it. Maybe I caught her on a bad day."

"You must've had questions," I insisted.

"I asked why she put up with it. She said that some marriages were built on things other than love. They were built on comfort ... and safety. Basically, she said that she was married to Dad but didn't love him. They were still determined to live a happy life together, she said. She said she knew when she married him that he was incapable of being loyal."

"Did you leave it at that?"

"Maybe for a week or two." Katie looked thoughtful now. "I thought about it a lot. I started watching my father more closely. He wasn't even subtle about it. He'd go to Mrs. Kramer's house across the road after dinner every night. He'd watch television with her and spend the night there sometimes."

Now we were getting somewhere. "Who is Mrs. Kramer?"

"Mom's friend. They're on the festival planning committee together. They hate each other, and yet they pretend to like each other."

"Because your mother knows that Mrs. Kramer is sleeping with your dad. What happened to Mrs. Kramer's husband?"

"He spends his nights with Mrs. Clarke two streets over."

"Of course he does." I rolled my neck until it cracked. This was getting very convoluted. "Did you ever ask your dad about any of this?"

"That's how I ended up here. When I brought it up, he told me to shut my mouth and mind my own business. I was annoyed and didn't do either, so he got frustrated and sent me here."

"Does your dad know that your mother knows about his affairs?"

Katie shrugged. "I don't know how he couldn't know, but there are times I don't think my dad is all that bright. I think ... I think maybe that he tells himself what he wants to hear and that's all that matters."

"Does your mom do that too?"

"Yeah." Katie blew out a sigh. "I thought she would stop him from sending me here. She didn't even try. She just accepted it. It's like she's too focused on him being a bad husband, and her place in all of it to think about anything else."

"Did you ask your mom to step in?"

"No, because I was over it too. I just wanted to be away from them. They're not normal parents."

My heart skipped at the way she said it. That created an opening for my next question. "Katie, I need you to look at me."

She glanced up and waited.

"My next question is going to be difficult, but I have to ask," I warned.

"Okay." She rested her hands in her lap and stared at me. It was as if she was resigned to the worst.

"Is it possible your mother found out about Mrs. Walters and killed her?"

"Absolutely not." Katie forcefully shook her head. "No way."

"How can you be certain?"

"My mother is a walking doormat. She might freak out for a second when another mistress pops up, but then she accepts it. If she had it in her to kill someone, she would've gone after Mrs. Kramer. She was supposed to be her friend. She wants to pretend it's not happening."

It made an odd sort of sense. "One more question: were you aware your father was seeing Bianca Golden?"

Katie's eyebrows moved toward her hairline in tandem with those of Autumn and Violet. "No way. Are you kidding me?"

"I wish I were."

"We didn't know that," Autumn said. "We knew about Ms. Walters, but not Ms. Golden. Is Ms. Golden behind this?"

"She's dead too," I replied. There was no sugarcoating it. "I don't think she was responsible. Can you think who it might be?"

Katie didn't consider it long. "I promise you it wasn't my mother. It had to be someone else."

I believed her, but hoped it wasn't because I pitied her mother. "Okay." I pushed myself to a standing position. "Thanks for your time."

"What will you do now?" Violet called out.

"Try to figure out who we're dealing with. It's the only thing I can do."

27
TWENTY-SEVEN

Landon found me in the upstairs hallway staring out at the campus an hour later. The last time I'd seen him, he'd had his head bent together with Chief Terry, whispering to one another.

"What are you doing?" Landon asked as he moved behind me, his arms automatically coming around my waist.

"Aren't we supposed to be working?" I leaned back and rested my head against his shoulder, looking up to see his profile. "I thought the rule was 'no funny business on the job' when we were on official business."

He chuckled. "Do you see me doing my mime routine? Nothing is funny about this." He pressed a kiss to my cheek. "What do you want to do, Bay? Obviously, you didn't get anything actionable from Katie. Otherwise, you would've tracked me down."

I didn't get anything from Katie. I was still bothered at how beaten down the girl seemed. "I've been thinking," I said, my hands landing on top of his on my midriff. "I don't understand how these kids fell through the cracks the way they did."

"Not everybody loves the same, Bay. Not everybody parents the same either."

"But … Katie's father sent her to this school to keep her mouth shut. Why didn't her mother step in and do something about it?"

"Isn't it possible her mother has been beaten down by circumstances and simply doesn't realize what a bad mother she's being?"

"I don't care how upset you are, you don't ship your kid off to be locked away in a school. You wouldn't do it."

"I'd like to think I wouldn't," he confirmed. "I don't know for sure. I mean … what if we had a problem child, and I couldn't handle her?"

"You still wouldn't do it." I was certain. "Joanie has completely failed Katie. I'm willing to bet she's failed her other kids too. And why? Because her husband has a wandering penis. I'm going to hex that thing so it falls completely off before this is over."

"Can you do that?" Landon looked intrigued … and a bit frightened.

That nudged a smile out of me. "Are you afraid?"

"No, because I love you and would never give you a reason to use that spell."

"You'd better not." Even as I said it, I couldn't work up any righteous indignation. He wasn't a cheater. "Why do you think Joanie puts up with it?"

"I can't answer that." Landon rested his cheek against the side of my head. "Maybe her father cheated on her mother, and she grew up thinking that's normal. Maybe she has terrible self-esteem and thinks that's what she deserves."

I pressed my lips together, debating, then sighed. "Why do you think the others do it?"

"The mistresses?"

I nodded.

"Kevin sounds like the sort of guy who knows how to charm a woman and make her believe a specific narrative. They see what they want to see in him."

"But they beg him for what they want, and he never does. Why don't they realize he's a lost cause?"

"Maybe they think they're the exception and not the rule."

"They believe they're special. That they're somehow different from the others. It's kind of like narcissism ... but on a really pathetic scale."

"It's sad," he agreed.

"I feel sorry for them."

"You shouldn't." Landon was strangely calm. "They have the power to change their lives. They have the power to walk away from him. Instead, they hold out hope that he will confirm they're special. Why not make themselves special?

"Let's say one of them actually gets what she wants," he continued. "Let's say Kevin finally does decide to leave Joanie and he even proposes to one of them. What do they have now? They have a husband they can never trust. How is that winning?"

"They think they'll be the special one," I replied. "They believe he won't cheat on them, that he only cheated with them because there was some sort of kismet at work."

"And how does that work in Kevin's case?" Landon asked. "He cheated with multiple women. I'll bet we've barely made a dent in the number of women he's cheated with."

I turned and buried my face in his chest. "We need to figure this out, Landon. Something doesn't feel right."

"A lot of things about this don't feel right," he confirmed, his hands moving up and down my back. "We need to start figuring things out. That starts now."

He was serious enough I stiffened. "Meaning?"

"Terry is having the uniforms call all the parents. The girls will be picked up tomorrow."

"What if they don't have someone available to pick them up?" I thought of Katie, of how embarrassing it would be for her parents to be one town over and to leave her here.

Seemingly reading my mind, Landon managed a reassuring smile. "I already talked to your mother. If we have kids left at the end of the day tomorrow, they're going to the inn for Christmas."

That was a relief and a surprise. "Who decided that?"

"It just worked out that way. Your mother and aunts are horrified that these girls were left alone. They want to dote on them. That works out for us because we can't leave them alone tonight."

I'd been wondering about that. "We're spending the night here?"

His smile was enigmatic. "Do you see another way around it? Your mom and aunts are staying here in the dorm. Apparently, there are a few empty beds. The girls seem thrilled with the idea of a slumber party. They're even talking about doing makeup."

"That actually sounds kind of fun."

"You can stay here with them if you want."

I opened my mouth to respond and then snapped it shut. I wasn't certain what to say.

"Or you and I can head to the administration building," he said. "The girls said there are sofas in the teachers' lounge. I've always wanted to romance you in a teacher's lounge—and while we're getting freaky, we can also go through the files in the headmistress's office. Perhaps we missed something in the other files she was keeping."

"We didn't even look at those files," I argued.

"Speak for yourself. I looked at them, but there was nothing much of interest. It was all basic information—including what the girls might have done to get in trouble."

"You think she took the files home as a way to throw someone off," I realized out loud.

"It's possible, right?"

"If she knew about Bianca, it's possible they were working against one another."

"While somebody else was working against both of them," Landon added. "I thought it would be worth a shot. We'll be in sight of the dorms but still have some privacy. Plus, it's just weird for me to stay in the dorm with teenage girls."

"Sounds like a kinky plan."

"I thought you'd like it." He cupped my face and planted a loud kiss on my lips. "We're eating here before we head over. I love you. I'm looking forward to the dirty teachers' lounge stuff, but I need sustenance first."

He was so earnest when he said it, I burst out laughing. When he kissed me again, a trio of sighs drew my attention over his shoulder. There, Katie, Autumn, and Violet watched us.

"It's so romantic," Autumn gushed as she pressed her hand to the spot above her heart.

"It's amazing," Violet agreed. "You're amazing." She took a tentative step toward Landon. "Do you have a brother?"

"Screw a brother," Katie argued. "There's no topping him."

"That's true." Autumn looked momentarily philosophical. "Are you guys sure you're going to make it? Maybe this is just a temporary thing."

"Ugh. You sound like the women who go after my dad," Katie chided. "Just ... don't." Her eyes moved to me. "Some people are happy. That gives me hope."

I moved closer to her, my gaze never moving from her face. "Keep the hope," I ordered. "It's good for you." I flicked my eyes to Autumn. "I'll squash you like a bug if you move on my man."

She giggled. "Just wishful thinking."

Landon slung his arm around my shoulders. "We're going to all have a meal together. Then we're leaving you with Winnie and the others and heading to the administration building. Out of curiosity, would you guys say that Enid Walters and Bianca Golden were friends?"

"Absolutely not," Autumn replied on a laugh. "They were mortal enemies."

"They pretended to be friends," Violet said. "It was important to them that they come across as friends. Why do you care?"

Landon sent me a significant look. "Come on. Let's go downstairs. You guys can fawn over me a little longer and tell me how handsome I am."

"Who says you're handsome?" Autumn challenged. "Maybe it's the way you love her that makes you handsome." She jerked a thumb toward me.

Landon considered it, but not for very long. "You know what? If that's what people remember me for, I'm okay with that. If loving Bay is my legacy, I'll be revered forever."

I swallowed the odd lump in my throat. "And here I thought you couldn't possibly get more schmaltzy," I gritted out.

He shrugged. "I'm good at what I do, sweetie."

AFTER A DINNER OF ROSEMARY CHICKEN, SCALLOPED potatoes, and fresh vegetables, we took one of the pies Mom and the girls had spent the afternoon baking and headed to the administration building.

Chief Terry had called in the county to clear the main parking lot and the sidewalks between the three primary buildings, so we didn't have trouble cutting across to the administration building. Still, I was restless as I took in the darkness surrounding us.

"What are you doing?" Landon asked when he realized I'd stopped walking and was staring into the nothing between buildings. "Is something there?"

I shook my head. "No, but I can't shake the feeling that something is coming."

"I'm guessing that something isn't good." Landon looked resigned. "And here I was hoping that we would have time for nookie in the teachers' lounge. My luck sucks."

I snorted despite his serious expression. "Who uses the word 'nookie' in this day and age?"

"Me, Bay. I like nookie."

"Of course you do." I used my magic to get us inside the administration building. We had to turn on all the lights to figure our way around. The first floor looked to belong to a secretary, complete with a waiting room. There wasn't much of interest to garner our attention.

The second floor, however, proved much more fruitful.

"Well, will you look at this?" Landon stood between two offices. The offices—and the desks inside—faced one another. Because of how everything was arranged, the people inside would've had no choice but to look at the individual in the opposite office if they dared to look up.

"That's kind of combative, isn't it?" I mused.

"It's very 'let's see which one of us can stare longer,'" Landon said. He moved toward the office on the right and tried the door. It was locked. "Bay, my love, can you do me a solid and open this office, so I don't have to kick in the door?"

"I kind of find it sexy when you kick in doors," I admitted as I pulsed the lock and listened to it click open.

"There's no need to damage such nice woodwork when new owners are likely coming in."

"Do you really think someone else will come in and run the school?"

"Don't you?"

I shrugged. "I don't particularly like the message behind this school."

"The girls are mostly happy, Bay. You might not like how they got here, but that doesn't mean this place isn't good for them. Maybe someone else will come in and do an even better job."

"Maybe." I wasn't convinced. "This looks like Bianca's office," I noted. "That means the one across the way belongs to Enid. How about you take this one, I'll take that one, and then we'll meet in the teachers' lounge for nookie?"

"Don't tease me," he warned. "I want the freaking nookie enough that I'll be crushed if you don't come through."

"I would never tease you." I left him with a kiss on the cheek.

"Winner gets the spoils and all that jazz. Or, rather, winner gets the trophy."

"I love when you try to talk sports metaphors, Bay."

"Yeah, yeah, yeah."

We settled into the offices and started digging. There was nothing overt—at least not immediately—and then I noticed the potted plant in the corner of the room. It was angled weirdly enough that I went over to check it ... and found a hidden door in the wall, just big enough to hide something.

"Weird," I muttered as I dropped to my knees and opened the door. I was careful when reaching inside—Aunt Tillie had told me enough horror stories about sticking my hands where I couldn't see to give me pause—and came back with a huge book. It was more like a scrapbook, and when I opened it, I found a wealth of information.

"Well, well, well," I drawled as I turned the pages. "Unbelievable."

"What did you find?" Landon asked as he appeared in Enid's office. He craned his neck to get a good view of me on the floor. "Is that a little door in the wall? There weren't elves living back there, were there?"

I shook my head without looking up. "It's a grievances book."

"I don't know what that is." He sat next to me, his forehead creasing as he took in the page I was studying. "Is that Bianca?"

"It is," I confirmed. "Enid was keeping track of all of them. There are quite a few in here." I flipped between pages to show him. "For example, apparently this woman—one Cherie Corner—was 'dating' Kevin when he first got involved with Enid. She kept track of who Cherie was hanging out with, and she even tracked when Cherie decided to move on from Kevin and started dating someone else. She followed Cherie after the fact to make sure she was really done with Kevin."

"That's a little creepy." Landon rested his shoulder next to mine. "Is there anyone in there we should be worried about?"

"Yeah." I'd already figured it out, I realized. Or Enid had shown me the truth from beyond the grave. "Georgie Hamilton." I flipped to that page. "She's the one we're looking for."

"How do you know that?" Landon's forehead creased as he read the entry. "I'm seriously confused."

"Georgie was originally born in Hawthorne Hollow, where there is a nexus. Enid kept track of a few odd things that happened around Georgie when she realized Kevin was sniffing up her skirt. Almost everything Enid noted was magical in origin."

"Like?"

"Like cars blowing up ... and people ending up dead."

"Who died?"

"Georgie's mother-in-law, Kevin's sister, and Bianca's aunt. All of them were poking their noses in Georgie's business. All of the deaths were ruled accidents or natural causes, but Enid thought otherwise. She was keeping track ... and appeared determined to confront Georgie."

"Do you think that's what happened?" Landon asked.

"According to this notation, Enid confronted Georgie the day before she died." I tapped the book. "She said it went about as well as expected and left it at that."

"So ... Enid told Georgie she knew what she was doing, including killing people, and Georgie decided to kill Enid to keep her quiet," Landon surmised. "Why kill Bianca, though?"

"Maybe Bianca knew too. Maybe Enid couldn't keep it quiet."

"And you think Georgie's ties to Hawthorne Hollow suggest she's magical."

"Yup, and she would know about us, about my family, if she was magical and raised in this area."

"Okay ... what do we do next?"

That was a good question. "I don't know, but something tells me we're going to find out before the night is out."

"Why do you say that?"

"I have a feeling."

Landon didn't push back on the statement. "Do we have time for teachers' lounge nookie before that feeling comes to fruition?"

I nodded. "I think something can be arranged."

"Then I'm good."

28
TWENTY-EIGHT

Landon got his nookie and then we got comfortable in the lounge. I couldn't be certain why they called it a teachers' lounge with no teachers in the building, but I wasn't in the mood to be picky. We pushed two couches together, so it was like sleeping in a weird little couch crib. Then I got dressed enough so the only thing I had to do was pull on my pants and boots in case there was an emergency, which I was anticipating. I was out like a light the second I curled into Landon.

It might have been early—way too early to sleep—but I knew we'd be awakened.

I wasn't disappointed.

It was right around midnight when I felt the zing. My eyes came open in an instant, and when I looked around the room, it took me a moment to get my bearings.

I felt it again.

The room wasn't familiar, but I remembered where we were. Where was the zing coming from?

"Where are you going?" Landon asked in a sleepy voice as I pulled away from him. He seemed lost in his own little world—the fact that we weren't in our own bed didn't bother him at all—and I knew if I could keep my voice even, he would slip back into dreamland.

"She's here," I replied evenly.

Landon bolted upright, his eyes seeking mine in the darkness. There was a bit of ambient light flitting through the window thanks to the lights that dotted the campus. It wasn't much, but it was enough to be able to read the fear crawling across his face.

"What do we do?" he asked.

"You're not going to do anything," I replied. "You're going to stay here."

"Try again."

"There's nothing you can do," I insisted. "I have to handle this."

"Bay, no." He vehemently shook his head. His hair was mussed from sleep, but his face was deadly serious. "We're doing this together."

"We *are* doing this together," I agreed. "You're doing your part from inside."

"I'm not leaving you."

"Of course you're not." I kept my voice light and easy. "You would never leave me."

His eyes narrowed into suspicious slits as he waited.

"I have to be the one to go outside." I had a plan. "I need you to call the other building and get Aunt Tillie up."

Landon made a face. "And just why would I want to do that?"

"I have a way for her to get rid of the Christmas decorations and end this at the same time."

Landon looked caught between annoyance and intrigue. "I'm all ears."

I told him, quickly, as I tugged on my pants, coat, and boots. "Do you understand?" I asked as I moved to the door that led downstairs.

"I do," he replied. "I just ... I don't like this, Bay. I'm afraid."

"Just do as I ask. Please. We can end this now."

I knew I'd won when his shoulders slumped. "Fine. You're going to owe me, though."

"You can have all the reindeer."

"I don't care about that. I just want a weekend of you and me and nothing else. No family. No monsters. Just us."

I thought about his Christmas gift. It would be a three-person weekend, but something told me he would be fine with it. "I can arrange something you're absolutely going to love."

"Fine." He grabbed me and planted a loud kiss on my lips. "Don't get hurt. You'll be in big trouble if you do."

"I've got this," I promised him. "Trust me."

IT WAS COLD WHEN I EXITED THE BUILDING. I scanned the parking lot, my gaze inadvertently landing on the spot where Enid's body had been found. Then I moved to the middle of the sidewalk. It was bright enough where I stood that there was no missing the fact that I'd emerged from the building ... or that I was alone.

"You can come out, Georgie," I called out. I wasn't in the mood for games. It was too cold, and too close to Christmas. I wanted this finished. "There's no point in playing coy."

She emerged from the darkness at the far end of the sidewalk. She was closer to the administration building than the dorm, for which I was grateful. The shadow was also close. I could feel it. It remained hidden in the trees ... stalking my every move.

"How did you know?" she asked on a light laugh. She looked genuinely surprised. "I thought for sure I'd convinced you I didn't have a motive."

"You did a good job," I confirmed. "You were off my radar."

"What changed?"

"A few things. The first of which was Bianca. You probably shouldn't have killed her so quickly after you offed Enid."

"She didn't give me much choice. Apparently, even though she and Enid hated one another, they liked to gossip."

I tried to picture the scene she was painting and cringed. "That is altogether terrifying."

Georgie made an exaggerated face. "Why would they spend time bonding when they were both in love with the same man?"

"Why would you kill them over a man you can never have?" I challenged.

Georgie's expression shifted. "You don't know what you're talking about. He's already mine. We're just working out the details."

It was hard to tell if she grasped the truth of her situation but refused to embrace it, or if she was truly delusional. "Enid kept a book of all her competition," I volunteered. "She tracked everyone, including you. She had some interesting thoughts on your mother-in-law, and Kevin's sister, and Bianca's aunt, among others."

Georgie's smile disappeared in an instant. "I figured she had the information written down somewhere. I was kind of hoping she gave it to Bianca—and only her—and we were done with this. Obviously not."

I found it interesting that she didn't deny the charges. "What's the plan, Georgie? How do you think you're going to get away with this?"

"I'm going to get away with it the same way I got away with it before. I'm going to do it and trust the universe is on my side. I deserve my happily ever after."

She sounded absolutely nutty. "I take it your happily ever after isn't going to come at the hands of your husband?"

"Andrew? He's not involved. Quite frankly, if he'd take the kids and get out of my hair, I would actually consider him something other than a complete waste of time. He keeps saying therapy will help. He just wants to get past this." She mock-clutched at her chest. "It is beyond annoying. I've told him that what we had was a mistake, but he refuses to accept it."

"Perhaps he sees what you don't."

"What's that?"

"That you're throwing your life away on a man who will never care for you."

Georgie's expression turned dark and sharp. "And you know that how?" she challenged. "How are you such an expert on something you have no actual knowledge of?"

"I've talked with Kevin." I could feel the shadow watching me from the trees.

"You talked to Kevin?" Georgie let loose a light laugh. There was anger rippling beneath her seemingly tranquil surface. "Should I be worried that you talked to him? Do you think that he wants you more than me? Let me guess, you're in love with him." She took a centering breath. "Honey, you're hardly the first woman to fall in love with him. He's a powerful man. They fall for him all the time. He'll never love anybody but me."

Yup. She truly was delusional. "I'm not in love with him. I don't even like him. I have my own husband. Even if I didn't, Kevin would pretty much be the last man on earth I wasted my time on. He's a piece of crap."

"I'd be very careful what you say about him," Georgie growled. "He's a good man, and I won't listen to someone disparage him."

"He's a piece of crap who gets his jollies hopping from woman to woman," I replied. "He's not a good anything. There's a rumor that he's a good father, but given the fact that he's shoved his daughter in this school because she called him out regarding his extracurricular activities ... well ... I'm going to call foul on that."

Georgie's forehead wrinkled. "I don't understand."

That was hardly surprising. "You didn't know? Well, let me break it down for you." I wasn't particularly worried about making Georgie see the light. She'd killed people to lay claim to a man who wasn't worth it. I needed to give the decorations time to arrive. The fact that a gnome had appeared and was breakdancing at the far end of the lot indicated I wouldn't have long to wait.

"Katie has known about her father's need to ... *adventure* ... outside his marriage for years," I started. "She heard her parents arguing about it when she was younger but didn't say anything for a long time. Several months ago, she *did* say something. And father of the year that he is, Kevin locked her away here to shut her up."

To her credit, Georgie looked taken aback. "That's not right." She shook her head. "Kevin said she'd been misbehaving."

"His version of misbehaving was calling him out for being a piece of crap. What's really terrible is that Joanie didn't do anything to save her kid. She sat back and let Kevin do what Kevin does. I'm guessing it was because she didn't feel she could deal with anything else on top of Kevin screwing around, but it's not okay."

Georgie pressed her lips together, seemingly considering. Then she shook her head. "No. Kevin said Joanie doesn't know what's going on, and he can't tell her because she's emotionally unbalanced and might do something terrible."

"I don't disagree about Joanie being emotionally unbalanced," I admitted. "She's a total mess. That doesn't change the fact that she let her daughter down, because she does, in fact, know. Kevin did it for purely selfish reasons—he wanted to keep having sex and not have to explain his actions—but Joanie did it because it was easier than dealing with the truth."

"I don't believe you," Georgie argued. "Kevin said Joanie can't handle the truth. That's why we can't be together. It's only a matter of time before she finds out, though. I've set certain things in motion. It has to happen at the right time, otherwise Kevin will blame me ... even though it's not my fault."

"Kevin is so good at gaslighting that a lot of this really isn't your fault," I agreed. "But you've been murdering people, and I don't have any sympathy for you."

As if on cue, the gnome—which had been joined by another gnome—began to sing.

Joy to the world, the witch is come. Let earth receive her queen.

I stilled. Aunt Tillie had changed the lyrics to put herself at the center of this fight.

"I'm not sure about etiquette here," Georgie said. She was

choosing her words carefully. "I happen to know a bit about your family. I've always been a fan. And while I find the dancing gnome absolutely delightful, perhaps now isn't the time."

I forced a tight-lipped smile. "I believe the gnome is about to co-opt a Christmas carol and put my great-aunt at the center of it, but I have no control over those things. It's not my spell."

And Heaven and nature sing.

"You're here," Georgie pointed out. "Obviously, you called it to distract me."

I narrowed my eyes as I regarded the gnome. "It really doesn't matter. The gnomes will be your smallest concern in about three minutes."

Georgie looked annoyed.

And Heaven and nature sing.

I knew the moment the shadow was going to attack, but not because I was a super witch. The gnomes telegraphed it with their eyes, which were tracking the shadow's movement.

When the shadow exploded from the trees, I was ready.

"*Destruo*," I hissed, calling on my necromancer power. The ghosts I called—including Viola—intercepted the shadow and proceeded to rip it apart with no further instructions.

And He-a-eh-ea-van and nature sing.

Georgie's eyes went wide as my ghosts incapacitated her shadow. One second it was there, the next it had been ripped to bits and scattered on the bitter wind.

"I think there's been some sort of mistake," Georgie quavered. "Um ... I'm not here to cause trouble. I'm just here to talk."

As the gnomes ramped up their song, the decorations finally made their appearance.

She rules the world with truth and grace, they bellowed, the night exploding with sound as bears, Santas, Grinches, reindeer, and the continuously bouncing ornaments appeared.

"What in the...?" Georgie trailed off.

And makes her enemies shake, the decorations shrieked. They were truly off the song now, singing Aunt Tillie's refrain.

"You were never going to win this one," I told Georgie. "Your plan to kill anybody who got in your way and claim Kevin as your own was never going to come to fruition because you were missing the most important piece of the story."

The glories of her righteousness!

"And what's that?" Georgie looked beside herself ... and maybe a little sick to her stomach.

And wonders of her love.

"Kevin never wanted to be with you, no matter what he said," I replied. "He told you he was never going to leave his wife right from the start, but you didn't believe him."

"But he showed me he wanted to be with me," Georgie insisted. "He loves me. I know he does."

And wonders of her love.

"He doesn't," I argued. "He never did. He doesn't love anyone but himself. That won't change. You never had a chance of getting everything because he was never going to be the man you thought. Why can't you see that?"

And won-uh-uh-nders of her love.

"If he doesn't love me, I have nothing!" Georgie screeched.

That's when the stripper elf that looked strangely like Mrs. Little arrived, whip in hand and heading straight toward Georgie.

"Oh, geez!" I threw up my hands. "This is unbelievable."

Georgie let loose a scream and ran into the woods.

"Go after her," I ordered the decorations. "Bring her back!" I extended a warning finger toward the sexy elf. "Don't use that whip on her. I have no idea where it's been."

The elf almost looked sad. Along with the others, she tore off into the woods. They sang the whole way as they gave chase.

When the noise died down, the sound of applause drew my eyes to the second floor of the administration building. There, Landon hung out of a window.

"Well done, sweetie," he called out as he popped something into his mouth.

"You'd better not be eating those reindeer without me," I warned.

"Then you'd better get moving and take the nasty witch into custody," Landon replied. "Did she tell you where she got the magic?"

I shook my head. "It's not very good magic. I really don't care."

"It still can't hurt to ask."

I gave him an extended glare before starting after Georgie and the decorations. I had to collect her before this could be considered finished. "I won't be long."

"I already miss you. Have I mentioned that you're my Christmas wish?"

I went warm all over despite my irritation at him eating all the reindeer. "You're my Christmas wish too. You, and I want Chief Terry to propose to my mother."

"That's a weird combination."

"It's what she wants, and there's no harm in making it official. He's already the father that counts."

"He is," Landon agreed. "Something tells me you might get your wish yet again."

Something told me he was right. "Give me fifteen minutes to track down Georgie. She should be sufficiently traumatized by the time I find her. Then I say it's time to embrace Christmas and leave the strife behind."

"That, my beautiful wife, is the best offer I've had all day."

29
TWENTY-NINE
CHRISTMAS EVE

I sat in the dining room, nursing a glass of wine and staring at the Christmas tree. Mom and my aunts had gone all out decorating it—they wanted a lot of photos for Calvin's first Christmas—and I had to say they'd outdone themselves. I couldn't remember the tree ever looking this pretty.

It somehow made the holiday all the better.

"There she is." Landon jolted me out of my reverie. He kissed the top of my head before removing his gloves. He seemed to be in fine spirits.

"Did you see Georgie?" I asked.

"I did." Landon glanced around to make sure we were alone. The inn was devoid of guests for a change, and the only sound was the music playing in the corner. Thankfully, because of how things had played out, we'd all agreed Christmas music was unnecessary, and we were going the boyband route this year.

"How much do you want to know?" he asked.

"All of it," I replied without hesitation.

He sat in the chair next to me. "Okay, I'll tell you. Then you're going to let it go and enjoy Christmas.

"Georgie claims you're evil and that you used magical Christmas gifts to take her down," Landon started. "Terry and I happen to know that's true. The other officers saw the Christmas decorations when they were running rampant around town. They're obviously curious, but they are not pointing fingers at you."

I wasn't particularly worried about any of that. "Has Georgie tried using her magic?"

"She has but without success. Whatever spell you cast to bind her powers worked."

"What about Kevin? Did he visit her?"

"You know the answer to that." Landon's lips twitched. "He's nowhere to be found. She's accusing us of keeping him from her—she's specifically blaming you for his absence—but I think reality is starting to set in. Right now, she's just a very sad woman."

"And all the girls?"

"They're home. No stragglers. As for the school ... I don't know. Enid owned the property, but nobody can find a will. There could be a battle for the property, if not the school, in the near future."

"So the school is essentially no more," I mused.

"At least for now," he confirmed. "I don't see it coming back this year, Bay. Maybe next year ... and maybe with a different yardstick for entrance."

"I just don't want it to be a place to shove girls who don't do what their parents want."

"You've made your feelings on the school well known. We'll have to see how that plays out."

I leaned closer to him and lifted my lips for a kiss. He was happy to oblige. When I spoke again, my voice was softer. "Have you seen Katie since her mother picked her up?"

Landon's smile diminished. "No, but you know you can't fix that situation. Kevin and Joanie have to repair their own family. You can't be Katie's savior."

"I just hate knowing what she's likely dealing with."

"You can't fix everything."

Rationally, I knew that. I was bothered, nonetheless. "I guess I should take it as a win—it was an easy fight given all the others we've faced—and not complain."

"You wouldn't be the woman I fell in love with if you didn't complain."

I opened my mouth to tell him exactly what I thought of that, but he kissed me senseless. I was a bit breathless when he pulled back.

"So, as I was saying," he said after stealing my glass of wine for a sip. "I stopped at the guesthouse long enough to make sure our tree was lit and pretty. Santa might have made an early visit. There are gifts under the tree that weren't there this morning." He looked pretty proud of himself.

"I knew you were hiding them in Chief Terry's office. I think Mom broke in and took a look a few days ago."

"She had better not have. Terry has been fretting over that ring for weeks. If she snuck a peek, he's going to be mad."

I stilled. "He bought a ring?"

Landon shot me an incredulous look. "It's a proposal. You can't have a proper proposal without a ring. Unfortunately for you, no matter how many times I insisted it would mean the world to you to witness the blessed event, he refuses to do the proposal in public. He has it planned for just the two of them later."

"I want to see it," I admitted.

"I figured, but he made me promise not to tell you his plan."

I narrowed my eyes. "You know?"

He puffed out his chest. "It's going to be amazing."

I didn't realize my lower lip had started quivering until he flicked it with his finger.

"If someone were to sneak out to the field around ten o'clock tonight—and be quiet—she might see something that will make her a very happy daughter," he said in a soft voice.

Tears sprang to my eyes. "You found out so I could spy."

"I found out because I'm a busybody. The fact that you'll be so happy you want to jump me after you spy is only a tangential reward."

I burst out laughing, and he swallowed the sound with another kiss.

When he pulled back, his eyes were a little glassy too. "I love you, Bay. I want this to be the start of our merry Christmases. Terry doesn't realize that this is important to you beyond the fact that you're a busybody. He won't put up a fight when you show yourself after the fact."

"Thank you." I snuggled in at his side.

"Don't thank me yet. I plan to go with you so I can participate in the festivities. There's a blanket in that field for a reason. You can thank me then."

That was going to be difficult given his Christmas gift. "Well..." Before I could explain to him, the sound of nails clacking on the hardwood floors had Landon's eyes moving to the doorway.

I followed suit, smiling when the black puppy appeared. It was a mutt—I didn't see the need to pay for a puppy when so many needed to be adopted—and it reminded me of Tramp from the old Disney cartoon. Except that he was black.

"Who is this?" Landon crooned as he dropped to the floor. The puppy enthusiastically rushed to him and started licking his face. "Who is getting a puppy for Christmas? Is it Calvin? I'm so jealous."

I watched him roll around with the puppy. I could've dragged things out, but he'd already given me my biggest gift. It only seemed fair.

"He's yours. I got him for you."

"What?" Landon went still. When he finally looked at me, there was surprise—and maybe a little worry—in his eyes. "You got me a dog?"

"I thought we could practice for a bit, because I'm not quite ready for those kids you so desperately want."

"So ... you got me a dog."

"I got *us* a dog, though he's mostly yours. When you're at work he can go to the newspaper office with me. Marcus volunteered to take him at the petting zoo."

"He'll be a working dog when I have him at the petting zoo," Marcus volunteered. "He'll be earning his keep."

"And Mom has agreed to serve as a babysitter too," I added. "She thinks Peg will love the puppy, and it will keep them both busy."

When Landon sat up, he was near tears. "I can't believe you got me a dog."

"I told you I was thinking about it."

"You did not."

"I asked if you wanted a dog."

"What did I say?"

"You didn't say anything. You turned into a big pile of mush."

Landon hugged the puppy as the little ball of fluff wriggled and danced, lavishing his new dad with kisses. "What's his name?"

"He's your puppy. You get to name him."

"You'd better not name him anything stupid," Aunt Tillie ordered as she breezed into the room with her combat helmet in place. She had a stick in her hand and a gleeful garden gnome chasing her.

"Where are you going?" I demanded as I watched her stroll toward the front of the inn.

"I have one more visit to pay to Margaret's house," Aunt Tillie replied. "It's my Christmas too."

"Do you want company?"

"Not this time," she replied. "This one is all me ... and the Christmas elf from the roof. She's tagging along for the ride."

That was both terrifying and a relief because I didn't want to go out into the cold. "Please tell me nobody will be arrested."

"Of course not," Aunt Tillie scoffed. "It's Christmas."

"That doesn't mean you can't be arrested."

"Then I guess we'll just have to wait and see." With that, she disappeared. I heard her whistling a jaunty tune as she exited the inn.

"Should we follow her?" I asked after a beat.

Landon was on the floor with his puppy, and there was no tearing him away from the dog anytime soon. "She's grown," he replied as the dog showered him with kisses. "She'll figure things out."

"True." I flopped down on the floor with him. "What should we name him?"

"It's going to take a great deal of thought, but something good."

"No food names."

"It's my puppy. If I want to name him Brisket, you don't get a say in the matter."

I should've seen that coming. "Maybe this is something we should do together."

"No. He's mine. I'm naming him."

Resigned, I flopped back on the floor and let the dog wiggle his way over. "You're going to name him Bacon."

"I guess you'll just have to wait and see."

Printed in Great Britain
by Amazon